AN ARTFUL CORPSE

HELEN A. HARRISON

Poisoned Pen

PRESS

Published by Poisoned Pen Press, an imprint of Sourcebooks
P.O. Box 4410, Naperville, Illinois 60567-4410
(630) 961-3900
sourcebooks.com

Library of Congress Cataloging-in-Publication Data

Names: Harrison, Helen A. (Helen Amy), author.
Title: Artful corpse / Helen A. Harrison.
Description: Naperville, IL : Poisoned Pen Press, [2021] | Series: Corpse trilogy
Identifiers: LCCN 2020001062 | (trade paperback)
Subjects: LCSH: Benton, Thomas Hart, 1889-1975--Fiction. | GSAFD: Biographical fiction. | Mystery fiction.
Classification: LCC PS3608.A78345 A89 2021 | DDC 813/.6--dc23
LC record available at https://lccn.loc.gov/2020001062

Printed and bound in the United States of America.
SB 10 9 8 7 6 5 4 3 2 1

To Roy
Always

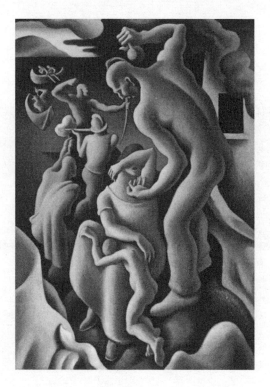

THE ART STUDENTS
LEAGUE OF NEW YORK

WEDNESDAY, NOVEMBER 1, 1967

The solitary studio on the top floor was in darkness when the monitor, Christopher Gray, opened the door at 6:45 p.m. A tall, slender young man of twenty-five and a full-time student at the League, Chris was responsible for preparing the room for Raymond Breinin's seven o'clock life drawing, painting, and composition class. Students would soon be arriving, and he needed to check that everything was in order.

Only a faint urban glow was visible through the grimy windows, since the sun had gone down more than two hours earlier. Chris switched on the lights and squinted at the sudden glare. As his eyes adjusted, he saw the easels arranged in a rough semicircle around the model stand, on which lay a pile of crumpled fabric—an old banquet tablecloth salvaged from a catering service. Some instructors liked to partially drape the figure in it. Some used it to disguise a chair or stool in a seated pose. But it wasn't supposed to be left in a heap on the stand.

"Damn," Chris muttered, "that should have been folded and stashed in the closet," silently blaming the monitor from Charles Alston's afternoon life class for leaving things in disarray. Grumbling under his breath, he stepped onto the low platform and bent down to tidy up the mess. He grasped the cloth and pulled it toward himself, expecting it to come easily, but it was held down by something wrapped inside. He bent over and untangled it, then jumped back in alarm.

He had uncovered the body of a man, curled up knees to chest, hands tucked under his chin. He might have been asleep, except that he hadn't moved at all when Chris tugged on the cloth.

Chris stood still for a moment, stunned. Then he knelt beside the man and looked at his face. He recognized him, in fact had seen him in the cafeteria at lunchtime.

He reached out his hand and touched the man's neck, hoping to find a pulse, but there was none.

One

The Thursday evening life drawing, painting, and composition class, held from seven to ten o'clock, started in the usual way. The monitor, Bill Millstein, whose tuition was forgiven in exchange for housekeeping duties, arrived fifteen minutes beforehand, just as the sun was setting. With the skylights no longer adequate, he turned on the overhead lamps in the ground-floor studio, at the end of the hall that led back from the main lobby. Its atmosphere was heavy with the odor of oil paint and turpentine, so he flipped the switch to activate the ceiling fans, hoping to dissipate some of the art funk. He unlocked the storage closet and took out a long wooden pole, which he leaned against the wall by the model stand. He wiped down the bench easels and checked the uprights to make sure none were broken. He found a rickety one and replaced it with a spare from the closet.

Just before seven the model arrived and began disrobing behind a privacy screen. Students started drifting into the large classroom, greeting one another amiably. Those who had paintings in progress took them out of the racks, set them up on their easels, and laid out their palettes. Those who were there for life drawing carried their Morilla No. 36 sketch pads and boxes of Grumbacher charcoal sticks, or removed them from the rented lockers where they stored their supplies. One of them was Timothy Juan Fitzgerald, TJ to his friends, a sophomore at John Jay College of Criminal Justice, the newly established training ground for law enforcement officers. At nineteen he stood head-to-head with his five-foot-ten father, whose ginger hair and high Irish coloring he shared, though he had inherited his mother's eyes, the warm brown of Spanish sherry.

Two weeks into the fall term, each student had already staked out a favorite location in the large studio. The model held the same pose for a month, so it was necessary to get into position and stay there for the duration. Since the class met only once a week, consistency was especially important. Once you started on a full-figure painting or drawing, you were expected to finish it in detail, complete with hands and feet. No fudging the fingers and toes, not in Edward Laning's class.

Among the most popular of the League's instructors, Laning believed in drilling the fundamentals into his students before encouraging them to experiment. To him, regardless of where one's training ultimately led, figure drawing from life was the cornerstone of art education.

After studying at the League in 1927–1930 and teaching there for a year when he finished his coursework, Laning had gone on to a distinguished career. He was a prolific muralist, best known for *The History of the Recorded Word*—from Moses's graven tablets to Mergenthaler's linotype machine—a huge mural cycle that graced the second-floor lobby of the New York Public Library's flagship building on Fifth Avenue, where it was seen by every visitor to the main reading room. Those who looked up could marvel at Laning's trompe l'oeil ceiling, lifted straight from the Tiepolo playbook, depicting Prometheus bringing enlightenment to humankind. This impressive achievement was completed in 1942 under the auspices of the WPA Federal Art Project, which supported Laning and many of his contemporaries throughout the Great Depression.

He returned to the League in 1952 to become a fixture, teaching drawing, painting, anatomy, and mural painting. Although he was personally devoted to Renaissance-inspired naturalism, he was not doctrinaire or dictatorial like those instructors who churned out younger carbon copies of themselves.

"It's important to master the basics of pictorial representation," he would tell his students, "but at the same time you mustn't neglect the problems of composition, structure, form, and design that must be solved in every picture, regardless of style. Try different mediums and techniques. Go to the museums and galleries, study the antiquities, the old masters, and the moderns firsthand. Take what you need from them, but don't just repeat it, make it your own."

Laning's flexibility was perfectly suited to the League, which was founded in 1875 by rebels from the National Academy of Design. Too rigid, they complained, too stuffy, and besides the Academy was in debt and cutting back on instruction. So a few of them jumped ship, rented the top floor of a piano warehouse at 103 Fifth Avenue, at the corner of Sixteenth Street, hired a model, and opened an independent art school run by the students themselves. Iconoclastic from the start, the school caught on and, rather surprisingly, was supported by some of the bigger names of the day, including William Merritt Chase, who advocated an impressionistic painting style, and Kenyon Cox, a strict traditionalist in the academic mold.

By the time the twentieth century rolled around, the League occupied studios in the imposing American Fine Arts Society building on West Fifty-Seventh Street. With no overriding aesthetic philosophy, an open admission policy, and a faculty that covered the whole artistic spectrum, it attracted an equally diverse student body, from dabblers and hobbyists to hard-core aspiring professionals and those who, like TJ, were considering a career in art but not fully committed.

———

Ever since he was eight years old, TJ had been fascinated by art and toyed with the idea of becoming an artist, but he was well aware of the drawbacks and pitfalls. When he first broached it to his father, Deputy Chief Brian F. X. Fitzgerald of the New York City Police Department, and his mother, Detective Inspector Juanita Diaz, they had howled down the suggestion. Not that they pressured him to follow in their footsteps and join the force—they both believed in letting him make up his own mind about that—but they were adamantly against his getting serious about emulating his friend and mentor, the painter Alfonso Ossorio.

The scion of a Philippine sugar baron, Ossorio met TJ back in 1956, when the boy and his family were on holiday out on eastern Long Island and became involved in a murder investigation. In fact Ossorio had been under suspicion. But after he was cleared and the crime solved, he and the Fitzgerald family became friends. In the following years they made annual visits to the artist's East Hampton estate, The Creeks, with its collection of outsider art and exotic artifacts from various cultures, as well as Ossorio's own Surrealistic creations and abstract paintings by his friends.

Even as his initial astonishment wore off and the artworks became familiar to him, TJ enjoyed discussing them with Ossorio and his life partner, Ted Dragon, a former ballet dancer. Returning from a stroll around the estate's spacious gardens or a paddle in Georgica Pond, which the house overlooked, Fitz and Nita might find the three of them deep in conversation before an impenetrable canvas by Clyfford Still, a grotesque figure by Jean Dubuffet, or one of Jackson Pollock's perplexing drip paintings. After a while, what had begun as curiosity evolved into appreciation, understanding, admiration, and, much to his parents' dismay, a desire on TJ's part to follow in Ossorio's footsteps.

After all, they reminded their son, Ossorio was rich and could afford to paint whatever he wanted all day, every day, without worrying about selling anything. Unlike TJ, who would have to work for a living, which for most artists meant a real job, like teaching or carpentry or working in a gallery or as a museum guard. So after high school, they suggested, if he went to John Jay and decided that law enforcement wasn't for him, he might go into security at the Met or the Modern, where he could spend the day among the masterpieces he admired while holding down a steady job with benefits.

TJ actually saw the wisdom in that, but he still longed to try his hand at creative work. "Just to see if I could do it," he explained. "Maybe I don't have what it takes anyway."

Fitz and Nita thought it over and decided to humor him. "You could go to night school," they suggested, "but you'll have to pay for it yourself."

His weekend job in Brother's Candy & Grocery, the convenience store on East Fourteenth Street, around the corner from the family's Stuyvesant Town apartment, paid only a dollar fifty an hour, but even after he contributed his room and board there was more than enough left over to pay the twenty dollars a month for Edward Laning's Thursday evening life class.

Two

"Hi, there, TJ," called Bill Millstein, a young man about his age, dressed in faded jeans and a rumpled work shirt. A head of shaggy brown hair framed a square-jawed, friendly face that always wore a pleasant expression, though there was something intense behind the genial façade.

"Waddaya say, Bill," replied TJ. He had taken an immediate liking to this character, who'd been attending art classes at the League since he was in grade school. So far all he knew about Bill was that, like TJ, he lived at home with his parents and was passionate about art, but, unlike TJ, Bill was determined to make it his life's work despite the hardships.

"Hangin' in there," Bill told him. "Still feel like I've got a long way to go."

"You can't be a monitor forever," said TJ. "They're going

to kick you out eventually, then how'll you be able to afford classes? You'll have to get a job."

"I think I can wangle a gig with one of the instructors," Bill said, "especially the sculptors, they're always looking for assistants to do the dirty work. Everybody knows I'm reliable. Look how nice I keep this studio, and it ain't easy. You guys are slobs. Crumpled paper all over the floor after every class, broken charcoal sticks, coffee cups, you name it. And the painters are worse."

"Better make sure your enrollment is current," advised TJ. "Don't want to lose your student deferment. If the League cuts you loose, Uncle Sam will have your ass for sure. Then it's off to Vietnam, and you won't have to worry about the future 'cause you probably won't have one."

Bill's expression suddenly changed from warm to cool. "Don't say that," he murmured, and TJ realized he'd made a faux pas.

"Hey, I was only kidding," he said hastily, eager to smooth over his gaffe. "I know guys who've been there and come back in one piece. Anyway, maybe you won't make the cut. As long as you're in school you should be okay."

"I've been lucky so far," Bill replied, "but if I get called up I don't think the draft board will accept the League. It's not accredited. I applied to Cooper. They have a BFA degree program, and it's free."

Founded in 1859 by the inventor, industrialist, and philanthropist Peter Cooper, The Cooper Union for the Advancement of Science and Art was among the most prestigious institutions for training in art, architecture, and engineering—and one of the hardest to get into. Not like the League, which had no entrance requirements. Full tuition scholarships for all undergraduates made it highly attractive to applicants, but the acceptance rate was less than 10 percent. Bill was facing very stiff competition.

"Well, good luck with that," said TJ. "From what I hear about Cooper, you'll need plenty of it. Me, I'm okay as long as I'm full time at John Jay. I got three more years, and the war will be over by then for sure."

Just then the model, wearing only a G-string, emerged from behind the screen and mounted the stand. TJ looked around the studio and saw that his fellow students were settling down.

He gave Bill a friendly poke and turned away. "Hey, I'd better get to my spot before somebody grabs it." His motivation was not strictly artistic. On his first night in class, when he had found himself at a bench easel next to Ellen Jamieson's, he resolved that he'd return to that place every week.

Ellen's long, straight ash-blond hair cascaded down her slender back. Bright-blue eyes and a ready smile animated a round face with a naturally peachy complexion unspoiled by makeup. Her outgoing personality made casual conversation easy. She was what TJ classified, precociously, as his kind of woman. He took his place and greeted her.

"Hi, Ellen. How's the drawing coming along?"

She rolled those bright blue eyes. "It's a disaster. I just

can't seem to get the proportions right. And it looks like he's made of rubber." She flipped back the drawing pad's cover to expose the sheet of newsprint she'd been working on.

TJ studied the drawing with mock concern. It was pretty bad, he had to agree, but he certainly wasn't going to say so, and he didn't really care whether it was any good or not. It gave him an excuse to express interest in her indirectly by pretending to be interested in her work. It was an old ploy, but an effective one.

"You've only been at it for a week, so you mustn't be discouraged. I don't think it's so awful. You want to see a disaster, just look at mine." He showed her, and she flashed that ready smile and told him he was right.

Far from being offended, TJ was charmed by her honesty. He laughed and promised to work harder if she would. She agreed. He shook her hand earnestly. They grinned at each other and turned their attention to the subject at hand.

The model, Walter Green, known to all as Wally—a former football player who had aged out of the team—knew the pose well. After disrobing behind the screened area where models could hang their clothes and relax during breaks, he had resumed the position assigned on the first day of class. It was the classic standing figure, legs slightly astride, one arm on hip, the other raised and holding the pole for balance. Masking tape outlines on the platform marked LANING-THU indicated the location and direction of his feet. With a trained athlete's strength and discipline, the ex–running back could hold the pose without flinching for twenty minutes. Then a ten-minute break for a stretch or a smoke or a trip to the restroom, then another twenty minutes in position.

After the first hour, Laning appeared and went around the room inspecting each student's work. Some were busy with paintings and drawings they had begun the first day and were now refining. Others had scrapped their initial efforts and started over. Still others were making series of quick sketches or focusing on a particular feature.

One reason Laning was such a popular teacher was his approach to criticism—always encouraging, never dismissive or disrespectful. He tailored his remarks to the individual and didn't insist on a particular style or technique.

There were instructors who grumbled loudly when a hapless student didn't follow their way of doing things, snatched the brush and made corrections with humiliating abruptness, ridiculed inept drawings, or even tore them up in disgust, but Laning wasn't one of them. Patience was his watchword, and he seemed to find something admirable in even the most tentative scribble.

The way he criticized Ellen's drawing, for example. She was struggling with the upper body, erasing and starting over several times, before Laning arrived at her easel.

"You're getting something there," he said, squinting in concentration, "but perhaps give a little more thought to how the head and neck connect to the body. Your handling looks a bit vague, don't you think?" She nodded in agreement. Then he approached Wally and pointed out how his prominent trapezius muscles sloped up from the shoulders, how the slight twist of his head gave each sternocleidomastoid a different definition.

"Why not make a detail sketch of that area, and I'll have a look at it at the end of class?" he suggested. Again she nodded and thanked him quietly. He gave her an encouraging smile in return and moved on to TJ, who had stuck with his original attempt to capture the full figure.

"Fitzgerald, isn't it? Well, you're making progress," said Laning, raising TJ's hopes, then deflating them. "You're a beginner, aren't you?"

"Yes, sir," replied TJ. "I guess it's pretty obvious." He slumped a bit as he contemplated his maiden effort. But Laning reassured him.

"Don't be discouraged, son. It's a good start, a very good start."

Three

At eight thirty, it was time for another break. As Wally stepped down and the class relaxed, Laning made an announcement.

"Listen, everyone, I want you to know that we'll be having a distinguished visitor next Thursday evening. Thomas Hart Benton will be in town, and I've invited him to drop by and observe my class. I'd like you all to make him feel welcome."

There was a crash from behind the screen as Wally knocked over the low stool he used as a side table next to his armchair. "Sorry," he called out, "I tripped. I'm okay."

This dramatic punctuation was in marked contrast to the class's reaction. Laning got blank looks from most of the students, while others raised their eyebrows at each other and shrugged.

"You mean to say you don't know who Thomas Hart Benton is?" he asked no one in particular. Bill was the only one brave enough to reply out loud.

"I remember Chris Gray mentioning his name once," he said. "Wasn't he a famous mural painter years ago, back in the Depression?" Gray, an aspiring muralist himself, had studied the work of his illustrious predecessors and, thanks to Laning's recommendation, had just won the Edwin Austin Abbey Memorial Scholarship for Mural Painting.

"Of course Chris would know," replied Laning, casting a withering gaze around the studio, "but it's shocking that the rest of you don't recognize the name of one of America's foremost living artists. His paintings have been hanging in the top museums since long before you were born, and his murals decorate important buildings around the country, including right here in New York City. Oh, and by the way, he taught right here in this building for some ten years." His voice had risen to an unusually strident pitch.

"Ever hear of Jackson Pollock?" he asked rhetorically and got the expected sheepish nods in response. The renowned abstract expressionist painter had recently been much in the news, thanks to a comprehensive exhibition of his work at the Museum of Modern Art that spring.

"Well, there would have been no Jackson Pollock without Thomas Hart Benton! Everything Jack knew about drawing, painting, and composition he learned here at the League from Benton. I mean *everything*, except the drip technique. That he learned from David Alfaro Siqueiros, the Mexican muralist, another great artist whose name you probably don't recognize. Benton and Siqueiros are the giants whose shoulders Pollock stood on."

Laning took a deep breath and let it out slowly. "Sorry, I didn't mean to come on so strong. But it makes me angry to think that someone as influential as Benton is not better known today. I guess I shouldn't be surprised, since he's spent the last thirty years in Kansas City. He hasn't had a New York show in twenty-five years, and the last one was only his prints. But that's going to change."

"What do you mean, Mr. Laning?" asked Bill.

"The reason he's coming to town is because the Whitney is mounting a full-scale retrospective. Lloyd Goodrich, the director, tells me they're pulling out all the stops, getting major museum loans, even borrowing back the murals he painted for the Whitney's old building on Eighth Street. They were removed and sold to the museum in New Britain when the Whitney moved uptown in the '50s. Of course they can't get the ones that are permanently attached to buildings, but they'll show preparatory sketches and photographs."

Laning's spirits lifted as he described the exhibition's scope. "It's going to cover his whole fifty-year career to date. Just wait until you see what he's accomplished. It's only because he chose to put New York behind him and base himself in the Midwest that he's been eclipsed. It's high time he got the recognition he deserves, and this show is going to make that happen. As soon as Goodrich told me about it, I wrote to Tom and asked him to come visit the League, and damned if he didn't accept."

Ellen raised her hand. "Mr. Laning, you said there are Benton murals in New York, but the ones he painted for the Whitney went to Connecticut."

"That's right," he answered, "but there are others still here. In fact they're the first murals he ever painted, and they're in the New School, down on Twelfth Street. They're called America Today, today being 1930, when the building was brand new and the Depression hadn't yet devastated the economy. The theme is the people at work and play in the city and the country, full of vitality and optimism."

"However," he continued, "by the time the murals were finished in 1931, things were looking bad, and Tom was criticized for ignoring the idle factories and foreclosed farms, the unemployment and the breadlines. His answer was that he wanted to show the positive forces at work in America, the energy that made this country great and would pull us through hard times. That argument contradicted the murals' title, but Tom held his ground. He's always been a contrary cuss."

"So you know him?" Ellen asked.

"Oh, yes," said Laning, "I met him when he was teaching here and I was a student, and got to know him a bit when I taught for a year, from '31 to '32. I never took his class but I got friendly with several fellows who did—Joe Meert, Pete Busa, Charlie Pollock, and his brother Jackson. They idolized Tom, and he treated them like family. He and his wife, Rita, would have them over to their place all the time. Rita was like a den mother. She's Italian, very warm and welcoming. She'd feed them spaghetti and play the guitar for their musical evenings. Tom played the mouth organ."

Laning was clearly enjoying this look back to his salad days. "They used to sing folk songs, long before it was popular in the city, but that was part of Tom's celebration of what he saw as the real America. I went to the sing-alongs a couple of times but I didn't really fit in, even though I'm from the Midwest. It seemed old-fashioned to me. I didn't appreciate Tom's paintings, either. I thought of myself as too sophisticated for that hick stuff. Shows you the arrogance of youth."

He grinned and looked pointedly around the room. Not all the faces that looked back at him were as young as he had been in the early 1930s, but they all took his self-deprecating point.

"Moral of the story is, when you examine Benton's paintings—and I want you all to go to the Whitney show, and to see his murals at the New School—ignore the subject matter, which may seem corny, and the style, which is very out of fashion. Look at their solid structure, their superb composition, their complex organization. If you want to learn how to build a picture, representational or abstract, you can have no better example than a Benton."

Four

I'm just not getting it," muttered Ellen to herself as the class broke up at ten p.m. Hands on hips, she studied her drawing, made a face at it, and shook her head. She pulled the sheet of newsprint off the pad, crumpled it up, and tossed it at the wastebasket, which she missed. It landed at Bill's feet.

"Don't worry," he said amiably, as he scooped up the errant wad of paper and dropped it in the basket, "I'm used to picking up the rejects. You'll do better next time, and you won't have to can it—or try to, that is." He winked and treated her to one of his most disarming smiles.

"You're sweet," she told him, "but I'm hopeless. Maybe I should quit this class and go to bookkeeping school instead. That's what Mom wants me to do."

TJ realized it was irrational—after all, this was only their second class together—but her exchange with Bill annoyed him. Not only did he resent Bill's flirting with her, he was also alarmed by the suggestion that she might stop coming to class. He'd just been working up to asking if she'd like to ride home with him on the subway. During one of the breaks, she had told him that she lived on East Fifteenth Street, off Union Square, which was his stop, too. She and a roommate shared an apartment—the "Up 'n' Down," she called it: a walk-up that's run-down.

"The stairs creak, the banister's rickety, and the hall smells like a garbage pail, but we love it," she said. "It's great being out of the house and on our own. My mother doesn't really approve, but I'm nineteen and earning a living, so she can't complain. And she knows Michele, my roomie, is a good kid." The two girls had been friends since childhood and, according to Ellen, always intended to share an apartment when the time came. They both relished their independence and felt very grown-up.

She worked as a nickel thrower—a cashier in the Horn & Hardart Automat across the street from the League. From inside a glass booth, she made change for the customers who bought prepared food out of the windowed compartments that lined the restaurant's walls. When the required number of five-cent coins, or a token for the more expensive items, was inserted into a slot next to the window, the compartment would open and the food could be removed. The Automat was famous for cheap and nourishing meals, making it a favorite haunt of the art students, who were especially fond of the fifty-cent hot dishes of macaroni and cheese and baked beans.

After a few months on the job, Ellen had made friends with some of the League regulars, who often came in for lunch or dinner as a respite from the limited fare in the school's cafeteria. One of them was Bill. He invited her to cross the street after work and offered to show her around the place, which captivated her with its bohemian atmosphere and comfortable camaraderie.

She had always enjoyed going to the museums on school field trips and continued to visit them on her days off now that she was a working girl, but she'd never taken an art class and certainly never considered becoming an artist. When she shyly asked what it was like to draw pictures of naked people, Bill chuckled and told her she should find out for herself.

"Why not try it, just for fun?" he suggested. "Sign up for the Thursday night class with Laning, he's a good teacher for beginners."

So she did.

Being a sociable type, not afraid to start a conversation or ask a question, Ellen had no trouble breaking the ice with her classmates. Several of them were greenhorns like herself, and she gravitated to one in particular, a handsome redheaded boy who she guessed was about her own age.

She first bumped into him in the art supply store off the main lobby, where they were both trying to decide what they would need for the class.

The man behind the counter was being helpful. "The Laning class that starts at seven? Will you be painting or drawing?"

"Drawing," they both said at once, and Ellen giggled.

"There's an echo in here," said TJ, and they introduced themselves.

The counterman recommended a large pad of newsprint and a box of charcoal sticks for each of them. "Better get a kneaded eraser as well," he said with a grin. "Mistakes will happen."

Five

TJ took his time packing up, loitering by his locker in the hope that Ellen would stop chatting with Bill and head out to the lobby, where he planned to intercept her. His patience was rewarded when she broke off their conversation with a smile and a toss of her head. "'Night, Bill," she said as they parted, "see you at the Automat."

"You bet," he replied.

Their easy familiarity gave TJ a sinking feeling. At least Bill wasn't taking her home. That would be his gambit.

He caught up with her as she reached the inner door that led to the vestibule. Holding it open with gentlemanly courtesy, he waved her through.

"Headed to the subway?" he asked, and got "Uh huh" in reply. "Let me walk you," he offered. "I'm going there, too."

They turned east, entered the BMT station on the corner

of Fifty-Seventh Street and Seventh Avenue, and boarded the downtown N express. It was only three stops to Union Square, where TJ would offer to escort Ellen to her door. Her place really was on his way home, so it would seem perfectly natural, as well as chivalrous.

On the short ride downtown, Ellen told him about her job. "It's kind of boring just making change all day, but the artists from the League liven things up. I'm not allowed to talk to them while I'm on duty, but I can sit with them on my breaks. That's how I met Bill, and he talked me into signing up for the life class. He's a really cool guy."

TJ had to ask the question that obviously arose from this information. It was none of his business, and it might even seem forward, but he needed to know.

"Are you going out with him?"

Ellen answered without hesitation. "Oh, no, silly. Bill's... well, he's not my type." She corrected herself. "I mean, I'm not his type."

TJ gave her a quizzical look. "I don't get it. I think you're...that is, who wouldn't want to...oh, hell." Mentally using stronger language to curse his ineptitude, he lapsed into embarrassed silence.

She laughed and cocked her head. "You're telling me you don't know? Bill's gay."

How could he have missed that? TJ was hardly unfamiliar with homosexuals. Before his father was promoted, he worked out of the Sixth Precinct. Any visit to the station house on Charles Street meant a walk through the heart of the gay bar scene. And two of his close friends, Alfonso Ossorio and Ted Dragon, where what gays used to be called back in 1956 when he first met them: pansies. But they were older men and an established couple, not like someone his own age, single, and not at all swish. Bill definitely didn't fit any of the Christopher Street stereotypes. He looked and acted straight.

"How do you know that?" TJ blurted, rather rudely, but Ellen answered frankly. She realized she'd surprised him and didn't want to rub his nose in his naiveté.

"Well, I won't kid you, I was interested in him," she admitted. "He's good-looking, fun to be around, and he seemed to like me a lot, so I hoped it might go somewhere. I don't have a steady boyfriend, and I thought he might be a candidate. But he never took it any further than pals, so I began to get suspicious. A girl can tell when a guy's not, how can I put it, not inclined. So I just up and asked him if he was queer, and he admitted it. We were both actually kind of relieved. He told me not to use the word queer, because it's considered derogatory. He said, 'I'm glad you know I'm gay, so you don't think I was stringing you along.' He was right. At that stage, it was just a crush, but if I'd fallen in love with him it would have been terrible."

Ellen's revelations had stirred up a variety of feelings in TJ: annoyance with himself for failing to realize that Bill was gay, gratitude to Bill for convincing Ellen to take the life class, and relief that she wasn't serious about anyone else. He was also feeling respect for her level-headed response to Bill's admission. He wondered how he'd react if a girl he fancied turned out to be a lesbian.

He wanted to tell her how well she'd handled it, but before he could come up with an appropriate way of phrasing it, the train squealed to a halt at the Union Square station.

———

As they emerged onto Fourteenth Street, they heard someone with a bullhorn addressing a crowd of about a hundred people massed under the equestrian statue of George Washington. The general's right hand, raised in a farewell gesture that signaled the departure of the British from New York City at the end of the Revolutionary War, seemed to be a symbolic benediction to the group that had gathered to protest the military draft.

Many held homemade placards with slogans like *END THE WAR NOW* and *HELL, NO, WE WON'T GO.*

In front of a banner that read Vietnam Veterans Against the War, a man wearing army fatigues was ranting at the assembly.

"I enlisted," he shouted. "I went willingly on the scenic tour of tropical resorts and combat zones in Vietnam, all expenses paid. That was my choice. I'm not saying it was right or wrong, but I made the decision. I wanted to be a war hero, doing righteous battle against an evil enemy. Instead I saw villages in flames, rice paddies turned into graveyards, innocent people massacred, victims of American arrogance and stupidity."

The crowd answered with cries of "Right on, man!" "Fuckin' A!" and "You tell it, brother!"

The veteran continued, his voice rising even higher. "The same arrogance and stupidity are forcing a whole generation of young men to sacrifice themselves against their will! The war is wrong, and the draft is wrong! I'm calling on you to resist conscription! If you're eligible, don't register! If you have a draft card, burn it!"

Someone had dragged a trash barrel to the center of the rally and set fire to it. A couple of long-haired youths approached it, each holding a Selective Service System Registration Certificate high above his head for all to see. Amid encouraging cheers and applause, they solemnly consigned their draft cards to the flames. Others stepped forward, and soon a dozen or more cards had been incinerated.

On the periphery, as they walked north through the square, Ellen and TJ watched the spectacle with apprehension. Two years earlier, President Lyndon Johnson had signed legislation that made the burning of a draft card a federal crime punishable by up to five years in prison or a $10,000 fine. If the cops showed up, which they were likely to do given the size of the crowd, the noise, and the burning trash barrel—a misdemeanor in New York City—those protesters, who believed they were exercising their rights of free speech and public assembly, would wind up in jail.

Union Square was the Thirteenth Precinct's responsibility. "I'm glad this isn't happening in my dad's jurisdiction," said TJ, "or my mom's."

"How's that?" asked Ellen, unaware that both his parents were police officers. He explained that his Irish American father was a deputy chief assigned to headquarters at 240 Centre Street, and his Cuban-American mother was a detective based at the Twenty-Third Precinct in Spanish Harlem.

"Cops on both sides, you see. That's why I'm going to John Jay. Don't get me wrong, they didn't push me, not hard, anyway. I'd say they encouraged me, but they want me to make up my own mind."

"And have you?"

"No, not really. It's too early to say. I'm only a sophomore. I'm thinking of majoring in forensic psychology. Professor Morales got me interested in it. He used to be my mother's boss at the Twenty-Third. He was her mentor, really believed in her and helped her get promotions, which isn't easy for a female cop. When I was little I called him Tío Hector—that's Spanish for uncle. He's retired now, and he teaches at John Jay. Anyway, as far as a law enforcement career goes, I haven't decided. Ever since I was a kid I've wanted to be an artist. That's why I started taking class at the League."

"Far out," said Ellen as they reached the door of her building. "Where did you get that idea? Not from your folks, I bet."

TJ looked at his watch. "I'd better explain another time.

It's almost eleven o'clock, and I have an early class tomorrow. And you have work." Not that he was eager to say good night, but a postponement gave him the opportunity to make a date.

She beat him to it. "How about tomorrow? I get off at five thirty. Meet me here at six and I'll show you the Up 'n' Down. Then maybe we can catch a movie at Cinema Village."

A big smile lit up TJ's face. "It's a deal," he agreed.

Six

The building at 332 East Fifteenth Street was every bit as shabby as Ellen had described. The stoop steps were worn and cracked, paint peeled off the outside door, and several tiles were missing from the vestibule floor.

"This is just the beginning," advised Ellen as she unlocked the inside door. In the dimly lit hall they were greeted by the promised fragrance of uncollected garbage.

"Wait 'til you see the staircase. We're on the fourth floor, so you'll have plenty of time to appreciate it. Just don't lean on the banister," she cautioned. The groaning treads slanted off at an alarming angle, suggesting structural as well as aesthetic deficiency. TJ was relieved when they reached Ellen's door safely.

She unlocked it and called out, "Anybody home?"

"Only me" was the answer from her roommate, who popped her head out the bedroom door. A thick mop of unruly strawberry-blond curls fell over her face as she darted back into the room. "Here and gone," she announced from inside. "Gotta run. I'm late for work." Out she came, and TJ did a gaping double take.

To say that Michele Kendall was imposing would be an understatement. Even without her high-heeled boots she was six feet tall, with a build somewhere between a Valkyrie and a linebacker. She towered over the five-foot-three Ellen, and, counting the boots, had at least four inches on TJ. Her wayward hair billowed around a pretty, heart-shaped face that seemed out of place on such a formidable body, made all the more impressive by a black leather miniskirt and a V-neck floral blouse that showed off her ample cleavage.

"I see you didn't warn him," said Michele to her roommate, and to TJ, "Don't worry, I only bite people I don't like, and I think I like you already." Before he could apologize, she grabbed her jacket and shoulder bag and was through the door, treating them to a hearty laugh followed by "Don't wait up for me."

Trying hard to suppress her own laughter, Ellen gave TJ a few minutes to process Michele. She took his coat, removed her own, and hung them both on hooks behind the door.

"She is pretty amazing, isn't she? I've known her since we were both this high, though it's hard to imagine her ever being little. She certainly has, ah, blossomed."

"You're not kidding. What does she do that she's off to work at this hour?"

"She's a waitress at The Bitter End, that's a folk club on Bleecker Street," said Ellen. She moved into the tiny kitchen, and TJ followed. She opened the icebox and asked, "You want a beer, or would you rather have a Coke?"

He saw a couple of bottles of Knickerbocker on the shelf. The New York beer had always been his parents' drink of choice, but the brewery had gone out of business two years ago. He asked where she'd got the Knicks and was told that they were in the icebox when she and Michele moved in last March.

"There used to be six," she said, "but we opened two to toast our arrival and drank two on Michele's birthday in August. Let's kill the last two while you tell me about your artistic ambitions."

She took the bottles, a church key, and a couple of glasses into the sparsely furnished living room that doubled as a dining area. No sofa, no television set, just a couple of well-worn armchairs with a coffee table between them, a round dining table with two mismatched chairs, a bricks-and-boards bookshelf, and a small cabinet with a portable record player on top. In one corner were a couple of guitar cases and a music stand, which attracted TJ's attention.

"Do you play?" he asked. "Or are they Michele's?"

"We both do," she answered. "We took lessons together when we were in high school. In fact, we have a regular gig at The Bitter End's Tuesday night hootenanny. That's how she got her job there. We went to the audition and the manager not only put us on the bill, he said they were looking for a part-time waitress to work Friday through Sunday and asked if she would be interested. She goes to Hunter during the week, so it worked out really well for her."

Ellen opened the beers and poured them. "Why don't you come down and catch our act next Tuesday night?" she suggested.

"Sure," said TJ, "I've never been to The Bitter End. Sounds like fun." *What a hypocrite I am,* he thought. He was not a folk music fan—like Laning, he considered it old hat, not to mention patronizing when sung and played by city slickers who knew nothing of its cultural roots. But, as with Ellen's awkward drawing, it didn't matter to him whether he liked it or not, as long as he would be there as her date.

"Let's get back to your story," prompted Ellen as she sipped her Knick. "I want to know why you're so keen to be an artist."

He told her about his youthful adventures in East Hampton and his friendship with Ossorio and Dragon. "Remember what Mr. Laning said about Thomas Hart Benton's student, Jackson Pollock? Well, Alfonso and Ted were close friends of his. We visit them every summer. They have Pollock's paintings hanging in their house. I even have one of his prints. I won it in a raffle our first summer out there, when I was eight. That's when Pollock was killed in a car crash, and my folks and I were there when it happened. His car almost hit us before it veered off. We saw it run into the woods and flip over. Actually, to be honest, I didn't see it. I was asleep on the back seat and woke up when my dad hit the brakes."

"Gosh," said Ellen, "that must have been scary."

"It was a shock, all right. But there was a lot more to it. I'll tell you the whole story some time. Point is, my folks helped with the investigation, and that's how we met Alfonso and Ted. Alfonso taught me to interpret Pollock's work, and his own paintings, too."

He leaned forward earnestly. "It's fascinating, Ellen, the way artists can communicate without words. And I don't mean by illustration, like storytelling with pictures. I mean something deeper, on an emotional level, the way Pollock and Alfonso and other abstract painters can. I want to do that, too. Of course I know I have to learn the basics first, like Mr. Laning says, just like Pollock learned the basics from Benton. If I can't do that I'll give it up, but I have to try."

Ellen reached across the table and put her hand over his. Her warm touch made his heart jump, but he kept his composure. Her eyes met his. She smiled her endearing smile and spoke softly, reassuringly.

"We have an agreement, remember? We shook on it. We're both going to work harder. After all, we've only been at it for two weeks, and then only one night a week. We can't expect miracles."

Oh, yes we can, thought TJ. *One just happened.*

Seven

Since it opened in 1961, The Bitter End, at 147 Bleecker Street, had been one of Greenwich Village's most popular music clubs. It was a coffeehouse, with no liquor license—that thirst could be quenched next door at the Dugout. The owner, Fred Weintraub, had stripped one wall down to the bare brick and enhanced the bohemian flavor by papering the other walls with enlarged reproductions of Surrealist collages from Max Ernst's 1934 graphic novel, *Une Semaine de Bonté*.

The stage was a low platform in front of the brick wall, with a few lights slung from a ceiling rack. No wings or backstage area, and a minuscule dressing room. The sound system was rudimentary, but amplification wasn't really a problem in the intimate 150-seat club. There were a couple of booths, but the main seating consisted of recycled church pews. The place had a funky, makeshift vibe that meshed perfectly with the entertainment: classic folk singers like Pete Seeger, Odetta, and Josh White, and younger singer-songwriters carrying on the troubadour tradition, as well as stand-up comedy from newcomers Woody Allen, Richard Pryor, and Bill Cosby.

By 1967 the club had changed with the times. Straight folk music was on the wane. As the manager, Paul Colby, put it dryly, "How many times can Michael row his fucking boat ashore?" Amid great controversy, Bob Dylan had transitioned from acoustic guitar to electric, from folk to folk-rock, and taken a generation with him, so The Bitter End was now booking more rockers than folkies. But the Tuesday night hootenanny continued as a showcase for new talent that sometimes hit the big time. Agents and managers would drop in to scout the acts. Artists like Simon and Garfunkel, Carly Simon, Richie Havens, and many others were "discovered" at the Bitter End hoots.

On this particular Tuesday night, as TJ, Ellen, and Michele settled into one of the pews, Ellen explained the setup.

"The hamburgers are pretty good, and they have coffee, soft drinks, and soda fountain specialties like the Frosty Freud, that's coffee with an ice cream float." She signaled the waitress, and they ordered Cokes. The girls didn't want to eat until after their performance, so TJ said he'd wait, too.

"Michele and I will probably go on early," Ellen said. "Unknowns like us usually do the warm-up spot. Or we might go on late, after the main acts. It depends on who shows up. Ed or Oscar will let us know."

"Who are they?" asked TJ.

"Ed McCurdy is the emcee, and he lines up the acts. Oscar Brand is a sort of folk-music impresario. I'm surprised you haven't heard of him, he's had a radio show on WNYC for years. It's called 'Folksong Festival,' and a lot of the singers he has on the show also perform here." TJ had neglected to tell her that he was not a folk music fan. His favorite deejay was Cousin Brucie on WABC, New York City's premier rock station.

She pointed to a group in one of the booths. "That's Brand in the black turtleneck. McCurdy is the guy with the goatee. We call him Dirty McCurdy because he loves to sing songs with off-color lyrics. The guys on the other side of the booth are Paul Colby, the club manager, and Theodore Bikel, the actor, the one with the full beard. I'm sure you've heard of him, he's on Broadway right now in *Fiddler on the Roof.* He's also a terrific folk singer. He and Oscar started the Newport Folk Festival. Looks like they're working out the lineup now."

"That's funny," said Michele, "Theo shouldn't be here now. He only comes in after the theater. I see him late on Saturday nights. Must be some reason why he took off from Fiddler tonight."

As if that were his cue, McCurdy detached himself from

the booth and headed toward them. Instead of his usual warm smile, his face wore a troubled look. Ignoring TJ, he bent low to speak to Ellen and Michele in a voice just above a whisper.

"Listen, girls, there's been a change of program. Woody Guthrie died this afternoon, so we're going to devote the whole evening to a memorial tribute. A lot of his old friends will be dropping in, so I don't know whether I can put you on."

Their disappointment took a back seat to their sorrow. Michele reached out and took McCurdy's hand.

"Jeez, Ed, that's terrible news. I guess it wasn't unexpected, he's been sick for so long, but it's still a blow. It's okay if you can't use us tonight. We understand." Ellen nodded in agreement.

"I knew you'd say that," McCurdy replied, "but hang around just the same. It'll be a night to remember, and I'll call on you if I can. I know you have some of Woody's songs in your repertoire." He squeezed Michele's hand, managed a meager smile, and returned to the booth.

In spite of his lack of interest in folk music, TJ had heard of Woody Guthrie. Bob Dylan had revived some of his protest songs, anthems of the Great Depression, and his son, Arlo Guthrie, was active in the anti-war movement.

"Oh, wow," said Ellen, turning to look at two young men carrying guitar cases who had just entered the club. "It's Arlo. And that's Dylan with him." The crowd, unaware that the elder Guthrie had just died, greeted them with shouted hellos, waves, and victory signs. They politely waved back and made their way to a table at the rear, off to the side of the stage, reserved for musicians. Once they were seated, McCurdy signaled for the house lights to go down and walked onstage to the single microphone.

"Today," he began, "America lost the voice of its conscience when Woodrow Wilson Guthrie passed away after a long battle with Huntington's chorea." There were gasps and groans from the audience, and someone cried out "No!"

McCurdy waited for the hubbub to die down. "Woody never stood on this stage," he continued, "but his music has often filled this room. And it will again tonight! His son Arlo is with us to pay tribute to his dad in the best way, the only way that makes sense."

Arlo opened his carrying case and removed a venerable instrument—his father's Gibson, famously festooned with the motto "This Machine Kills Fascists." He mounted the platform, stepped to the mike, raised Woody's guitar, and began to sing "So Long, It's Been Good to Know Yuh."

The entire audience, many of them in tears, joined him in a reprise of the chorus.

"What's that? Do I hear somebody bawlin'? Better cut it out," Arlo scolded, "Woody don't like that. No siree, we're gonna make some *joyful* noise tonight! I see Mary Travers over there—come on up here, Mary. How about you, Bobby?" He turned to the musicians' table and beckoned Dylan to join them, which he did. So did Brand and Bikel.

"Wait for me, Arlo," came a voice from the door, and

Pete Seeger entered the club, brandishing the vintage banjo he played as a member of The Almanac Singers back in the 1940s, when Guthrie was the group's guitarist and chief songwriter.

"Let's give 'em a rousing version of 'Ain'ta Gonna Grieve', in the key of C," he called out as he hopped on stage, already playing the opening notes. Arlo quickly picked up the tune, and he and Seeger sang the first verse.

"Everybody on the chorus," shouted Seeger, and the room erupted in song.

That was just the opener. As word of Guthrie's death and the memorial hoot spread through the Village, more and more musicians stopped by to pay their respects. Ellen and Michele sat enthralled as some of the biggest stars in the folk world took the stage, and TJ was unexpectedly moved by the outpouring of admiration, affection, and respect for the man and his music, which he had to admit wasn't the cornball stuff he thought of as folk songs.

As performers came and went, those who had known Guthrie personally told anecdotes, some poignant, some hilarious. Everyone had his or her favorite Woody song, whether familiar, like "Pastures of Plenty," "This Train Is Bound for Glory," and "The Sinking of the Reuben James," or obscure. He had written hundreds of them, so there was no shortage of material.

When each musician came forward, Arlo whispered a brief comment, and at evening's end, it was apparent why. He wanted to save one particular number for the finale. As one a.m. approached, he stepped to the mike and thanked everyone for the great send-off.

"Woody's upstairs enjoyin' the concert, but it's past his bedtime, so I think we'd better wrap things up." He played the last eight notes of Guthrie's most famous song as, despite hands already sore from clapping, thunderous applause filled the room.

"Everybody, now," he prompted, and the crowd joined him: "This land is your land…"

———

Walking home through Washington Square Park, still bustling with activity on a mild autumn night, TJ, Ellen, and Michele reflected on the remarkable experience they'd just shared.

"I have a confession to make," said TJ somewhat sheepishly, "I don't really dig folk music, at least I didn't before tonight. I didn't realize that it's not just old-timey ballads and sea shanties. Guys like Guthrie were writing about what they were going through, and a lot of it was pretty rough. He wasn't afraid to speak out about war, poverty, injustice, racial prejudice, the kind of social and political problems we still have today. I can see why young guys like Dylan look up to him."

"You should read his autobiography, *Bound for Glory*," suggested Michele. "Dylan calls it his Bible. I'll lend you my copy if you like. Some of it's a little, well, embellished, but he's a great storyteller and he did lead a really colorful life."

"Thanks," he said, "I can get it the next time I visit the Up 'n' Down." It was pretty obvious that he was angling for an invitation.

"How about Thursday night after life class, on your way home?" said Ellen.

"You bet," he replied, encouraged.

Eight

Not long after the second break, Laning entered the studio with his guest, a short, stocky man in his seventies, dressed in a checkered flannel shirt and jeans that sagged under a sizeable paunch. His deeply creased face, like that of a weather-beaten farmer, scowled out from under a head of thick grizzled hair. His matching moustache pursed as he looked around the room, his intense gaze taking in the entire class in one long unblinking sweep.

"So this is your latest crop of geniuses," he said, addressing the students rather than their teacher, his voice sharp with sarcasm.

"That must be Benton," whispered Ellen to TJ. "Mr. Laning warned us he'd be intimidating, and he wasn't kidding."

"Gosh, he looks familiar," replied TJ under his breath. "Wasn't he at The Bitter End on Tuesday night?"

"Yeah, I think you're right. Didn't he come in right after Pete Seeger? He was wearing a lumber jacket, red and black check. I remember because it wasn't cold enough for such a heavy coat, so he looked out of place. I don't think he stayed long."

Laning spoke, his warm tenor lightening the mood cast by Benton's gruff baritone.

"This ornery fellow is Thomas Hart Benton, who has very graciously agreed to give you the benefit of his criticism. As I told you last week, Mr. Benton is in town for a major exhibition of his work at the Whitney, and I just learned that he's also being honored by the American Academy of Arts and Letters, which has elected him to membership."

"Reelected, you mean," Benton corrected him. "I quit that musty mausoleum a couple years ago when I got into a little spat with the management. Now they want me back. Can't think why." He grinned and winked at Laning, who good-naturedly took the bait.

"Why, Tom, you old rascal, of course they want you back. You're one of the country's top painters. The way I heard it, it was just a difference of opinion."

"Damn right it was. The goddamn president was supposed to be welcoming us to the spring meeting, but instead, he started mouthing off against the war, trashing the government, calling our policy immoral. I wasn't going to sit there and listen to that shit. I told him he had to take it back, or I'd quit. He didn't, and I did."

The Academy's president, Lewis Mumford, was a leading public intellectual, a humanistic philosopher, prolific author, and critic of modern technology whose ideas about the artist's role in society coincided with Benton's. In fact, the two men had long been friends, but Mumford's outspoken opposition to America's involvement in Vietnam—including a strongly worded open letter to President Johnson condemning the bombing of North Vietnam in 1965—caused the rift that prompted Benton's resignation.

Benton snorted a laugh. "Now I'm in and he's out— had to resign when they reinstated me over his objections. Serves the bastard right for foisting his bleeding-heart politics on us. Those commies in Indochina deserve everything we can throw at 'em."

Ellen leaned over to TJ. "Not shy about letting us know where he stands, is he?"

"Or what he thinks of people who disagree with him," he answered. "Can't wait to hear what he has to say about my drawing."

"Anyway," said Benton, striding toward the center of the room, his heavy boots resounding on the bare wood floor, "I'm not here to talk politics, don't want to get riled up. Truth is, I'm feeling nostalgic. Ain't been back to this drafty ol' barn in decades. It's over thirty years since I packed up and put New York behind me with no regrets. But me and the boys, we had some great times here. Yes sir, great times, in and out of class." His gaze softened for a moment as he reflected.

The bluster returned quickly. "Speaking of class, let's see if Ed here has managed to knock any of his wisdom into you." He approached one of the painters, a man in his late twenties, whose canvas was well advanced.

"Too flat," he barked. Gesturing at Wally, he continued, "That fellow is made of three-dimensional flesh and blood, solid muscle and bone. You've turned him into a paper cutout."

The painter, who was no novice, defended his approach. "I wasn't aiming for a literal depiction, Mr. Benton. I'm interested in the relational planes, the intersecting forms, the—"

"Bullshit," roared Benton. "You sound like a fucking Cubist. I got that nonsense out of my system before you were sucking your mother's tit. Warmed-over Parisian modernism is a dead end, totally irrelevant. It's empty, it has no meaning or purpose beyond aesthetics. American art should deal with reality—real life, real people—and appeal to ordinary folks, not to dipshit collectors and the nancyboys who run the museums. Climb down from your ivory tower and come back to earth, sonny."

Grabbing the startled painter by the arm, Benton pulled him toward the model stand and mounted the platform, dragging the man along with him.

"Feel this thigh," Benton demanded, pushing the student's hand onto Wally's leg. "Unlike your pathetic painting it's *real*, it has a *pulse*, it has *strength*." Wally winced, and the muscles in his jaw visibly tightened, but he remained still as Benton ran the student's fingers up and down his leg. "See what I mean? Feel the bump here, and the hollow there. Go back and paint that."

Now the whole class was startled. Laning often pointed out anatomical details on his models, but he never actually touched them, whereas Benton thought nothing of manhandling them. Laning was reminded of a quip from his student days: Benton's models better not be ticklish.

As soon as Benton relaxed his grip, the luckless painter retrieved his hand and retreated behind his easel, his dignity in shreds. Benton then turned his attention to the rest of the class, who were clearly dreading his critique. Laning decided to follow in his wake and do damage control if necessary.

Fortunately, Benton seemed to have vented all his spleen on his first victim. With the rest he was largely dismissive, grunting a few generalizations at the men's efforts and pointedly ignoring the women's. TJ got a whiff of bourbon fumes as Benton muttered something about lack of rhythm, then moved on past Ellen without a word.

His rounds completed, Benton swaggered toward the door, surveyed the room again, and shook his head. "Well, Ed, you've got your work cut out for you. I don't see a winner in the bunch."

Ever the diplomat, Laning replied, "It's early days for most of them, Tom. You wouldn't want to discourage them just yet, would you?"

"Why not? They're either inept or caught up in airy-fairy

theories, like your pseudocubist over there." He flipped his hand dismissively toward the object of his disdain. "Most of 'em wouldn't know a Cézanne from a Chardin, and the ones that do could never hope to paint like Chardin. The best they could manage would be clumsy Cézanne imitations, and he was a goddamn clumsy painter himself."

This antimodernist heresy was met with silence from the class. Even Laning was momentarily at a loss for words, then he rallied.

"I'm not ready to give up on them just yet, Tom. And I hope you don't mind my disagreeing with you about their potential." That got another scowl and snort from Benton, but Laning continued. "I seem to remember that you had a few unpromising students who went on to make names for themselves in the art world. I can think of one on particular." He grinned widely, and instead of taking umbrage Benton let out a guffaw.

"Hah, you got me there, Ed! Yeah, I have to admit Jack Pollock didn't have much goin' for him in the beginning. Couldn't draw worth shit, but by God he worked at it. Never missed a life class, studied the old masters, even made clay models like I did, to get a feel for the volumes and masses. He had such a desperate need to learn that I was sympathetic, and I flatter myself that I gave him the confidence to stick with it."

"No doubt about that," Laning agreed. "He told me himself that he'd have been lost without you."

"He was lost," said Benton, "a lost soul. He only found

himself in his painting, and when he stopped painting it was the end of him." He shook his head and made for the exit.

"Well, Tom, I'm sure the class is grateful for your guidance," said Laning, rather lamely, as he opened the door for Benton, who left without another word.

"Go ahead and take your break, Wally. I'll be back in a moment," he told the class as he followed his guest into the hall. "I'm just going to get Mr. Benton a taxi."

Benton had slumped down on one of the wooden benches that lined the hallway. One hand held the large bandanna he used as a handkerchief. The other held a hip flask. Alternately wiping his eyes with the bandanna and swigging from the flask, he grumbled, "Goddammit, Ed, I wish you hadn't mentioned Jack Pollock. Course you were right, he was the silk purse I made out of a sow's ear. We never lost touch, you know, even after he got famous. He's been dead for more than ten years, but I still miss the son of a bitch."

He blew his nose loudly and took another hit from the flask. "C'mon, let's go tie one on, get a real drink." Laning reminded him that the class was in session until ten.

"Fuck 'em," Benton croaked. "They don't need you to tell 'em how useless they are."

"You're right," said Laning. "You took care of that for me."

Nine

J esus, what a performance!" Bill was shaking his head in disbelief. "Swearing like a sailor, putting everybody down, embarrassing Mr. Laning. I wonder if he was just as offensive years ago when Pollock was in his class."

"He was tight, you know," said TJ. "I smelled liquor on his breath when he leaned over my drawing and gave me a two-word critique. 'No rhythm,' he said, that's all. Not much help."

"That's two words more than he gave me, or any of the other girls," Ellen pointed out. "It seems he's not interested in women." She realized that her statement had a double meaning. "Oh, I wasn't implying that he's gay. Mr. Laning said he's married."

Bill chuckled. "That doesn't mean anything. Lots of gay men have wives and children. Not that I'm saying Benton is one, but he does play the macho role way too strong, strutting around like he's trying to convince everyone, including himself, what a he-man he is."

Knowing that Bill was gay made TJ more receptive to his implication. He'd probably be able to recognize the closeted homosexual beneath the manly bluff and bluster.

"Look how he was groping Wally, forcing poor Al Schwartz to feel him up," Bill continued. "That's not normal. Bet he doesn't do that to female models."

Before they could speculate further, the studio door opened and Laning returned. He had managed to pour Benton into a cab and direct the driver to take him to the Hotel St. Regis, where the Whitney was putting him up. He doubted that the artist would head straight to his room, since the hotel's King Cole Bar, renowned for its Bloody Marys and its whimsical Maxfield Parrish mural, was open until one a.m.

Laning hastened to apologize on Benton's behalf. "I hope you'll pardon our distinguished guest," he began, "he wasn't himself tonight. I think he's having trouble adjusting to New York again after so many years away."

"As Benton would say, bullshit," whispered TJ to Ellen. "Didn't he mention that he comes to the Academy meetings, or did until he left in a snit? I bet he's been back to New York any number of times since he quit the League."

Ellen was more generous. "I'm sure Mr. Laning is just trying to make excuses for Mr. Benton's rudeness," she whispered back. "He couldn't have been expecting it, and he tried his best to get him to tone it down. He certainly wouldn't have invited him if he thought he'd behave like that."

Laning continued his conciliations. "I have to hand it to Tom. He's got that Midwest hayseed character down pat, but it's just an act to get a rise out of you. He loves to come on strong about how American he is, but he's a lot more cosmopolitan than he lets on. He was in Paris before the First World War and did some pretty radical abstract paintings. They'll probably have a few in the Whitney show, and you'll see how he carried over those principles into his figurative imagery."

"Here comes Wally," he said as the model removed his robe and mounted the platform. "Let's get back to business. As I'm sure you know, I don't believe you're all hopeless, far from it. And I don't think Tom Benton believes it, either. He was just being provocative, testing your resolve. Remember what he said about Pollock. Such an unpromising beginner, but look where his hard work and determination took him."

He paused. "If only Jackson could have controlled his drinking, he'd still be alive and painting masterpieces. Speaking of which," he added, lightening the mood, "let's see what my 'latest crop of geniuses' has come up with so far." He pointedly singled out the so-called pseudocubist whom Benton had humiliated.

"You've been here for a couple of years, Mr. Schwartz, so I know you've mastered figure study well enough to paint representationally if you want to. The real question is, are you satisfied with the way this figure is going?" The painter expressed some reservations.

"The planar quality is actually very good," Laning observed, "but I do see a problem with the proportions. It's really a matter of compositional balance, rather than any lack of naturalism. The integrity of the picture itself is the most important thing, regardless of the style." He gave Schwartz a reassuring smile, which was returned with gratitude.

———

On the subway ride home, Ellen and TJ couldn't help wondering about Benton's motivation. "Do you think it was just the liquor talking, or is he always so aggressive?" she asked.

"He'd certainly had a few," he replied, "but I'm betting he's just as belligerent when he's sober. Maybe fewer curse words, but just as confrontational. He strikes me as the kind who burns his bridges, then accuses the folks on the other side of setting the fire."

"That's a good way to make enemies," she said. "I wonder if his personality will affect the reaction to his Whitney show."

"What do you think?" he asked, though it wasn't really a question.

As they approached Ellen's building, she reminded TJ that Michele had offered to lend him Woody Guthrie's autobiography. Not that he needed reminding—he'd been planning to remind her so he'd have an excuse to go up to the apartment.

They entered the fragrant hallway and trudged up the creaking stairs. Walking behind Ellen, TJ appreciated her graceful navigation of the questionable staircase and admired the long blond hair that managed somehow to shine in the dim light. He kept his own ginger hair unfashionably short to avoid the taunts of the cadets who shared the Police Academy building on East Twentieth Street with John Jay College. Any male student with hair that reached below his earlobes would be called a fucking hippie or a flaming faggot, or hear a voice behind him ask, "Is that a guy or a girl?"

When they got to the fourth floor, Michele greeted them with her usual ebullience.

"Thank God you're here at last," she cried, jumping up from her chair and embracing them both, as if she'd known TJ forever. "I was dying of existential loneliness, and Kierkegaard gives me the creeps." She indicated the philosophy textbook open on the dining table. "We have a quiz tomorrow or I wouldn't be reading that depressing stuff. I'm sure you'll find *Bound for Glory* a lot more entertaining." She marched to the makeshift bookshelf and retrieved it.

"It came out in 1943, when he was living in New York and involved with the Almanac Singers, but it's all about his childhood, growing up out West, riding the rails, and surviving the Dust Bowl," said Michele as she handed the book to TJ. "He illustrated it himself. He could draw as well as write songs, sing, and play the guitar."

TJ thanked her and flipped through the book, enjoying

Guthrie's charming sketches drawn from life on the road. Crude but vigorous, they captured the playful aspects of his ramblings as well as some of the darker, more perilous episodes. Meanwhile Ellen brought in two Cokes and set them on the dining table. Michele already had one going.

"Time for a break, you bookworms," said Ellen as she popped the bottle caps. "I want to tell Michele about our so-called distinguished visitor to class tonight, Thomas Hart Benton. Turns out he was at The Bitter End on Tuesday. Don't know if you remember him, he was the little old guy in the lumber jacket. Came in right behind Pete Seeger."

"I didn't notice anyone like that," said Michele. "Maybe if I saw him again I'd remember. Who is he anyway?"

"TJ and I will probably never forget him! He's a famous painter—at least he used to be famous maybe thirty years ago—in town from the Midwest for a show of his work at the Whitney. Mr. Laning invited him to talk to our class, but instead of words of wisdom and helpful criticism we got curses and insults. He'd been drinking, and his language would have made a sailor blush."

"Sounds like a real charmer. What did you do?"

"What could we do? We had to sit there and take it. Actually I got off light because he paid no attention to me or my work. The men had to deal with the crap he was dishing out by the carload. Poor Mr. Laning was so embarrassed, but he managed to get him out the door before he did too much damage to our egos."

"You know," interjected TJ, "our friend Bill said something

interesting after Benton left. We were all kind of in shock, but Bill said he thought maybe it was a cover-up act."

"Cover-up for what?" asked Michele.

"That maybe Benton is gay, and was putting on a tough-guy act to mask it. Actually it was Ellen who started us down that road. She said something about him not liking women, and Bill picked up on it."

"Interesting," mused Michele. "Think there's anything to it?"

"I know somebody who I bet can give me the lowdown on Benton," said TJ. "My friend Alfonso will know if there's anything to what Bill was suggesting. I'll give him a call tomorrow."

Ten

After he determined that the body curled up on the model stand in Studio Nine was in fact dead, Chris Gray experienced what he later described as bewilderment, quickly followed by foreboding. Once his initial shock wore off, he thought maybe the man had been taken ill, collapsed, and died. The way he was huddled, it looked like he'd had a cramp or a spasm. But Chris dismissed that right away, since the body was completely obscured by the drapery. Even if the fellow had tried to cover himself—maybe he got the chills, didn't that happen with a heart attack or a stroke?—he couldn't have wrapped himself up like that. No, it appeared that someone else had deliberately covered him. Who would do such a thing, and why?

With a sinking feeling, Chris realized he knew the answers to those questions.

Eleven

Returning home from John Jay on Friday afternoon, TJ found the apartment deserted. Both his parents were still on the job. He dumped his books on the hall table, hung his jacket in the closet, sat down at the telephone stand and dialed 516-324-1472. The call was answered, "The Creeks, Dragon speaking."

"Hi, Ted, this is TJ. How are you?"

"Well, my young friend, this is a surprise, and a very pleasant one. I hope you're calling to invite yourself for a visit. It's been weeks since we had the pleasure of your company."

"I miss you, too, Ted, but I'm not angling for an invitation. What with college during the week and my job at the candy store on the weekends, I don't have even one day off.

Actually I'm calling because of something that happened in my Thursday night class at the League. I need to ask Alfonso about it. Is he around?"

"He's in the studio, finally. He has a New York show coming up in November, and as you know he wasn't working on it when you and your charming parents were visiting in August. He spent two weeks doing nothing but entertaining the Fitzgeralds, who are a bad influence on him," teased Ted. But TJ wasn't falling for his good-natured ribbing.

"Well, I'm gonna continue the family tradition and interrupt him again," he said. "Will you please buzz the studio and ask if I can to speak to him? It won't take long, I promise."

"I am here but to serve," offered Ted with mock humility. "Hold the phone while I see if my master deigns to be interrupted."

Moments later the call was switched through to the studio extension. A delighted Ossorio greeted TJ warmly.

"No, no, don't apologize, Señor TJ. It's long past time for a break. I lose all track when I'm working. In fact, I forgot to eat the lunch Ted left for me in the anteroom. If you don't mind I'll put down the phone for a moment and retrieve it. And perhaps you'll forgive my bad manners if I work on my sandwich while you tell me why you're calling. Otherwise my rumbling stomach may drown you out."

As Ossorio belatedly tucked into lunch, TJ described Benton's visit to the life class and the impression he made on the students. His goal was to find out if Ossorio thought

Benton was gay, but not wanting to offend his mentor, he chose his words carefully, starting with a generalization.

"What do you think of Benton?"

Having finished half his sandwich, Ossorio took a sip of the iced tea that had long since lost its chill and cleared his throat.

"Never met the man," he began, "but Jackson spoke of him often. And of course he has a reputation that lingers in the New York art world long after his departure. Evidently, from what you tell me, he hasn't mellowed."

"What was Pollock's opinion?"

Ossorio addressed the artistic aspect of the relationship. "Publicly, Jackson discounted Benton's influence. He called him 'a strong personality to react against.' That was disingenuous, to say the least, but perhaps understandable for an artist whose work seemed, on the surface at any rate, so antithetical to everything Benton represented. To Benton's credit he has never repudiated Jackson, and in fact has been very generous in acknowledging his student's innovations and surprisingly modest in refusing to take credit for them.

"His chief complaint about modern painting, Jackson's included, is what he perceives as its lack of content, that it doesn't communicate what he calls 'human meanings.' He goes on about such things at great length in his books, articles, and interviews. He's an excellent writer, quite the opposite of what you'd expect from someone who presents himself as anti-intellectual. He's also, I'm told, an eloquent speaker. Unfortunately he doesn't always show up sober, so his public appearances are sometimes, shall we say, problematic."

"He and Pollock had that in common," remarked TJ, whose own momentary brush with the late artist, driving drunk, was soon followed by the car crash in which he was killed.

Ossorio continued, "Jackson once told me that the only thing Benton taught him was how to drink a quart of whiskey a day. That was nonsense, and I must say I expressed my disagreement to him. As I said, I've never met Benton, but I can see echoes of his aesthetic principles even in Jackson's most abstract compositions. And there's another important aspect of Benton's influence that's usually overlooked, something that Jackson did own up to when I confronted him."

"What do you mean?" asked TJ, intrigued.

"Benton insisted that his students draw on personal experience—practical knowledge rather than theoretical principles—for inspiration. Of course he was talking about the kind of fieldwork he does himself, cross-country road trips, hanging out with the dirt farmers, coal miners, stevedores, and such. Jackson bought into that American Scene rhetoric in the beginning, but it didn't sustain him. He soon realized that a more valid form of personal experience was subjective, looking inward for meaning.

"You and I have often talked about the influence of nature on Jackson's work, not in terms of subject matter but as an elemental force that motivates the spontaneous outpouring of imagery. Few people appreciate how that relates to Benton's experiential philosophy because his results and Jackson's are so different."

TJ realized that the discussion was ranging far from the issue he wanted to address. How to take Ossorio back to Benton's personality, and by extension get to the fraught question of his sexuality?

"I remember your telling me that Pollock often acted very macho, but that it was a pose to cover up his extreme sensitivity. Do you think he learned that from Benton, too?"

"No, I think that came from his youth out West, though Benton certainly reinforced it. Things are different now, but back in the early 1930s, when Jackson was a student, artists were considered effete. To call someone 'artistic' was almost an insult. The popular image was either a female dilettante painting insipid landscapes en plein air or a limp-wristed male in smock and beret, head in the clouds, toiling away in a garret.

"Mind you, another common stereotype is the sexually promiscuous artist, male or female, someone who lives outside the social norms of morality. The parties known as artists and models balls that many art schools and societies used to throw annually were viewed as little better than orgies. Who knew what sort of deviant behavior was tolerated, even promoted?"

This gave TJ the opening he was after. "You mean guys like Benton and Pollock would act tough so no one would think they were deviants?"

"Yes, I believe that has a lot to do with it. Especially for

Benton, whose family didn't approve of his becoming an artist. Jackson's mother encouraged him and his brothers, and his father went along, but Benton's father was dead set against it. He was a hard-drinking, two-fisted politician who wanted his son to follow in his footsteps. They were at loggerheads from the time young Tom learned to talk, which meant talking back, one stubborn Missouri mule to another. He wrote about his rebelliousness quite candidly in his memoirs."

"But is Benton's macho act a cover-up? You should have seen him barging around the studio, swearing a blue streak, offending everyone in the class, especially the women. He more or less ignored them and spent his time belittling the men."

"That's his reputation in a nutshell," said Ossorio. "He seldom has a good word for anyone except his abject followers and those who agree with his jingoistic politics. He plays offense and defense simultaneously, and it's made him plenty of enemies."

This information merely confirmed what TJ already knew or supposed and didn't get to the question at hand. Ossorio was one of the art world's most formidable gossips, but apparently all he knew about Benton was common knowledge. TJ realized he'd have to look elsewhere if he wanted to satisfy his curiosity. Maybe it wasn't worth pursuing, and in fact he wondered why he was so curious in the first place. What difference did it make if Benton was gay or not?

He checked his watch and realized he needed to leave soon to meet Ellen at the New School, a short walk from his apartment, where they were planning to visit the murals Laning had told them about.

"Benton's certainly a peculiar character. I've never met anyone like him, and it's been helpful to get your insights. I really appreciate your taking the time, Alfonso. I apologize for imposing on you. I know you're busy getting ready for your show next month, so I won't keep you any longer."

Ossorio was his usual gracious self. "No imposition at all, Señor TJ. You know how much I enjoy discussing art with you. You must keep me apprised of your progress at the League. We haven't spoken of that at all, so we shall have to save it for next time, which I trust will be soon. Until then, buenas tardes y buena suerte."

Twelve

TJ left a note for his parents to let them know he'd be back in an hour or two. They didn't monitor his comings and goings, but he was a thoughtful son and didn't want them to worry about him when they expected him to be at home. An only child, he could sense that they were protective, though they kept it well concealed. He'd never given them cause for concern, but they felt it nonetheless. In their line of work they'd encountered too many nice, respectable parents who'd lost their children to gangs or drugs to believe it couldn't happen to them.

He caught up with Ellen as she walked down Fifth Avenue from the Union Square subway station toward Twelfth Street. Late afternoon was turning into early evening, and the setting sun's rays slanted along the crosstown streets, bathing them in the most appealing form of urban daylight. It backlit

Ellen, stopped at the corner of Fifth and Thirteenth, as she turned to acknowledge TJ's call. "Wait up, Ellen, here I am," he said. Twilight brought out the sheen of her lustrous hair and framed her slender silhouette. Her shapely legs emerging from her plaid miniskirt completed the delightful image, and TJ silently thanked the sun for this visual benison.

She smiled a greeting, followed by "Hi, there, TJ." He resisted the urge to kiss her and decided not even to take her hand, just to say hi and return her smile. Their relationship was at that awkward early stage when a false move on his part could spell disaster. He wanted desperately to be more than a friend, but knew that moving too quickly risked putting her off. Then she might decide to quit the life class, and he'd never see her again.

He sensed that Ellen wasn't what was known in the locker room as "easy." Even in those days of counterculture rebellion, when girls were on the pill and boys thought nothing of asking for sex on the first date, he was still a virgin and he assumed she was, too. Of course that was just a guess.

He really knew nothing about her, except that he was quickly falling in love with her—just like his father had fallen for his mother, more or less at first sight, back in 1943. But they'd been older, both in their midtwenties, and had had other lovers before each other. Their life experience had helped them recognize the signs of mutual attraction, whereas TJ was very much at sea.

His relationships with other girls had been platonic or never went beyond soul kissing and heavy petting. Not that he would admit it to his male friends, all of whom, to hear them tell it, had been rutting like stags since puberty. He suspected that much of their talk was just empty boasting, but not all of it for sure. He was too innately honest to indulge in outright fabrication, but he did hint at romantic encounters that went beyond third base. At least he hit home runs in his dreams, which now featured Ellen as the player who embraced him at the plate.

Walking together, they turned right on West Twelfth Street toward number sixty-six, the New School for Social Research's sleek International Style building. With an open enrollment policy and progressive philosophy, the New School was a sociopolitical counterpart of the Art Students League. From its inception in 1919 it was devoted, as its motto had it, "to the living spirit." After the rise of Fascism and Nazism in Europe, many intellectuals fleeing persecution found a safe haven on its faculty.

The founding director, Alvin Johnson, was responsible for commissioning Joseph Urban, a Viennese-born modernist architect, to design the building, and a Mexican muralist, José Clemente Orozco, to decorate its dining room and lounge. Orozco's art dealer and lover, Alma Reed, got him the job, and when Benton found out he was furious. Although he admired Orozco, both as an artist and a friend, he envied the Mexican's reputation as one of the foremost muralists of the day. Reed was Benton's dealer, too, and she knew very well that after several unsuccessful mural proposals he was itching for such an opportunity.

Never reticent about self-promotion, he lobbied Johnson and was rewarded with an offer to decorate the walls of the school's boardroom. Like Orozco, he did the job virtually for free, demanding only an unlimited supply of eggs for the tempera paint he planned to use, in emulation of the old masters. Orozco painted in buon fresco, another age-old European mural medium that had also been used by indigenous Mesoamericans, but Benton had no expertise in that demanding, labor-intensive technique. In fact, notwithstanding his failed schemes, he had no mural experience at all. Yet, with typical grandiosity, he wanted to stand alongside acknowledged master muralists, up there with Giotto, Piero, and Cennini, so he chose egg tempera, the medium they favored.

———

An inquiry at the reception desk directed Ellen and TJ to the third floor, where, they were told, Mr. Benton was leading a small party on a tour of his murals. They almost turned away, somewhat relieved at avoiding another encounter with the obnoxious artist, but the receptionist suggested they go on up and ask if it was all right to join the tour.

"After all," she said, "it isn't every day you get to hear the paintings explained by the man who painted them." She had a point, and after a brief consultation they decided to take her advice.

They found the group gathered outside the boardroom awaiting Benton, who was said to be in the men's room.

They approached the leader, a New School board member, mentioned that they were art students eager to see the murals, and were invited to join the tour as his guests.

"I'm sure Benton won't remember us," said TJ confidentially to Ellen. "I doubt he even remembers visiting the class, considering his condition."

Before she could reply, Benton rounded the corner and came toward the group. His gait was just a bit unsteady, and TJ and Ellen glanced at each other and nodded, as if to say, looks like he's in the same condition now.

The artist bowed ceremoniously and, with a flourish, waved a hand above his head and pointed to the boardroom door. "Right this way, ladies and gentlemen," he bellowed, "the show is about to begin. The three-ring spectacle that is America awaits you!" Then he marched on in, and the tour trailed along in his wake.

Those in the party who had not seen the murals before were visibly stunned by their effect. The pictures stretched almost from floor to ceiling and circled the room, broken only by the entrance door and two windows in the opposite wall, where the largest panel, a montage of so-called instruments of power, from a speeding locomotive and soaring plane to a hydroelectric dam driving a piston engine, fairly pulsed with energy. The main program, in six sections of overlapping vignettes separated by strips of silver molding, was a kind of travelogue around the country, depicting life-size American character types—the steelworker, the farmer, the coal miner, the lumberjack—engaged in manual labor.

As TJ scanned the scenes, he realized that all the workers were male. Muscles bulging, bodies poised for action or straining at their tasks, they toiled productively, building a strong, confident nation full of steaming trains, bustling docks, roaring blast furnaces, and fertile fields. Only in the miners' slumping bodies and downcast faces were there any signs of fatigue. When TJ mentioned this to Ellen, and pointed out that women were conspicuously absent, she directed him to a small detail at the bottom of the panel dominated by a huge oil derrick and a welder.

"Look," she whispered, "there's a working girl." It was a prostitute, vamping a dejected Indian—both victims of westward industrialization.

After taking in this dynamic panorama, those who looked behind them saw two even more action-packed panels representing city activities in the Roaring Twenties, where women finally figured prominently. Their labor, however, involved burlesque dancing and circus acts, with a little Salvation Army psalm singing thrown in. Except for a bored subway straphanger with incongruous arm-wrestler muscles, the ladies were enjoying themselves at a revival meeting, the movies and a dance hall, flirting at a soda fountain, and necking on a park bench. Apart from a portrait of Benton's wife, Rita, holding their son, who raised a hand as if to bless his teacher, the female presence was distinctly déclassé. For that matter, so was the artist's self-portrait, emerging from the lower right corner of the urban entertainment scene. With his sleeve rolled up to expose a sinewy

arm holding a paintbrush, he towered over the seated figure of Johnson—in life a much larger man. Clinking glasses of bootleg whiskey, they toasted the mural's completion.

Surprisingly, Benton had remained silent while the group dispersed to study and discuss the various panels. Now he was ready to hold forth.

"What you see around you," he began, "is a true portrait of America, the America I know from firsthand experience. Not only the Midwest of my childhood, but the whole she-bang, city and country, coast to coast. Before I touched a brush to the canvas, I spent thirty years studying the places and the people you see on these walls. Every square inch is true!" He crossed his arms, and his dark eyes swept the room with the same intensity he had directed toward Laning's life class, as if daring anyone to contradict him.

Most of the group remained politely mute, but there were a couple who could not let such a blanket statement go unchallenged. The New School board member, for one.

"As you no doubt recall, Mr. Benton, there was a lot of controversy when the murals were unveiled." Benton snickered, but didn't interrupt. "Critics took you to task for painting too rosy a picture when the economy was in a slump. They said the title should be *America Yesterday*, not *America Today*."

"Poppycock," rejoined Benton. He had evidently decided to clean up his language for the occasion. "The picture isn't all that rosy. Look over there. Didn't I show a Negro chain gang, and the backbreaking labor of cotton pickers and a dirt

farmer stooped over his harrow? Ask them if that's a rosy picture." He gestured toward the opposite wall. "Look at the beaten-down coal miners, not only exhausted but now out of work because the mine is on fire. Look at their flimsy houses clinging to a slag heap and tell me that picture is rosy!"

The board member continued to press. "That doesn't answer the charge that your overall program depicts prosperity and ignores the very real economic hardships brought on by the Great Depression."

Benton jabbed a finger at his challenger. "Don't forget, sir, that the downturn was barely a year old when these murals were painted. How was I—how was anyone—to know it would become a decade-long economic, social, and political catastrophe? The spirit I captured in these pictures was, I felt, strong enough to get us out of the slump. With hindsight, maybe I was wrong to be so optimistic, but I had faith in the American spirit, and I still do." He swept his arm around dramatically. "People like these brought us back to prosperity. I believed in these people, and they didn't let me down!"

"Why did you make them look so distorted?" came a question from the back. The group turned to look at Ellen, who had voiced what several others thought but didn't dare say out loud.

"My, my," said Benton, cocking an eyebrow and breaking into a grin, "you're a spunky gal, and a lot prettier than most of my critics. Stuart Davis, the cookie-cutter Cubist, had a face that could stop a clock, and Alfred Stieglitz, a jumped-up Jew from Hoboken, was as ugly as the abstract art he promoted." Both men were safely dead, so he could insult them with impunity.

Such ad hominem attacks were routine for Benton, but they shocked his audience, especially his reference to Stieglitz. One onlooker decided not to let it pass.

"I understand we'll be treated to a graphic demonstration of your attitude toward Jews when your *Arts of Life* murals return to the Whitney later this month," he remarked, prompting a blustering reply from Benton.

"Nothing against the Hebrew race. Plenty of fine, upstanding citizens among 'em. Why, my own lawyer is a Yid." Perhaps forgetting where he was, he continued, "Got no time for the pretentious ones, though, the phony intellectuals who run the so-called institutions of higher learning and shove their left-wing philosophy down the students' throats. Their anti-war rhetoric is poisoning the minds of our young men and undermining the government. Ought to send 'em all back to the commie countries their people came from, see how they like it there."

Benton's tirade had thinned the crowd, several of whom had departed as soon as they heard the word "Yid." Rather than thank Benton, the board member opted to express appreciation for his time and wish him success with the Whitney show. Then he and the rest of his party retreated, leaving Benton alone in the room with TJ and Ellen.

"Glad to see not everyone's afraid of plain talk," he growled. "So, spunky gal, is this your boyfriend? Handsome young fella, looks healthy, too. How come he's not in uniform?"

"I'm a full-time student at John Jay College," replied TJ bravely, "training for a career in law enforcement. Someone's got to keep the peace on the home front."

In view of the reservations he had expressed only last week, Ellen was surprised to hear TJ describe his future plans with such certainty. Then she realized he was mollifying Benton to avoid a confrontation. It did the trick. Beaming, the artist strode over and clapped the young man on the shoulder. Once again TJ caught a whiff of alcohol as he exclaimed, "Good for you, sonny! You micks make the best cops." Turning to Ellen, he condescendingly patted her cheek. "He'll look even more handsome in blue, dearie. Be a good girl and take him home now. I want to spend some time alone with my old friends here."

Benton turned and, swaying slightly, slowly approached the steel-mill panel. "See that big, brawny worker up front?" he said, speaking to the mural rather than to the couple behind him. "That's Jack Pollock, age eighteen. Strapping lad, like you, sonny. He was too green to be a painting assistant, but he did action posing for me, helped prime the canvases, fetched and carried, never complained. Christ, I loved that boy."

Out came the bandanna, and Benton dabbed at his eyes. Quietly, Ellen and TJ left him to his memories.

Thirteen

I guess the preview went smoothly," said Bill to the others gathered at the lunch table in the League cafeteria. "According to this morning's *Times*, the Whitney is still standing, though I gather Benton took the place by storm." He was sitting with his fellow full-time student Al Schwartz, instructor Charles Alston, whose afternoon life class was due to start at one, and Edward Laning, who would be teaching mural painting at the same time.

"He was actually very well-behaved," remarked Alston, who had been at the previous evening's reception for Benton's retrospective. "For once he was stone-cold sober, and he stuck to soda water all evening. His wife had him under control. You should have seen him, all duded up in a monkey suit, black tie, cummerbund, the works. I had to chuckle—not to his face, of course. But if he was uncomfortable he didn't show it. In fact he was eating up the adulation, and Rita was in her glory. She's the real force behind his success, you know. She handles all the negotiations with the dealers and the bureaucrats who commission his murals. If it were up to him he'd never sell a thing. Doesn't have the patience to deal with the business end."

"Or the temperament," added Laning, who was also at the opening. "He's way too volatile. You never know when he might say something to offend the guy who's writing the check."

"Paper says he made a bit of a fuss outside," said Bill, opening the *Times* to the story at the top of the society page. Skipping the lede, which recited the who, what, when, and where, he read: "Emerging from a limousine in front of the Whitney's imposing new building, designed by the Hungarian-American architect Marcel Breuer, Mr. Benton was heard to opine that it looked more like an artillery emplacement than an art museum. 'I've seen prettier prisons,' he said loudly as he and Mrs. Benton, the former Rita Piacenza, stepped under the concrete canopy that juts out over the Madison Avenue sidewalk."

"Shows you he can be just as cantankerous sober as drunk," said Alston.

"That's what I heard from his students, back in the early '30s," said Laning. "A few of them transferred to my class, and they told me why. They said he was always sober when he was teaching, but sobriety didn't improve his disposition. Short-tempered, impatient, foulmouthed, played favorites, that sort of thing. Not everyone's cup of tea."

Schwartz, who was facing the cafeteria entrance, suddenly sat up and stared.

"Speak of the devil! Damned if Benton didn't just walk in. I'd better make myself scarce."

"Stay put, Al," said Laning. "He won't remember you. It was over a week ago that he gave you those helpful pointers, and frankly I doubt if he remembered it the next morning, if you know what I mean." He rose and went to greet Benton, who was wearing his hillbilly uniform—the plaid lumber jacket, flannel shirt, dungarees, and work boots—and looking around the room somewhat vacantly.

"Why, Tom, this is a surprise, and a pleasant one," said Laning affably. "Come on over and set a spell. Charlie and I are off to class soon, but we'd love to hear your impressions of last night's shindig. With all the admirers crowded around you we couldn't get near you."

"Bunch of fucking brownnoses," grumbled Benton as he made his way to the table. Unwilling to risk a conversation that might spoil their afternoon, Bill and Al excused themselves and left Benton to the company of his colleagues.

Alston asked if he'd like coffee and Benton nodded. "Yeah, that's a good idea. Truth be told, I'm a little bit under the weather. When we finally made it back to the hotel, and I got out of that straitjacket Rita made me wear, I headed for the bar. Jesus, I was dyin' of thirst! 'Fraid I closed the place."

"Wouldn't be the first time, right?" Laning chided him, while Alston went for the coffee. "I'm sorry I wasn't there with you to toast your success. The show is a triumph, Tom. I mean it, no brownnosing. The Whitney has done you proud."

"Thanks, Charlie, you're a lifesaver," said Benton as Alston placed the mug in front of him. He winced as he sipped the brown liquid. "For Chrissake, you'd think they'd have learned how to brew decent coffee since I was here last, what, thirty years ago. This stuff's weak as eyewash, just like in the old days. Better add some hair of the dog." Out came the hip flask, and a healthy dollop of bourbon went into the mug. Benton downed a mouthful of the spiked coffee, sucked his moustache and smacked his lips. "Now it's got some flavor! Join me, boys?" He offered the flask, but his tablemates demurred.

"Too early in the day for me, Tom," said Alston. "Besides, Ed and I have to teach in a half hour or so. Got to be on our toes."

Benton grinned, leaned over and, in a friendly way, punched Alston lightly on the arm. "Good for you, Charlie. Keep clean in the classroom, that was always my motto. And here I am leadin' you down Satan's path. Shame on me!" His grin widened to a full-blown smile as he took a bigger swallow of the doctored java.

"Lemme ask you something, Charlie, and no offense meant. I don't know if you heard it, but at the opening some people were sayin' that my *Arts of the South* mural is disrespectful to Negroes because I show 'em shootin' craps and singin' spirituals. What do you think?"

This question put Alston, an African American, on the spot. In *Arts of the South*, the central figure, life-size, was a barefoot black man surrounded by his family and a pile of trash, his hands clasped prayerfully and his eyes turned to heaven as he sang. To the left, in the middle ground, three black men crouched in the dirt over a dice game. To many viewers, the painting depicted rural Negroes as backward and shiftless.

Arts of the South was one panel of the *Arts of Life in America* murals commissioned by the Whitney in 1932. As Laning had told his class, the murals were sold to the New Britain Museum of American Art in 1954 when the Whitney left its original building on West Eighth Street in Greenwich Village and moved to West Fifty-Fourth Street, adjacent to the Museum of Modern Art. All five panels had been lent back to the Whitney for the Benton retrospective.

Even when they were new the murals were derided as ugly, vulgar, and inept. Critics complained that Benton's figural distortions and exaggerations created stereotypes rather than the real people he professed to represent. They were especially offended by the wicked caricature of a Jewish intellectual in the lunette panel. The "art forms," from bronco busting and religious revivalism to poker playing and drinking in a speakeasy, pictured in garish colors, were called crude, gross, and ungracious.

Well aware of these critiques, Alston personally agreed

with them. After an early career as a highly regarded figurative painter, he had transitioned to a modernist idiom, in effect going in the opposite direction from Benton. While he was receptive to Benton's conceptual approach—the fieldwork, the character study from life, the focus on ordinary people and their environments—the overwrought imagery often made him uneasy, especially when the subjects were Negroes, though he had to admit that everyone became equally grotesque when subjected to Benton's neomannerist stylizations.

In spite of his reservations, Alston had no desire to argue with Benton. He knew a fishing expedition when he heard one, so he opted for diplomacy.

"You showed it like it was back in those days, Tom. Black boys did shoot craps—white boys, too, come to that— especially if they had nothing better to do, being out of work like so many were during the Depression. And you can't blame folks for looking to religion for salvation. That's all the hope they had before the New Deal came along."

Benton took another gulp of his coffee cocktail and nodded emphatically. "Damn right, Charlie! I saw every one of those scenes with my own eyes. Nobody who ain't been there has the right to tell me they ain't honest, especially those self-righteous pinkos and simpering homos I left this benighted city to get away from. And I told them so to their faces last night!"

Fourteen

H ave you read the reviews of the Benton show?" asked Bill as he and Al set their canvases on their easels.

"Boy, have I!" Al replied with relish. "Both Hilton Kramer and John Canaday blasted it in the *Times*, and Emily Genauer did the same in *Newsday*. It's no surprise that Genauer and Kramer would pan it—she's a big Picasso fan, and he's all for modern art. But I was surprised by Canaday. He's usually so conservative, I thought he'd go for it. But he picked up on the clash of Benton's subject matter and style. How did he put it?"

Bill quoted from memory: "'The misalliance between Huck Finn and El Greco.' I love that. Whether or not I agree with Canaday, and I seldom do, I find some of his little nuggets stick in my mind."

"I'll bet that one is stuck in Benton's craw," said Al, "and I hope it's painful."

"Now don't be vindictive, just because he gave you a hard time. You've had it easy with Laning, Mr. Congeniality. You should try Ray Breinin's class, he's a real Tartar. I mean a genuine Tartar, straight off the steppes, with a temper the size of Mother Russia."

Al was not about to switch instructors. "Maybe I have a thin skin, but I prefer encouragement to badgering. I guess some people thrive on that kind of challenge, but it just puts me off."

"Breinin's okay, he's just a bit rough around the edges. But he's a good teacher, really knows his stuff, even if his own work is kind of illustrational. Lots of fanciful Russian folktales, like a darker, more mystical version of Chagall. Not my taste."

———

TJ and Ellen were also settling down at their easels, both ready to continue working on drawings they had started the previous week.

"Have you seen the Benton show yet?" she asked him as she propped her pad on the bench and donned her smock.

"No, not yet. I had a day off on Columbus Day, but the museum is closed on Mondays. I'll have to try to get there one day next week, even if I have to cut a class. I'm sure Mr. Laning is going to ask us all what we think of it."

"I went on Saturday, and it was packed. The weekend isn't the ideal time to go, but that's when I have off. Not that everyone there was an admirer. The reviews brought out both camps. It was fun to eavesdrop on some of the discussions. Perfect strangers were arguing back and forth, very entertaining."

"At least, if Mr. Laning asks, I can tell him I've seen the New School murals. I guess there's a lot more of the same at the Whitney."

"It's much more varied than you'd imagine," she told him. "His early stuff is pretty traditional, portraits and landscapes, a little Impressionism, a little Postimpressionism. He may have pooh-poohed Cézanne to us, but he did a pretty good imitation of a Cézanne still life when he was in Paris before the First World War. Then he went through Cubism and a more colorful variant called Synchromism, but when he got back to the States he dumped modern art and started on his American epic, as he called it. Of course that's the bulk of the show, but you can see where his formal and structural concepts come from, especially in his analytical drawings and preparatory studies. They're really interesting."

By this time Wally had adopted his pose, and the class was getting down to work. Ellen flipped open her pad and started a new drawing. Unconsciously taking a leaf from Benton's book, rather than trying to work from detail to detail, as she had before, she began by blocking the figure in rhythmic strokes, getting a sense of the entire body before concentrating on refining the parts.

TJ was impressed with her newfound approach and decided to try it, too. Sure enough, it gave him a better sense of the overall structure of the body and eliminated the fussiness of his earlier efforts. *Damn,* he thought, *maybe Benton isn't just full of hot air after all. The rhythm really is important, and now I see what he was driving at.*

When the break came, Ellen had some news. "Guess what? Benton showed up at The Bitter End on Tuesday night. I think he'd been next door to the Dugout before he came in, and he was in a good mood. Kind of surprising, considering the reception his show is getting in the press. Another surprise was that he recognized me from the New School. Called me 'spunky gal' and sat with me and Michele. You should have seen his face when she stood up!"

"I'm sorry I missed that," said TJ, who'd been grounded with homework that night and unable to take up Ellen's blanket invitation to accompany her to The Bitter End any Tuesday.

"I told him I'd seen him at the Guthrie evening," she continued, "and he said he'd been a longtime fan of Woody's, though he'd never met him. It was Pete Seeger who told him about it and brought him along. Pete's father and Benton were in a band together in the '30s—they even played at the New School when the murals were unveiled. According to Benton they were a big hit. He would say that, wouldn't he? Anyway, he plays the harmonica. He had it with him and he offered to accompany us when we went on."

"And did he?"

"He sure did. I asked Ed, and he said okay. He knew who he was, and so did Oscar, or at least knew of him from his music. He recorded a folk album, 'Saturday Night at Tom Benton's,' that Oscar had played on his radio show. Oscar invited him on the show, and Benton was pleased as punch. He said he'd be in town for another couple of weeks, until after the Academy meeting in early November."

She paused, looking a bit sheepish. "I was kinda nervous about performing with him. He really knows folk music from its roots in the hinterlands. Michele and I are from Queens, and I've never been west of Atlantic City, so I was afraid he'd think we were phonies and say so to the crowd. But Michele wasn't at all intimidated—as you can tell, she's pretty self-confident. She suggested 'Banks of the Ohio,' and he said that was one of his favorites, so that's what we sang. After we finished he actually complimented us, praised Michele's harmonies, and said I had a voice like an Ozark thrush. At least I think that's a compliment."

"Was that it? Just the one number?"

"Yeah, just the one. He said he couldn't hang around 'cause Rita, that's his wife, has him on a short leash, but I think he really wanted to go next door and wet his whistle. As you know, The Bitter End has no bar."

"Speaking of hanging around," said TJ, "Bill tells me Benton's been hanging around the cafeteria at lunchtime. Mr. Laning's not the only instructor who knew him from his League days. Bill says some of them were practically born here, so I guess he feels comfortable eating lunch with the old-timers."

"Probably more friendly than some places he could go. If he hung out in the Whitney's lunchroom he'd be liable to get an earful about the show, and at the Academy he might bump into the guys who kicked him out. Pretty far uptown, too."

"I see the League's appeal. The menu's not the greatest, but he's got a sympathetic audience and he can walk here from the St. Regis and not even be out of breath."

Fifteen

W here's Bill?" asked TJ, who had arrived fifteen minutes early to this week's class. Chris Gray, whom he didn't recognize, was opening the studio door. Gray, the aspiring muralist, usually monitored for Laning's afternoon mural painting and composition class, which met five days a week, and Breinin's evening life class on Wednesdays, so TJ had never encountered him before.

"He's off tonight," replied Gray tersely as he opened the door and flipped on the lights. "I'm Chris. I'm filling in for him."

TJ pressed him. "Is he sick? I hope not."

"No, he's okay." Chris hesitated, as if to continue, but turned away instead and started inspecting the easels.

That wasn't good enough for TJ. He followed Gray on his rounds. "Then what's the problem? Is there a problem?"

Chris stopped and turned, sizing him up. "You a friend of his?"

"Yes," said TJ confidently. "My name's Timothy, but everybody calls me TJ. I really like Bill, and I want to help if there's anything I can do."

Chris sat on one of the bench easels, and TJ sat opposite him.

"Last Saturday afternoon I went up to Studio Nine on the fifth floor to get something out of my locker. Nobody goes up there between classes, so I was surprised to find Bill all alone, sitting on the edge of the model stand with his head in his hands, looking really dejected. I asked him what was wrong, and he broke down crying."

"He has a really close friend who's in the infantry in Vietnam," Chris continued, and TJ assumed that really close meant more than just a buddy. "On Friday he got a long letter from this guy. Bill said it was a real horror story, all about the terrible things he'd seen, and that he'd done himself. Said he was afraid he was cracking up, thinking about going AWOL, or worse. I said I understood what the guy was going through. I'm a veteran, though I never went overseas. I was on permanent party at Fort Hamilton, in the admin office. But I had buddies who served in Nam, and some of them came back in bad shape."

Chris paused, deciding how much to reveal. He made up his mind and continued. "Then Bill told me the guy was his boyfriend. I kinda suspected he was queer, but I wasn't sure, 'cause he acts straight, and he never talks about his private life. But after the letter he couldn't hold it in, he felt so helpless and scared of what the guy might do."

"What did you say?"

"I asked him how much longer the guy's hitch was, and he said, 'He has another three months to go, and I don't think he can make it.' Bill was afraid he'd kill himself, even though he's Catholic, so suicide would be a mortal sin."

"Man, that's heavy," said TJ. "I knew Bill was gay—my girlfriend Ellen told me. She had a crush on him, so he warned her off. It sure isn't obvious. But what can he do about his boyfriend's state of mind? He must be going crazy himself."

"I told him the letter was clearly a call for help. If the guy really was hopeless he wouldn't have written it, he'd have just shot himself. I think that helped calm him down, not feel so desperate. He said he was gonna write back immediately, tell the guy how much he loves him and that he's praying for his safe return."

TJ digested this news thoughtfully as Chris continued. "So when he came in on Monday he said he felt a lot better. He wrote the letter, poured his heart out, and told the guy to talk to the chaplain. I worked with the army chaplain school at Fort Hamilton, and I know how much lots of soldiers rely on them for moral and spiritual support. I said that was good advice, and he seemed grateful to hear that. Not like the problem was solved, but at least he'd done what he could."

"So why is he out today?" TJ wanted to know. Chris explained that the next day Bill had been hit with a one-two punch. In Tuesday's mail he got a rejection letter from Cooper Union and a summons from the draft board. Without the student deferment he was classified 1-A, so in all likelihood he'd be sent to Vietnam like his boyfriend—only nowhere near him, and in for twelve months while the other guy's coming home in three, assuming he gets through.

"Yesterday," said Chris, "a bunch of us were having lunch in the cafeteria, and Bill came in. The desperate look was back, and I was worried that his letter might have crossed with bad news from Nam. I didn't want to say anything to, you know, let on about the boyfriend, but he told us he didn't get into Cooper and was about to be drafted, so that accounted for it. He said, 'Fuck it, I'm not going! I'll go to Canada before I let those baby-killers send me into hell! The fucking army can go to hell, but not me!' He was pretty agitated. Next thing we know he pulls out his draft card, grabs some matches off one of the smokers, lights up the card, and drops it in the ashtray."

"Does he know that's a federal offense?" asked TJ.

"He knows it now," replied Chris, "because Tom Benton told him so, at the top of his lungs. The old bastard was sitting at the next table. He's been holding lunchtime seminars on the glorious career of Thomas Hart Benton, America's answer to Michelangelo, practically every day for the past two weeks. When he saw that card go up in flames, I thought he'd bust a gut. Called Bill a lily-livered sissy, a sorry excuse for a man, and things I won't repeat.

"A couple of the fellows confronted Benton, told him to butt out, it was none of his business. If they thought that would shut him up, they were dead wrong. He called us all a bunch of draft dodgers and actually took a swing at Dan Forsberg, who's at least six-one and forty years younger. Fortunately Wally was sitting at Benton's table, and he got between him and Dan. Benton seems to have a soft spot for Wally, so he backed off. Then Jacob Lawrence, one of the other instructors, stepped in and calmed him down while we hustled Bill out the door."

By now Wally had arrived, and other students were beginning to appear. Chris excused himself, did a quick check of the easels, and found everything in order. Wally hailed him, "Hey, Chris, I need the pole tonight," and he retrieved it from the closet.

TJ got his supplies from his locker and took his place. Normally he would be watching eagerly for Ellen's arrival, but the story of Bill's dilemma had distracted and disturbed him. He tried to imagine what it would be like to know that your lover was in harm's way, not only in mortal danger physically but also mentally, and be powerless to help. And probably not be able to turn to your family for comfort.

That complication was especially hard for TJ to wrap his head around. *How would I tell my parents?* he wondered. *He said he lives at home, like me. Most likely his folks don't know he's gay, and would disown him if they found out. On top of that he faces jail for burning his draft card—Benton will probably rat him out, may have done so already—or becoming a fugitive. Neither one a great option.*

"Earth to TJ," said a voice that brought him back to the studio. Ellen had installed herself next to him without his even noticing. His embarrassment showed on his cheeks, an involuntary consequence of a sensitive nature coupled with a fair complexion.

He apologized for ignoring her, and said he'd explain during the break. When the time came he gave her a synopsis of what Chris had told him.

"Now I see why he keeps to himself so much," she said. "After he told me he's gay I figured he had a boyfriend somewhere. I never thought he'd be in the service. Don't they reject homosexuals?"

"He may not have told them," said TJ. "Lots of them don't admit it because of the stigma. On the other hand, if you say you're gay most draft boards will take you anyway. They assume you're lying—that you're what they call a hoaxosexual—to get out of serving, and besides the army needs the bodies. Some people want a military career, or really believe in the war, like the vet we heard in Union Square did before he wised up, so they're not going to tell. One gay guy I know from the neighborhood was gung ho like that. He kept quiet and enlisted in the marines because he wanted to prove he was just as macho as the straight men. He came home with a Purple Heart and a Bronze Star."

"So you don't think they'll reject Bill if he tells them he's gay?"

"Chris said Bill is 1-A. Either he didn't tell them, or they ignored it. I think to be 4-F these days you have to be practically dead."

Sixteen

WEDNESDAY, NOVEMBER 1

Inspector Jacob Kaminsky, commanding officer of the Eighteenth Precinct, arrived at the Art Students League with a photographer, a medical technician, and several uniformed police officers at 7:05 p.m. The station house was only a few blocks away, on West Fifth-Fourth Street, so there was no delay in response to a call from Stewart Klonis, the League's executive director, who reported the discovery of a body on the top floor.

Kaminsky, a twenty-seven-year veteran of the force, was among the 10 percent of the New York City Police Department who were Jewish. Defying his family's ambition for him to enter one of the favored professions—doctor, lawyer, accountant, businessman—his strong social conscience had led him to follow the concept of tikkun olam, to improve the world, and he saw a career in law enforcement as the ideal means to that end. He was among the distinguished Jewish graduates of the Police Academy class of 1940, who by the mid-1960s included a Chief Inspector—the highest uniformed rank—a female Deputy Chief Inspector, the Chief of Detectives, Chief of the Organized Crime Bureau and Chief of the Narcotics Division.

At six foot three, Kaminsky's muscular build carried his two hundred pounds easily, and his ramrod posture signaled his authority silently but effectively. His patch extended two-thirds of the way across the island, from the Hudson River to Lexington Avenue and Central Park south to Forty-Third Street. Among the landmarks under his jurisdiction were St. Patrick's Cathedral, Rockefeller Center, Carnegie Hall, and the Museum of Modern Art, all of which he had visited on various official and social occasions, in and out of uniform.

The League, however, was unknown territory. He had passed the Renaissance Revival building innumerable times, but had never been inside. More than once he'd thought about just dropping in for a look around, but somehow he'd never made the time. He often wondered just what went on in the imposing edifice, designed by Henry J. Hardenbergh, who based it on a sixteenth-century hunting lodge in Fontainebleau, France. His own building, known as the Midtown North station house, was a dowdy thing by comparison, built by the Work Projects Administration in 1939 in the Stripped Classical style typical of New Deal–era government construction. It was so generic that no architect was credited on the commemorative bronze plaque.

When the call came in, Kaminsky decided to satisfy his curiosity and head up the investigation himself. But when he got inside the League he was somewhat surprised by the smallness of the entrance hall and main lobby. Judging by the façade, he expected something grander, even palatial. Instead he found himself and his team in a cramped space filled with students milling about in confusion. At the sight of his uniformed men, the buzz died down and the crowd parted, allowing Klonis to step forward and identify himself to Kaminsky as the man who had placed the call.

A watercolorist of modest accomplishment and a League alumnus himself, Klonis had served as the Board of Control's treasurer during the Depression, when he was instrumental in saving the school from falling off a financial cliff. His reward was to be elected president in 1937 and director in 1946, after which his fiscal prudence and the advent of the G.I. Bill's education stipends ushered in a period of prosperity. Soon two-thirds of the students were veterans, and the number of instructors tripled. Twenty years later, the League was welcoming a new wave of ex-servicemen and -women.

Klonis's devotion to the place was total and all-consuming, which explains why he was still in his office at six fifty when a breathless Chris Gray, having sprinted down five flights, entered at a run and blurted out the news that Thomas Hart Benton was lying dead in Studio Nine.

———

As he met the police in the lobby, Klonis struggled to maintain a businesslike demeanor. Always impeccably groomed, a suit-and-tie island surrounded by a sea of bohemian informality, his dependable equilibrium had been seriously compromised by Chris's report. This was the first time in the League's history that a death had occurred under its stately mansard roof. Nervously, he motioned Kaminsky into the office where he could have a private word. Clearly flustered—wringing his hands, eyes darting this way and that—he explained the circumstances as Chris had relayed them, and told Kaminsky that the monitor had locked the studio door behind him so nothing would be disturbed.

Chris had stationed himself at the elevators and turned away Breinin's students, telling them only that class was canceled but they could squeeze into the Laning anatomy class on the first floor if they wanted to stay. Breinin himself wasn't due for at least another half hour, so Chris figured he could head him off before he got upstairs. Once Kaminsky was apprised of the situation, his men took charge of crowd control, and Chris was ordered to accompany them to the scene. Klonis volunteered to go along, which Kaminsky approved.

A uniformed officer was stationed at the elevators, denying access to all the upper floors, which meant dealing with a dozen canceled classes and scores of irate students. Another officer emptied Laning's studio, and two more were dispatched to check the other three floors and dismiss anyone they found there, so the school was shuttered for the night.

Only one of the two elevators went to the top floor. When Kaminsky and his party reached 5, they found a few students who had come up from the cafeteria, which had closed at seven, and were waiting to be admitted. They were surprised to find the studio locked, since people could usually come and go freely, and were even more surprised when the elevator door opened and a trio of uniformed police officers accompanied Klonis, Chris, and two strangers— one carrying a medical bag and the other a camera—into the narrow hallway.

"Stand back, please," ordered Kaminsky, politely but firmly. "Tonight's class is canceled, and the building is closed. Officer Jenkins will take you to the exit." Jenkins herded the disgruntled students to the elevator, bundled them inside, pressed 1, and escorted them down. The other cop was stationed outside the studio door.

When the hall was clear, Kaminsky signaled Chris to open the studio. Benton lay where Chris had found him, with the tablecloth pulled away to reveal the body.

"Did you touch anything other than the cloth?" Kaminsky asked.

"Well," said Chris, concentrating on remembering his movements, "I touched the doorknob and light switch, but I never got to any of the chores. I must have put my hand on the model stand when I bent over to check Mr.

Benton's pulse—oh, of course, I touched his throat, like this." He put two fingers under his jaw. "I guess I shouldn't have disturbed the body."

"That's fine, son. You didn't know just by looking at him that he was dead. Mr. Klonis told us you realized he wasn't asleep, so you'd want to know if maybe he was just unconscious. Could have had a stroke or a heart attack and needed a doctor. What he needs now is a thorough examination by the doc here," said Kaminsky as he gestured to his medical technician.

First the photographer took shots of the scene from various angles. Then the medic began to examine the corpse. He pressed his hand to the neck, and observed that the skin was cool but pliant, indicating recent death. Curled in on himself, Benton looked as if he had suffered a paralyzing cramp or seizure. But he was not gripping the tablecloth, so he had not wrapped it around himself. Someone else must have done that. But why conceal him if he had died of natural causes? Why not just call for help, as Chris had done?

The answer became evident when the medic turned the body on its back and laid it out. Embedded in Benton's chest, up to the hilt, was a knife with an ornate grip and pommel that Chris recognized from the prop cabinet. It was a nineteenth-century Russian dagger, intricately decorated with cloisonné enamel, which featured prominently in Breinin's still life arrangements. It added an exotic note to the standard fruit-bowl tableau and challenged his students' ability to render detail. But it was a valuable artifact, and, whenever it was used, Breinin always locked it securely in the cabinet at the end of class.

The medic motioned to the photographer. "Get a close shot of this, will you, Jim? There's something pinned under the crossguard. See if you can get a detail or two before I remove the weapon." Several pictures were duly taken while the medic made some observations.

"The knife was inserted under the rib cage, just to the left of the sternum," he said. "The blow was clearly aimed at the heart. I'd say the victim died within moments of being struck. Almost all the bleeding is internal, so I believe he was lying still when the knife went in. In fact I think he may have been unconscious. The autopsy should tell us, but it looks to me like he was knocked out first, then stabbed. The killer had plenty of time to find just the right spot. And something was attached to the knife blade beforehand. That takes planning. Looks like a picture of some kind. Let's find out." He reached for the exposed grip.

"I think I need to sit down," said Klonis, groping for a stool. Chris was also looking a bit green around the gills, so Kaminsky suggested that they both wait in the hall with the uniformed officer until the body was ready for removal. They gladly agreed.

Using the tips of his gloved fingers, the medic eased the dagger out of Benton's chest. It came away easily, revealing a double-sided blade about six inches long and about an inch wide.

"Charming little pig-sticker," remarked Kaminsky dryly. "What's that piece of paper on it?"

The blade had been neatly inserted through the center of a picture postcard. It showed the stylized figure of a Native American warrior attacking a white mother and child, with a battle between a colonial invader and Indians taking place in the background. The medic carefully removed it from the knife, which he put into a clear plastic evidence bag. He also bagged the postcard and handed it to Kaminsky, who frowned and grunted at it before flipping it over.

The back was smeared with blood, but the information on it was legible. Kaminsky squinted as he read the fine print. The Whitney Museum of American Art had published the card, and the image was identified as a 1925 painting by Thomas Hart Benton—a panel from the *American Historical Epic* series, one of his proposed mural projects that never came to fruition.

The title of this panel was *Retribution*.

———

Kaminsky left the medic to his work and stepped into the hall, where Klonis and Chris stood opposite the elevator. What might have been the scene of an accident or natural death was now clearly a crime scene, so he ordered the uniformed cop to go downstairs and radio for someone to bring over a fingerprinting kit. He told Chris that he'd be required to go with them to the station and give a formal statement, then he asked, "How did you recognize the dead man?"

"He's a well-known artist—that is, I mean, he was," Chris stammered. "He used to teach here, but he left New York years ago. He's back in town for a big show of his work at the Whitney, and he's been hanging around the League for the past few weeks."

"So he was not on the faculty?"

"Not for some thirty years," said Klonis. "He taught painting here when I was a student in the late '20s and early '30s. He took a year off for a mural job in Chicago, then quit for good in '35. Hadn't been back since, until last month, when he started dropping by almost every day, often for lunch, and sometimes in the evening as well."

"How many people knew he was here?" Kaminsky asked Klonis.

"Tonight, you mean? Or in general?"

"Both."

"Well, I don't know about tonight specifically, but anyone who was in the building when he was around would have been aware of his presence. He was a forceful character. What I mean is, he tended to, shall we say, announce himself loudly, and he often dropped into classes uninvited. He might offer advice or give an impromptu critique, that sort of thing."

"Did the teachers resent that?"

Klonis realized that was a leading question. "I doubt Mr. Benton would have disturbed any class enough to cause resentment. Our classes are not formally structured," he explained. "Some meet every day in the morning, after-noon, or evening, others are held once or twice a week. The instructors are not always present. They may give a talk or demonstration and then leave the students to work on their own, or they may come in part way through the session and give critiques, then leave."

"You know what I'm getting at, Mr. Klonis," said Kaminsky. "The man was murdered in this building, and I need to determine if anyone here would have a motive to kill him. Were there rivalries, jealousies, or other friction with him that you're aware of?"

"As you see," Klonis replied, "Benton was a small man, but he had an oversized personality that tended to antago-nize people. I'm sure any number of our faculty and students would have preferred that he left them alone, but I'm not aware of any outright animosity toward him. He'd been out of the New York art world for many years, and the Whitney show was his chance to revitalize his career. He wanted everyone to know that he was still important. I'm sure they realized he was just showing off."

Chris, on the other hand, was well aware that Benton had made at least one serious enemy at the League—one with intimate knowledge of the building and keys to many of its doors.

Seventeen

The elevator door opened to admit the fingerprint man with his kit, accompanied by an orderly from the medical examiner's office, who rolled a folding gurney into the studio. Behind them, an officer steered an irate Raymond Breinin toward Kaminsky. Wearing a broad-brimmed fedora, a red velvet jacket, a colorful paisley ascot, and a scowl as dark as his jet-black hair, the agitated artist demanded to know why he was being barred from his classroom. Gesturing dismissively at the officer, he complained, "This pitiful excuse for Cossack tells me nothing!"

Kaminsky scowled back at him and bristled. "Who the hell are you?"

Klonis made the introductions, giving both men time to dial down the temperature, while he explained to Breinin what had apparently occurred.

"You joke!" blurted an astonished Breinin. "So little

man's big mouth is now silent. There will be few tears, I fancy. I will shed none."

This remark alerted Kaminsky. "You were not a fan of Mr. Benton's, then?"

Disregarding the consequences, Breinin began to elaborate on his grievances against the late artist, which dated back three decades.

In 1934, he said, he was living in Chicago, where his family had emigrated from Russia after the revolution. With the economy in the dumps, there were few prospects for young artists—he had just turned twenty-five, and was not long out of art school—but the New Deal had come to the rescue. The Public Works of Art Project, a federal government employment program, hired him to paint a mural in the library of the Skokie School in Winnetka.

Inspired by the Mexican muralists and flush with youthful enthusiasm, he chose the idealistic theme, *Give Us the Unity of Men and We Shall Build a New World*. At the north end of the forty-foot composition, which pictured cooperative industrial and agricultural labor, was a section called *The Unity of the Races*, showing three men embracing— described by Breinin as a Caucasian worker in overalls flanked by a Negro and an Oriental. The subject matter, which had been approved by the school board and the art project staff, reflected the Roosevelt administration's aim of commissioning optimistic public artworks to counter the national malaise. The program also kept artists off the relief rolls by giving them something productive to do.

Breinin's work was almost finished when Thomas Hart Benton showed up at the Skokie School. Thanks to the nationwide publicity generated by his latest mural, a sweeping historical panorama for the State of Indiana pavilion at the Century of Progress Exposition in Chicago, where he was holding court, he was the most famous artist in the country. Thinking his populist views would make him sympathetic, and willing to lend his endorsement to the cause, the regional art project administration invited him on a tour of the public works they were sponsoring.

Benton took one look at Breinin's mural and pronounced it aesthetically derivative and politically socialistic, suggesting that the Russian-born artist was foisting Communist propaganda on innocent schoolchildren. As he was later told, Benton turned the school board against the painting. What they had once considered uplifting and inspirational was now deemed "sinister and threatening." No sooner had it been unveiled than it was whitewashed.

"Thanks to Benton, my mural was destroyed," fumed Breinin, still boiling mad more than thirty years later. "Where is body? I want to spit on it!"

"Now take it easy, Mr. Breinin," cautioned Kaminsky. "Your attitude does you no credit, and in fact it puts you in a bad light. Even more so, considering the murder weapon. It was your fancy knife that did him in."

"Splendid!" thundered Breinin. "Kinzhal is perfect weapon for revenge."

Kaminsky was taken aback by the man's attitude, which

seemed almost deliberately self-incriminating. But Breinin continued, "I regret that I did not strike blow."

"Are you saying you would have killed him if given the opportunity?"

"Perhaps. I have murder in my heart for him since many years. When he invade my class last week I throw him out. Tell him to go back to devil, where he come from."

At that moment the studio door opened and the orderly, followed by the medic, wheeled out the gurney bearing Benton's corpse. Kaminsky herded Breinin off to the side hallway, effectively blocking him while the gurney was maneuvered through the narrow passage and into the elevator. A stream of Russian invective followed it and continued even after the door closed and the car began to descend.

Kaminsky then turned his attention to the artist. "I'll need you to account for your whereabouts this evening, Mr. Breinin, so I'll oblige you to come with me to the station and make a formal statement. Mr. Gray here, who found the body, will come along as well."

"Will it take long?' asked Chris. "Normally I'd be home by ten thirty, quarter to eleven, and my wife will be worried if I'm any later than that."

Kaminsky understood, but given the circumstances Chris had to be considered a suspect. He might have killed Benton, then made up the story about stumbling across the body. He certainly couldn't be ruled out at this early stage.

"Where do you live, son?" he asked. Chris told him they had an apartment at 49 Morton Street in the Village. "I think we can get you down there in plenty of time. If there's a delay you can call your wife from the station."

"And me?" growled Breinin. "I have wife, too, and daughter. On Bethune Street, number Thirty-One. When do I go to them?"

"You'll be free to go as soon as we have your statement," Kaminsky told him. "The more cooperative you are, the sooner it will be."

———

As the party headed through the lobby to the waiting squad cars, Klonis took Kaminsky aside.

"I hope the school can reopen tomorrow," he said anxiously. The experience had shaken him badly, and he would have liked nothing better than to go home to a double whiskey and spend the next day in bed. But his responsibility to his faculty and students far outweighed personal considerations.

Kaminsky appreciated his position. "I see no reason why not. Of course the top floor will be closed. You'll have to cancel the classes in that room or find another place for them. Officer Gomez will remain there until I send a relief, and the room will have a police guard until further notice. No one is to enter it until the investigation is complete. I hope that's clearly understood."

Klonis was thinking of the students who had belongings in the lockers and paintings in progress stored in the racks.

He debated asking Kaminsky for permission to clear those things from the studio, but realized it wouldn't be possible. Studio Nine was now a crime scene, and everything in it was potentially evidence.

There was another practical matter to be dealt with.

"We need to notify Mr. Benton's next of kin," said Kaminsky. "Do you have that information?"

"Yes, I can help you with that," replied Klonis. "Come into my office, please." He led the inspector through a glass-paneled door, behind the registration counter, past the secretary's desk and into a cluttered sanctum lined with bookshelves. The director's desk was tucked into a corner. The remaining space was almost completely filled by a long rectangular table at which the monthly Board of Control meetings were held.

Motioning Kaminsky to a heavy oak chair opposite his desk, Klonis took his seat and located a pad and pencil. He wrote out the information as he spoke.

"Benton's next of kin will be his wife, Rita. They're staying at the St. Regis. They have two grown children, young Tom and Jessie, but they're not with them. Benton is—I beg your pardon, was—here for his Whitney Museum retrospective exhibition, which opened on October twelfth, and what was to have been his reinstatement ceremony at the American Academy of Arts and Letters next week. I daresay that will become a memorial tribute. Lloyd Goodrich, the Whitney's director, and George Kennan, the Academy's president, should be contacted. I can give you their numbers, or if you prefer I'll speak to them. I know them both personally."

"Yes," said Kaminsky, "I think it would be better coming from you." He took the information Klonis had written down, stood and thanked him, handed him his business card, and advised him to call at any time. Klonis reciprocated with his own card, rose politely, and escorted him through the lobby. As they reached the entrance, they could see through the outer glass doors that a crowd had gathered on the sidewalk. Apparently the students' mass exodus had attracted rubberneckers, including a couple of reporters, and on his way out Breinin had gleefully informed the world at large of Benton's demise. Flashbulbs popped as Kaminsky descended the steps, past Officer Jenkins, who was blocking admission, and headed to his car.

Klonis looked on with dismay. Better make those calls right away, he said to himself. This will be all over the front pages by morning.

Eighteen

"I'm sorry to disturb you at home, Lloyd, but I must speak to you right away," said Klonis into the telephone, eager to get the distressing conversation over with as soon as possible. Lloyd Goodrich also hoped the conversation would be brief. Klonis's call had interrupted him at dinner with his wife, Edith, and several guests, though the museum director was too gracious to say so.

One of the New York art world's most respected administrators, as well as a League alumnus, Goodrich had been associated with the Whitney since its founding in 1930, first as a curator and since 1958 as director. He was often called upon as Klonis's unofficial advisor and confidante, and was used to being asked for his opinion on governance matters and recommendations for potential instructors. But these requests were seldom, if ever, made at nine o'clock on a weeknight.

"What's the trouble, Stewart?" he asked with concern.

Fidgeting with a pencil as he spoke, Klonis explained the situation. There was silence on the other end of the line as Goodrich absorbed the news.

"So, as you can see," Klonis concluded, "this is not simply a matter of Benton's having died at the League. He was murdered. Possibly by one of our own students or instructors."

Goodrich had had several squabbles with the irascible artist, but he was having a hard time imagining Benton's behavior provoking someone to homicide. "Poor Tom," he sighed. "Oh, I know he had plenty of enemies, but who hated him enough to kill him?"

"How in God's name should I know?" snapped Klonis, who immediately apologized for his rudeness. "Please forgive me, Lloyd. I'm at my wit's end. I don't know what impact this will have on the League, how much adverse publicity it will generate, whether it will affect enrollment. Frankly, I just don't know how to handle it."

"Has Rita been informed?"

"The police will contact her as next of kin. I offered to let you and George Kennan know."

"Good. I'll get onto George as well, coordinate the memorials. Of course we'll do something at the museum. But for the moment, let's consider your position, and the League's reputation." Knowing Klonis's singular devotion to the school—matched by his own commitment to the Whitney—Goodrich understood how personally painful this calamity was to him.

"As you know, the museum has had its share of bad publicity. Nothing quite like this, of course, but in my experience the best way to handle it is to get in front of it. Don't wait for the papers to call you for comment. Draft a statement right away and get it to all the papers as soon as you can—tonight, if possible."

"Yes, yes, you're absolutely right, Lloyd. May I ask you to help me with it?"

"Certainly. I'll just have a word with Edith first, if you don't mind, then I'll be back with you right away. Stay on the line, in case a reporter is trying to call in. You need to prepare before you speak to the press."

As if on cue, the phone at the secretary's desk in the outer office rang. Goodrich could hear it in the background. "Is that the League's listed number?" he asked.

"Yes," said Klonis. "My office number is a private line. It's unlisted."

"Excellent. It will take them a while to find it, but eventually they will. Meanwhile, let's work out some wording. You'll have to run it by Everett before you release it." Walker G. Everett, the League's president, was also a member of the public relations committee and had final approval on all official communications.

"Naturally," replied Klonis. "I'd better call him right away. I can use the other line to dial out and leave this line open. Or perhaps I should wait until I have something to read to him. Oh, dear, this is complicated. What if he doesn't approve?" He was beginning to get flustered again.

Goodrich, an old hand at fending off unwelcome press inquiries and manipulating board members, assured his friend that it would all go smoothly. "Call Everett now, and tell him what you told me. Tell him you'll handle everything, and that you'll call him back as soon as you have a statement ready. You know he'll be only too glad to defer to your judgment, and the board will give you the credit for saving the day." Unspoken was the implication that if things went south, Klonis would be the one to take the blame.

———

An hour later, Klonis was on the line to the Associated Press office at 50 Rockefeller Plaza, reading the following statement to the New York City correspondent on night duty:

At approximately seven p.m. on Wednesday, November first, 1967, the body of Thomas Hart Benton, the noted American Regionalist painter, was discovered in Studio Nine at the Art Students League of New York, 215 West Fifty-Seventh Street. The cause of death has not been officially determined. The circumstances are being investigated by the New York City Police Department's Eighteenth Precinct, 306 West Fifty-Fourth Street, under the leadership of Inspector Jacob Kaminsky.

An Art Students League instructor from 1926 to 1935, Mr. Benton had lived and worked in Kansas City, Missouri, for the past thirty-two years. He was

> *a frequent visitor to the school since a retrospec-*
> *tive exhibition of his work opened at the Whitney*
> *Museum of American Art, 945 Madison Avenue,*
> *last month.*
>
> *The administration, faculty and students of the*
> *Art Students League wish to express sincere condo-*
> *lences to the artist's widow, Rita Piacenza Benton,*
> *and his children, Thomas Piacenza Benton of Acton,*
> *Massachusetts, and Jessie Benton Gude of Roxbury,*
> *Massachusetts. Memorial services will be announced.*
>
> *Inquiries should be directed to Stewart Klonis,*
> *Executive Director, Art Students League of New York,*
> *Circle 7–4510.*

"Give them lots of information," Goodrich had advised, "but don't say very much. Whatever you do say, don't lie. Be factual. Let the police take the next steps, after the autopsy. That will buy you some time."

Klonis was pessimistic. "Not more than a couple of days, I'm afraid. As soon as the cause of death is official, the press will be all over us. The police already know he was murdered, and a murder in our building has thrown suspicion on everyone associated with the League. No doubt the police will be a visible presence. Students and faculty will be questioned. Classes are sure to be disrupted. Enrollment for next term may be affected." He was audibly agitated by this bleak prospect, and Goodrich did his best to calm his friend.

"Your best plan is complete cooperation with the

investigation. If you know of anyone who might have had a motive, you must tell the police."

"When they were here, the inspector asked me about that and I said I didn't. But now that I think about it, some things were brought to my attention, more or less in passing. Several instructors mentioned to me that Benton had butted in on their classes, but that was mere annoyance. There was, however, an incident in the cafeteria a week ago that was more serious. Blows were exchanged, I was told. Perhaps I should advise Inspector Kaminsky of that."

"You know," said Goodrich, "we had something like that happen at the museum a couple of weeks ago. Tom was giving a gallery talk—he came in several times and did impromptu tours for whoever happened to be in the exhibition, and he always attracted a crowd. Very entertaining commentaries, they were, too. But one day, who should show up but Andy Warhol and his entourage. I'm sure it was a coincidence—Tom couldn't possibly have invited them, because no sooner did he recognize Andy than he started insulting him in the grossest terms. I got the story, in graphic detail, from one of the guards.

"Please pardon my language, Stewart, but according to the guard he called Andy a simpering queer and ordered him and his, pardon me again, bunch of butt-fuckers and dope addicts out of the building. Of course they laughed at him—Andy actually cracked a smile—and that made Tom even madder. He practically started a fistfight in the gallery, and the guards had to break it up. They brought him to my office, and I calmed him down, but not before he spent half an hour raving about how this Pittsburgh parvenu pansy and the whole Pop art contingent had hijacked the art world."

Klonis was taken aback. "Good God, Lloyd, it sounds like the man was out of control. I know the exhibition put a lot of pressure on him, and of course the largely negative reviews didn't help, thought the coverage seems to have stimulated attendance. He must have felt threatened by anyone who might challenge his position. Did the Warhol crowd do anything to provoke him?"

"On the contrary, that's what's so curious. Andy was very respectful. You know how he can be, sort of gee-whiz about things, and you do wonder if he's sincere or if it's some sort of ironic act. But on the face of it he was being complimentary. The guard told me Andy didn't know at first that Tom was in the gallery. He went over to one of the paintings and said something like 'Oh, gosh, isn't that beautiful? Look at the pretty colors. Aren't the flowers pretty?' He had his flock around him, and they do attract attention, so they were distracting people from Tom's monologue. Tom told them to pipe down, and that's when he recognized Andy. It went downhill from there."

This account made Klonis wonder if Benton's killer might be an outsider. "You'd better tell the police about that incident, Lloyd. Whatever you think of Warhol or his art, there's no question that some of the people around him are unsavory. Any one of them could have come in here and assaulted him. Some of them may even be former League students familiar with the building."

Goodrich was skeptical. "How would someone get him up to the fifth floor? What was he doing up there between classes anyway? As I recall, there's only the one studio on that floor, and it's usually empty when there's no class in session."

"I don't think that would have been difficult," replied Klonis. "Studio Nine was Benton's old classroom. He called it the penthouse—top floor for the top artist. He was up there several times during the past few weeks, dropping in on whatever class was in session. Charles Alston, who's in there five afternoons a week, apparently didn't mind, nor did Bob Brackman, who has the morning class. He started teaching here back in Benton's day. I think they got along fine. Ray Breinin, on the other hand, threw him out—he told us so himself. There's a history of animosity there, and he's definitely a suspect."

Nineteen

Well, I'll be damned," said Brian Fitzgerald as he read the front page of the *Daily News* at the breakfast table. He handed the paper, folded over to the headline, "Artist Found Dead at League," to his son and asked, "Isn't this the guy you told us about?"

"Who's that?" asked Nita as she poured herself another cup of coffee.

"Thomas Hart Benton, the artist," said her husband. "You remember TJ telling us how he disrupted his art class, and how he saw him at the New School. That's him, right?"

TJ took the paper and read the first paragraph. "It sure is. I wonder what happened. Says here cause of death not known. Says he was found in Studio Nine, that's up on the top floor, so I guess he didn't fall down the stairs. He was an old geezer, maybe he had a heart attack. I'll probably find out more tonight."

"Says Jacob Kaminsky is investigating," said Fitz. "That means it's not straightforward. Looks like they don't have much to go on, at least not yet. Most of the story is background about Benton's career and the show at the Whitney. Jake'll get to the bottom of it."

———

Inspector Kaminsky was already organizing his inquiries. But his first order of business was to inform the widow.

Rita Benton had not been at the St. Regis on Wednesday night. The management told Kaminsky that she was visiting her niece on Long Island for a few days and had left a number where she could be reached. He much preferred to speak to the next of kin in person, but he couldn't wait for her to return. By the time he finished with Chris Gray and Ray Breinin it was too late to call, so he tabled it until morning.

Early on Thursday he dialed the Mattituck number, which was answered by Maria Piacenza Kron. He identified himself and asked to speak to Mrs. Benton.

"Aunt Rita's right here, Inspector. Don't tell me Uncle Tom's gone and got himself arrested." Maria had apparently heard about some of Benton's recent antics.

No, I won't be telling you that, said Kaminsky to himself.

He ignored her prompt and asked her please to put Mrs. Benton on the line.

"Just a minute," she said, and laid down the phone. He heard her footsteps on the hallway's bare wood floor, and her voice call, "Aunt Rita, there's a policeman on the phone for you." A distant voice said something in Italian that he didn't catch, but from the tone it sounded like a curse. A chair scraped, and more footsteps approached the telephone in the hall.

"This is Rita Benton." The voice was richly accented and slightly exasperated. "No doubt you are calling about my husband. What has he done now?"

"Please sit down, Mrs. Benton. I have some very bad news for you." He told her, but not that her husband had been stabbed to death.

"Gesù, Maria e Giuseppe!" she cried. "Maria, Joe, Tommasso è morto! Mio amore!" She began to moan, and her niece rushed to the phone with her husband in tow.

"Take her back to the kitchen, Joe. Get her some brandy. Hello, Inspector, what did you tell her? Is my uncle dead?"

"Yes, he is, Mrs. Kron. Can you arrange for your aunt to return to the city as soon as possible?"

"What happened to him?"

"His body was found at the Art Students League. There will have to be an autopsy, and we need Mrs. Benton, as next of kin, to release the body to the medical examiner."

Maria Kron took charge. She told Kaminsky that she and her husband would drive Rita Benton to New York

City immediately. He gave her the address of the Eighteenth Precinct, and she said they'd be there by noon.

Thank God that's over, at least for now, thought Kaminsky. *I hope she doesn't break down here at the station. I'd better have a policewoman on hand when she gets here. She'll probably start howling when she identifies the body. Oh, well, that won't be my problem. And the guys at the morgue are used to it.* He called the New York City Mortuary at Bellevue Hospital to let them know that he would be bringing in Mrs. Benton early that afternoon.

Kaminsky now turned his attention to the statements taken from Christopher Gray and Raymond Breinin the previous night.

Chris had told him that Alston's afternoon class finished at four thirty, after which students tended to trickle out until about five. Then the room was vacant until a quarter to seven, when the monitor for the evening class went in to tidy up and do whatever preparations were required. He said the studio door was left open so students who wanted to work after class could come and go, but the top floor was usually deserted between classes.

He was the Wednesday evening monitor. He explained what was involved, depending on the type of setup. A live model might need drapery, a chair, a stool, or a pole, which were usually left out in the room or kept in the storage closet, while a still life arrangement required a table and props from a separate cabinet. The monitors had keys to all the doors.

When asked where he was during the hiatus between

classes, Chris said he'd gone to the cafeteria around six to grab a sandwich and stayed to chat with some of the other students. Then he walked up two flights and entered Studio Nine at six forty-five, his usual time.

"What about the time from four thirty to six?" asked Kaminsky.

"I was in Laning's mural class in Studio Sixteen on the first floor until half past four," he said, "and I stayed on to work on my project. I'm a full-time student, and I want to be a professional muralist when I finish my coursework. I just won a scholarship that'll begin in January, so between that and my G.I. Bill I won't have to monitor anymore."

"You say you were on the first floor all the time until you went to the cafeteria?"

"Yes, that's right. I'm working on a mural concept for a library, just a proposal, nothing specific. Sort of like what Benton did when he was first trying to get mural commissions. He made a proposal to the New York Public Library back in the '20s, but it was rejected. I guess I'll have to expect that, too, unless Mr. Laning goes to bat for me. He did the library murals in the main branch, you know, on Fifth Avenue."

Kaminsky took him back to the point. "Was anyone else there with you during that hour and a half?"

"No, I guess not. I think somebody came in to get something from a locker, but I wasn't paying attention. But nobody else stayed after class, if that's what you mean."

Kaminsky left it at that. He had the statement typed

up, and Chris signed it. The inspector thanked him for his cooperation and dismissed him with the usual caution not to leave town until the matter was cleared up. It was obvious to both of them that Chris couldn't support his account of his whereabouts during the period when the killing must have occurred. The time of death had yet to be officially determined, but the corpse was fresh when the medic examined it. Dead not more than two hours was his guess.

Meanwhile a homicide detective had been interviewing Breinin. This thankless task was given to Anthony Falucci, a veteran interrogator with a mild manner that concealed a razor-sharp instinct for obfuscation, mendacity, and all manner of cover-ups. His questions were not audible through the interview-room door, but Breinin's answers were, much to the amusement of the cops in the hallway.

"I was in studio all day! No, idiot, not League studio, my studio! Is there I paint my pictures. Alone? Of course alone! With pittance I get from League, you think I can afford assistant? What is corroborate? My wife has job, my daughter has school, they cannot what you call vouch."

The artist made no secret of the fact that he harbored a grudge against Benton. His statement reiterated the censorship of his mural, for which he held Benton responsible, and the deep-seated animosity that had led to his ejecting him from the classroom the previous week. These facts were embellished with many colorful epithets in two languages.

Eventually, under Falucci's persistent probing, Breinin constructed what amounted to an alibi. He remembered that he emerged from his studio—the converted front parlor of his Bethune Street apartment—at around four thirty, after the sun had set and he'd lost the light. His daughter was home from school, and they'd had a cup of tea in the kitchen and chatted until about five. Then she got busy with her homework while he cleaned his brushes and puttered around the studio. His wife returned from work at five thirty as usual, and the family had dinner together before he left for the League at seven, which was after the body was discovered. He would not have had time to leave home, go to the League, kill Benton, and return before his wife got home.

"Of course he has only his family to back him up," said Falucci, as he handed the signed statement to Kaminsky, "and the murder weapon belongs to him. You should have heard him, Jake. He was actually proud that it was his knife— what did he call it? Oh, yes, here it is, a kinzhal—we found in Benton's chest."

"I did hear him, loud and clear, when we first questioned him," Kaminsky recalled. "He called it the perfect weapon for revenge. Gray said it was kept in the studio prop cabinet, under lock and key. But I wouldn't be surprised if it's a skeleton key that opens all the cabinets, so anyone with keys could have access. We need to check on that. And since Breinin's only there once a week, other teachers must be using it, too."

"Breinin had the motive," said Falucci, "but if his story checks out, he's in the clear. I'll interview the wife and daughter this evening. Gray had the opportunity—he's in the building, can open the cabinet, is going up there anyway to set up for the class at seven—but why would he kill Benton? Okay, the guy was making a pest of himself, but that's not reason enough."

Even though Chris had seemed entirely honest, Kaminsky knew better than to accept his story at face value. "Could be there was something going on that Gray didn't mention? He told me he's training to be a muralist. That's kinda outside my area of expertise, but I bet you don't just walk out of art school into a career. You'd need recommendations, maybe an apprenticeship, to get started. He said he hopes his teacher, Laning, will help him, so maybe he approached Benton as a potential mentor. Suppose Benton saw his work, didn't like it, told him so, and threatened to derail him when the time came. Look how he sabotaged Breinin."

"So how does he get Benton up to the top floor?"

"He has a locker up there. Maybe that's where he keeps his stuff, not down on the first floor. Easy to find out. He could have arranged to meet Benton up there so he could show him what he was working on. Benton says it's a load of shit, and he's gonna blackball him. Gray gets sore and beans him."

Falucci liked that line of reasoning. "Maybe he hit him too hard, and that's actually what did him in. Or he had a heart attack as a result. How old did you say Benton was— late seventies, right? Anyway, he's dead, and Gray has to think fast. He remembers the knife, fetches it out, sticks it into Benton to make it look like that's what killed him. The autopsy should tell us whether he was alive or dead when he was stabbed."

Kaminsky wasn't buying that scenario. "That doesn't account for the postcard. Maybe I didn't mention that to you." He reached into the case file, extracted the clear plastic envelope containing the card and handed it to Falucci. "The knife pinned that picture to Benton's chest. No prints on it, unfortunately."

The detective let out a breath, half whistle, half sigh. "What the fuck, an Indian attack? You saying whoever killed Benton stuck the knife through this before they stabbed him? What the hell's it supposed to mean?"

"If you're asking me the significance, I can't tell you," said the inspector, "but one thing it means is that the killer wanted to send a message. It also means that the stabbing wasn't a spur-of-the-moment act. Look at the information on the back. It's one of Benton's paintings, and it's called *Retribution*. Not just any old Benton painting, I'm sure of that."

Falucci nodded. "Points right back to Breinin, doesn't it?"

Twenty

The intercom on Kaminsky's desk buzzed. When he flipped the switch, the clerk told him that a Stewart Klonis from the Art Students League was calling. "Put him through," he said, and picked up his phone.

Klonis informed him of Bill Millstein's fight with Benton in the cafeteria and provided the Millstein family's address, 310 West Forty-Ninth Street, only five blocks from the Midtown North station house. Kaminsky relayed the background to Falucci and sent him to investigate.

There were twenty doorbells at the entrance to the five-story building. Falucci found the name Millstein, one of the few Jewish ones among the largely Irish roster. His ring brought no response. Fortunately he bumped into a gossipy neighbor, who told him that Mr. Millstein was at work, Mrs. Millstein was out, and she hadn't seen the son for the past few days.

"Such a nice boy, so polite, not like the hoodlums around here," the yenta said as she rolled her shopping basket toward the entrance to the brownstone next door. "For their elders, they got no respect. But he wants to be an artist, so meshuga. 'What you gonna eat, paint?' his papa asks him, but his mama says, 'Let the kid alone, Sammy.' She thinks he's talented, whatever that means. So maybe he's Picasso, but it don't pay the rent."

Falucci thanked her and said he'd come back later. "You should maybe call first," she suggested, "they got a phone. In my apartment I can hear it ring, we got such thin walls." He said he'd take her advice.

———

Back at the station, the Krons had arrived with Mrs. Benton, who proved to be as formidably distraught as Kaminsky had feared. Backed up by Felicia Fisher, his most experienced female officer, he steered the trio into his office as quickly as possible. Chairs had already been arranged for them, and Fisher guided Rita Benton to the one directly facing Kaminsky's on the other side of the desk. Joe and Maria Kron sat slightly off to the side. Fisher asked if anyone wanted water or coffee, which were declined all around, then she stepped back and stood at ease by the office door.

Throughout the preliminaries, Rita kept up a steady stream of lamentations in Italian. Maria interjected soothing words, when she could get one or two in, but without effect. Kaminsky had no choice but to interrupt her.

"Please accept my sincere condolences, Mrs. Benton. Under the circumstances, your distress is understandable, but I must ask you to bear with me while I take some information from you. I don't speak Italian, so I hope you'll indulge me by answering in English."

Rita wiped her eyes with a large man's handkerchief, already quite damp and probably supplied by Joe, and squared her substantial shoulders. A heavyset woman of seventy-one, with short-cropped salt-and-pepper curls framing a face that still bore the evidence of youthful beauty, she was every inch the Lombardy matron. Although she'd arrived in New York as a teenager, her voice had never lost its thick accent, which could be sweet as honey or tart as vinegar, depending on her mood. Today it was not mellifluous.

"What has happened to my dearest Tommasso?" she demanded. "I cannot believe he is gone from me! I must see him or I will not believe it!"

"I have arranged that, Mrs. Benton," Kaminsky told her. "Your husband's body is at Bellevue Hospital, in the care of the medical examiner's office." He decided not to say it was in the morgue, which sounded so clinical and morbid. "You'll need to make a formal identification. Officer Fisher and I will take you there, and your niece and her husband are welcome to come along. First, however, please sign this release"—he slid a form and a pen across the desk to her— "authorizing the medical examiner to perform an autopsy."

She regarded the form with alarm, as if it were a poisonous snake. "It means you will cut into my Tommasso's body! No, I could not bear that. Why would you do that?"

Now came the part he was really dreading. "Your husband did not die of natural causes, Mrs. Benton."

She stared at him. "Not a heart attack? That is what I expect, he had one last year. He was pushing himself so hard, so hard. New York will kill you, I tell him, but he laughs, tells me not to worry, he can look out for himself. Old fool! He never looked out for himself, it was always me. Not to worry would be not to breathe!"

She had gone off track, and Maria reached over and patted her hand. "Take it easy, Aunt Rita. Let the policeman finish."

He told her what they had found in Studio Nine, and she let out a wail of misery. "Gesù Cristo! Orribile, orribile! Who would do such a thing?"

"I promise you we will find out, Mrs. Benton, but we need the autopsy to determine the cause of death. We think he may have been hit on the head before he was stabbed, and it's possible the blow killed him. Or he may actually have had a heart attack and been unconscious, or even already dead, when he was stabbed. Please let us have your cooperation." He pushed the release form closer to her.

"Go ahead and sign, Aunt Rita," prompted Maria. "They have to do their job."

Silent now, she crossed herself and signed the form.

"Thank you very much, Mrs. Benton," said Kaminsky,

collecting the document quickly and concealing his relief as best he could behind his matter-of-fact demeanor. "Officer Fisher, have the desk call the hospital and let them know we're on the way, and alert the squad car. You'll go in it with Mrs. Benton and I'll drive with Mr. and Mrs. Kron."

"Yes, sir," said Fisher, and left the room.

But Kaminsky did not make a move to leave just yet. He addressed all three of them. "One more thing before we go. Please tell me if you know of anyone with a motive to kill Mr. Benton. Anyone who threatened him, or had a grudge that made him, or her, seem dangerous. I understand he was a man who rubbed some people the wrong way. Did he antagonize anyone enough to provoke such an attack?"

"More than once I threaten to kill him myself!" said Rita with feeling. "We fight like cat and dog sometimes, then we make up. Yes, he could be impossible, but he was lovable, too. Nobody could stay mad at him for long."

In his peripheral vision, Kaminsky saw Joe roll his eyes and Maria poke him in the ribs. He rose and moved around the desk to escort them to the cars.

"Well, please give it some thought. It was not a random attack, that much is certain."

Twenty-One

An hour later Kaminsky returned from the morgue, having turned Rita Benton over to the personal care of Milton Helpern, the chief medical examiner, who assured her that he would handle the postmortem himself. Known as "Sherlock Holmes with a microscope," Helpern was famous for getting to the bottom of the most mysterious cases of sudden death, whether from natural causes or foul play. Some of his notable achievements in forensic pathology, including his widely reported criticism of the John F. Kennedy autopsy, had recently been described in the rather gruesomely titled book *Where Death Delights*.

In his thirty-six years with the Medical Examiner's Office, Helpern had performed thousands of autopsies and supervised thousands more. He assured Mrs. Benton that he would do only what was necessary to determine the cause of death, and his sympathetic manner helped ease her through the ordeal of identifying her husband's body. Fortunately they had arranged for a windowed viewing room separated from the autopsy theater. Kaminsky was sure that if she'd been taken in to view the body directly she would have thrown herself on it.

Afterward she was returned to the custody of the Krons, who said they would take her back to the St. Regis and inform the two Benton children, who lived in Massachusetts. There was also a funeral to arrange, but not a burial. The Benton family plot was in Neosho, Missouri, but Rita had no intention of interring him with the relatives who had overtly disapproved of her. According to his wishes, she planned to have him cremated and to scatter his ashes on Martha's Vineyard, where they had first summered in 1920, when he was wooing her. After they married in 1922, they spent every summer on the rustic island off the Massachusetts coast. For an artist so closely identified with imagery of the Midwest and the South, it seemed surprising that this Yankee stronghold was in fact the source of Benton's Regionalist aesthetic, but he credited the Vineyard, as it was known, as the locale that inspired him to begin his study of the American environment and its people.

On his desk Kaminsky found a note from Detective Falucci to say that the Millsteins were not home when he visited and that he'd go back later. Also that he'd interview the Breinin family after five thirty, when Mrs. Breinin was expected home from work.

There was another note informing him that while he was out a Mr. Lloyd Goodrich of the Whitney Museum had called and left his number. He flipped on the intercom and asked the clerk to call him back.

Goodrich's secretary connected him immediately. "Thank you for returning my call, Inspector," he said. "I understand you are in charge of the Benton investigation."

"That's right, Mr. Goodrich. Do you have information for me?"

"Frankly, I don't know that I do, but Stewart—Mr. Klonis, that is—said you want to hear about anything that may have a bearing on the case. It's just something that happened at the museum last week. At the time, I passed it off as a minor incident, but in light of what occurred, it seems worth mentioning. Of course it may have no bearing at all."

Stop shilly-shallying, dammit, said Kaminsky to himself. Out loud to Goodrich he said, "And what would that be, sir?"

"Have you heard of an artist named Andy Warhol?" Kaminsky said he knew the name. It would have been an oblivious New Yorker indeed who didn't know it, considering the publicity Warhol had received for his deadpan takeoffs of Campbell's soup cans and Brillo boxes, posterized portraits of celebrities, and grisly renderings of car crashes and other disasters. He was also getting plenty of ink for his coterie's outrageous behavior, and especially their provocative movies, some of which had been closed down by the police for indecency. His so-called Factory on East

Forty-Seventh Street, where the films were shot, had been raided more than once.

Goodrich told him about Benton's run-in with the Warhol entourage. "Tom's antipathy to Andy is somewhat ironic," he mused. "He had a similar group of devoted followers when he, too, was a provincial transplant making his reputation in New York, and in their own way they were just as iconoclastic. They were fueled by whiskey instead of drugs, and they weren't making pornographic movies, though in some ways their art was equally controversial. But Andy is gay, and a couple of his hangers-on are transvestites. Tom couldn't abide homosexuals, and he hated Pop art, which he thought was a corruption of his populist philosophy."

"From what you tell me, the animosity was all on the Benton side," said Kaminsky. "You say Warhol was making favorable comments about Benton's paintings, and no one in the group was contradicting him?"

"I wasn't there myself, but that's what I was told by the guards. But, you know, or perhaps you don't, Andy isn't always sincere. At least one always has to wonder if perhaps he's pulling one's leg. He'll say something like 'I love that,' and it makes you think, does he really, or is it an act? Most of the time he has a very bland affect, and even when he lights up he's a dim bulb. To put it another way, he's the static center around which his circle of manic misfits revolves. If he was praising one of Tom's paintings, and the others were echoing him sarcastically, Tom would naturally take it as mocking. That would be sure to get his goat."

"But then Benton would be the one with a motive for violence, rather than the other way around. You said he went after them in the gallery. Did he physically assault anyone?"

"No, the guards intervened before anyone got hurt, but he was using some very offensive language. There was a bit of pushing and shoving. I was told Tom went for Andy, and one of his boys got in the way before the guards broke it up. And one of the girls, a real one, that is, was screaming at Tom. She called him, please excuse my language, a scumbag and said he'd be first on the shit pile of men she planned to exterminate. She said she'd get him in the dark with a six-inch blade."

"You mean one of them actually threatened him?"

"It all seemed almost amusing at the time. At first they were laughing at Tom's bluster, which of course only made him more belligerent. Anyway, no real harm was done, and it gave the visitors something to talk about at their dinner parties. One of the guards got Tom to my office, and he blew off some more steam about the degenerate art world. Can't say I completely disagree with him. By the time he calmed down, the Warhol party was long gone. I walked him out front and hailed a cab for him."

Kaminsky circled back. "This girl who threatened him, any idea who she was?"

"As I told you, I wasn't in the gallery when it happened. Perhaps one of the guards recognized her. I can ask them. You don't think she was serious?"

"It's like you said, Mr. Goodrich, it may have no bearing

on the case, but it needs investigating. Was it just an angry outburst or a real threat? If it was real, was it acted on? You wouldn't have called me if you hadn't asked yourself those questions."

———

There were quite a few Millsteins in the phone book, but only one at 310 West Forty-Ninth Street—Samuel Millstein. Falucci placed the call at half past three and got Mrs. Millstein, who said her son was not at home.

"When do you expect him back?"

"Who wants to know?"

"This is Detective Anthony Falucci of the New York City Police Department, Mrs. Millstein. I need to speak to your son in connection with an investigation."

There was a pause, then she said simply, "He's out of town." She was not going to elaborate. He thought, *I wonder how much he's told her.*

"Then I'll need to ask you some questions," he said. "I'll be with you shortly. Please stay at home until I get there. It will only be a few minutes." He hung up before she could object.

On his way out of the station, he popped into Kaminsky's office and told him he'd spoken to Mrs. Millstein and was headed off to interview her. "I'll go from there down to Breinin's place," he said. "The wife is supposed to be home around five thirty. If I'm early I'll wait for her. Don't know how long I'll be at the Millstein place. The mother says her son's out of town. Probably on the run to Canada, only now he's dodging the law as well as the draft board."

"Shouldn't be too hard to trace him. I'll issue a warrant and alert the inspection station at Rouses Point. That's where the New York Central train goes through customs before heading into Quebec. There's only one train a day, and it won't have gotten to the border yet." He knew this because, on his vacation in August, he and his wife had taken that train to Expo 67, the world's fair in Montreal, and had been exasperated by the long delay passing through customs. No passport was required, but proof of identity was.

"He's sure to have a fake ID," said Kaminsky. "I got a pretty good description from Klonis over at the League, but see if you can get a photo of him from his mother."

Twenty-Two

By the time TJ arrived at the League that evening, the building was literally buzzing with apprehension. The top floor was cordoned off, and the police had been questioning the instructors and staff who were in on Wednesday. Other officers had been sent to interview those who had been there Wednesday but were not in today. The registrar had supplied a list of all students registered in Wednesday classes, and they were being checked for criminal records. It was obvious that they were treating Benton's death as a homicide.

Klonis had insisted that, despite the ongoing investigation, classes should be held as scheduled. Alternative accommodations had to be found for those usually held in Studio Nine—not a simple matter, since the large studio was used primarily by full-time students who left their canvases there and were now barred from getting them. They would have to start over in a different studio or with a different instructor if no vacant space could be found.

Fortunately Breinin taught only on Wednesday evenings, so he would not be returning to that studio for a week, by which time Klonis assumed the case would be solved. Of course if it turned out that, notwithstanding his denial, Breinin was the killer, he'd have to find another instructor. He could probably persuade one of the other part-timers to take on two evenings a week.

This logistical juggling act didn't affect TJ's once-a-week night class, which maintained its normal schedule. And the venerable building itself still sat sedately in its usual spot on West Fifty-Seventh Street, but that was where normality ended. The entrance was now guarded by a uniformed police officer, who turned away anyone not authorized to enter. Proof was needed, so a monitor also stood at the door checking everyone's identification against a long list of students, staff members, instructors, and models. No part-timers were allowed in if it wasn't their assigned day.

A chilly crosstown breeze blew in TJ's face, warning that fall would soon turn to winter. He turned up the collar of his jacket as he approached the entrance, and the atmosphere cooled further as he huddled with a group waiting for admission. "No one goes in who's not on the list," shouted the cop. "Get your IDs ready."

"What's going on?" asked a young man next to him, someone he didn't know from one of the other evening classes.

"Didn't you read about it?" replied TJ. "There was a body found here last night. The police are investigating." He filled in some of the story he'd got from the paper as they slowly made their way to the entrance.

While the cop gave TJ the once-over, a man with a clipboard asked him for his ID. He offered his draft card, which showed his 1-S classification as a full-time college student. The monitor, a hard-faced man whom TJ pegged as ex-military, looked at it and handed it back to him without comment. His name was checked off, and he was motioned through the outer door. Clearly the gatekeeper was not enjoying his job.

Once inside, he joined the general hubbub in the lobby, where another monitor was redirecting Rudolph Baranik's students, whose class in Studio Nine was relocated. Loud complaints were heard—"All my supplies are in my locker up on five," "I need to get my painting," and "What room did he say Baranik is in?" Baranik, a Lithuanian émigré, World War II veteran, and Art Students League alumnus, was an outspoken anti-war activist whose ongoing series of paintings he called *Napalm Elegies* was chronicling the human ravages of America's defoliation campaign. His Thursday evening life class attracted a fiercely loyal cadre of like-minded students, including those Vietnam vets who were also against the war. They would have gone to his class if it had been moved to the broom closet. Fortunately a vacant studio on the second floor was available, so that's where they were sent.

TJ made his way among the knots of students speculating about Benton's death. Theories ranged from apoplexy brought on by a fight, the most popular, to murder by one of the many people he had offended, not an unreasonable assumption.

"I bet Bill Millstein did him in," TJ was alarmed to hear one young woman suggest. "I was in the lunchroom when he called Bill a poor excuse for a man, then started cursing at him, said he must be a fucking pansy. I think he called him a kike, too. Bill picked up a knife off the table, and I swear he would have used it on Benton if a couple of the other guys hadn't stepped in."

"My money's on Breinin," said someone in another group. "I heard he was telling the world how he hated Benton's guts and was glad he was dead."

"Yeah," chimed in his friend, "but would you say that if you killed the guy? Not if you're smart. Breinin's impulsive, and he's got a temper, but he's no fool."

"Maybe they had an argument, and Benton blew a fuse," offered an advocate of the apoplexy explanation. "I'd say that loudmouth Russian's capable of riling him up enough." Apparently the fact that Benton had been stabbed had not yet leaked out.

When TJ finally reached the studio, he saw Ellen already inside. She usually went home to change after work, swapping her miniskirt for more practical jeans, but tonight she hadn't bothered. Instead she'd gone straight from the Automat to the League, a mere matter of crossing the street.

At first they wouldn't let her in—too early, the monitor said—but at half past six they gave her the okay. She was looking for Bill.

"Have you seen him?" she asked TJ anxiously. "He hasn't been to the Automat for over a week, and out in the lobby they're saying he may be mixed up in this Benton thing. What really happened, TJ? Did he just drop dead or did someone kill him?"

"Damned if I know," he answered. "My dad saw it in the paper this morning, that's the first report I got, and it didn't say much, just that he was found dead upstairs. Nobody outside has a clue, either, they're all just guessing."

The bottleneck at the entrance was thinning out, but some students had decided to turn around and go home when they heard what had happened. Others had probably read about it and simply stayed away. The only one who didn't seem perturbed was Wally, who came in late, apologized politely for the delay, and disappeared behind the screen.

At seven thirty the depleted class was far from settled when Laning appeared. Usually he would wait for an hour or so, giving the students time to accomplish something before he checked on their progress. But this was no ordinary night.

Remarkably, Chris had shown up for the afternoon mural class, which had also been sparsely attended, and went about setting up as if nothing had happened. But when the class finished he took Laning aside and told him the whole story, knife and all—except for the postcard, which neither he nor Klonis had gotten a good look at. He said only that something, probably a note of some kind, was stuck on the blade.

Laning was dumbfounded. "It's unbelievable. I've heard people say they'd like to wring Benton's neck, even threaten to punch him in the nose, but actually kill him? I know there was that fracas in the cafeteria, but surely it wasn't that serious."

"Things got pretty hot," Chris told him, "but Wally intervened and Mr. Lawrence calmed Mr. Benton down, and we got Bill the hell out of there. Dan Forsburg was pretty sore, but it was actually kinda comical the way Benton went after him, like a bulldog taking on a bull. I think he'd had a skin full, or he would've thought twice before he threw that punch. Dan shrugged it off afterward, but he was ready to deck him for sure."

"What about you, Chris? You've had a helluva time. The shock of finding the body, then trying to cope while the police were here, then being questioned at the station until late at night." Gently, he put his hand on his student's shoulder. "How are you holding up?"

Chris sighed, lowered his eyes, and shook his head. "Thanks, Mr. Laning, but I'll be okay. It only sank in when I got home and had to tell Arlene why I was so late. I called her from the police station, just so she wouldn't worry, but I didn't want to talk about it on the phone. She's afraid they'll think I did it, but that's ridiculous. I had no reason, none at all."

He looked up, and Laning saw a hint of uncertainty in his eyes. Was it simply hope that the police had accepted his statement, or a plea for affirmation? He decided it was the latter.

"Of course you didn't, Chris. No one I know had a reason to go that far. Anyone could have come in here and attacked him, the building is wide open—at least it was. The police will find him, don't you worry." Laning realized it was a foolish thing to say. Chris would be stupid not to worry.

———

Laning stepped onto the model stand and asked Wally, who had only been in position for a few minutes, to take an early break. He donned his robe and returned behind the screen, where an armchair and the sports page were waiting.

"I think you all know the cause of the disruption," Laning began, "but what you may not know is that Mr. Benton was murdered. Chris Gray found him, and he told me Tom was stabbed in the chest."

There were murmurs in the room, a few jaws dropped, and one of the women made a high-pitched sound that wasn't quite a scream, then quickly covered her mouth with her hand.

"If any of you would prefer to skip tonight's class, I will understand. I've discussed it with Mr. Klonis, and he has agreed to give everyone credit for a makeup session when this business is settled. Meanwhile those of you who wish to stay, please raise your hands." Only Al Schwartz, and a couple of the other painters did. Since Bill was absent, Al took attendance while those who were leaving packed up their supplies.

"I hate to miss class, but I couldn't have concentrated," said Ellen as she walked with TJ to the subway. "It just seems, like, unreal. Murder. Wow. Crazy. Just crazy." She was mumbling, distracted. Suddenly she stopped, reached out, and took TJ's hand. "Will you help me find Bill?" she asked earnestly. "I'm so worried, scared for him, really. I need to know he's okay."

Thrilled by her touch, TJ wanted to embrace and reassure her, but he held back. *Not now, when she's so upset,* he told himself, *she'll take it the wrong way.* Instead he contented himself with squeezing her hand, not too hard but firmly, and promising to do whatever he could.

Then he had an idea. "Come home with me, Ellen. We can ask my parents what to do. I told you they're both cops. My mom's a detective; she does this kind of stuff all the time."

"You really think they'd help?" she asked hopefully. Her hand tightened in his, causing his heart to skip a beat.

"I know it," he said. "Come on. Let's go."

Twenty-Three

Nita and Fitz had just settled down to watch *Bewitched* when the apartment door opened and TJ brought Ellen into the hall. Their other choices at eight thirty on Thursday night were the cowboy series *Cimarron Strip* or the crime drama *Ironside*, both of which were a bit too close to their line of work to be appealing. The fantasy sitcom featuring a beautiful witch turned suburban housewife was just the sort of escapism they craved.

TJ was used to seeing them snuggled on the couch in front of the television, but the sight of a middle-aged couple behaving like, well, like teenagers startled Ellen. She was sure her parents didn't cuddle that way, even when she wasn't around. Unlike teenagers, however, Nita and Fitz weren't embarrassed to be caught at it. They just smiled and took their time untangling.

"Home so early?" asked Nita rhetorically as she rose from the couch and approached them. "And who is this lovely young lady with you?" Fitz got up and turned off the TV, then followed his wife to welcome TJ's guest.

"This is Ellen Jamieson," he told them. "She's in the art class with me. We left early because of the disruption, you know, about Mr. Benton. Mr. Laning said we could do a makeup session later. It's kinda chaotic over there right now. Everybody's pretty freaked."

"I'm surprised they held the class at all," said Fitz. "Well, come on in, you two. Let's grab a beer, and you can tell us what's going on." He turned to Ellen. "Or would you rather have a soft drink? We have Coke and ginger ale."

"I'd love a beer, Mr. Fitzgerald. I'm kind of wound up, and it might help me relax. Actually, I have something on my mind that I'm hoping you can help me with. TJ said it was all right to ask."

Nita was quick to express concern. "Of course. Come on into the kitchen and we'll find out what the trouble is. This must be very distressing for you, for all the students, in fact. The faculty, too. I hope they get to the bottom of it soon. Here, let me take your coat."

They headed to the kitchen, where Fitz liberated four Rheingolds from the icebox and Nita fetched the opener, some glasses, and a box of pretzels while TJ directed Ellen to the table, pulling out a chair for her in a gentlemanly way. She thanked him politely and made an effort to smile in spite of her somber mood. Behind their backs, TJ's father nodded and his mother winked back, signaling approval of their son's good manners and of his new girlfriend.

Once they were settled, TJ told them what they'd learned about Benton's death. "They're saying he was murdered; stabbed in the chest. One of the monitors found him, and he told our teacher, Mr. Laning, and he told us."

Fitz got right to the point. "Any suspects?"

"That's what I'm so worried about," said Ellen. "I'm afraid my friend—our friend, that is—Bill Millstein may be involved. No, I don't mean that, I don't think he did it, but I'm afraid the police will."

"Why would they?"

"Bill had a fight with Mr. Benton last week. I wasn't there—I work during the day, across the street at the Automat, and it was at lunchtime, in the school cafeteria. But I got an earful later when some of the students came over after class. They said Bill was about to be drafted, and he told them he wouldn't go, that he'd run away to Canada. He got really upset, and right there at the table he burned his draft card."

"That's a serious offense," said Nita, "but what does it have to do with Benton?"

"Mr. Benton saw him do it and heard what he said about running away. He was there having lunch with some of the teachers and one of the models. My friends said he got furious, started shouting at Bill, demanded to know his name, said he'd just committed a crime and should go to jail. He was cursing him out, calling him a coward and a homosexual. Bill is gay, but he doesn't want people to know it, so he yelled at Mr. Benton to shut the you-know-what up. Then Mr. Benton called him an anti-Semitic name, which made him even madder. They said he almost went for Mr. Benton with a knife; they had to hold him back. When they got him out of the room and took him downstairs to cool off, he said 'I bet that blankety-blank is gonna turn me in.' That was last Tuesday, and I haven't seen Bill since."

She leaned forward and fixed her large blue eyes intensely on Nita. "Please, Mrs. Fitzgerald, can you help me find him? TJ says you're a detective. I'm sure the police will be after him, and I want to know he's safe. I hope he's already in Canada."

"Where does he live?" she asked.

"With his parents, somewhere on the West Side, in Hell's Kitchen, I think. Oh dear, I don't think he ever mentioned the address. He did say it's close enough that he usually walks to the League. Only takes the subway when it's pouring."

"The school will have his address," interjected TJ, "and if his fight with Benton was reported they've probably already given it to the police." He looked around the table and continued, "There's more to it. Chris Gray—he's the monitor I mentioned—told me that Bill's boyfriend is in the army in Nam, and the guy is in trouble mentally. Plus Bill was hoping to get into Cooper Union so he could get a student deferment, but he just found out he got rejected. All that on top of the induction order, and you can see why he went ballistic when Benton started in on him."

Ellen's distress was evident. "Oh, no, I didn't know all that! Why didn't he tell me?" The fact that he hadn't confided in her had hurt, but TJ was quick to reassure her.

"He never saw you after he got the news. According to Chris, he thought things were smoothed out with the boyfriend last Monday, then the next day came the double whammy—no from Cooper and yes from the draft board. The letters were waiting for him when he got home Tuesday night. Then things blew up with Benton on Wednesday, and he was gone—probably lying low while figuring out his escape plan."

"They usually give you a month or so to report," said Fitz, "so he'd have time to make arrangements. There are organizations that help draft dodgers get fixed up in Canada."

"If he's going to leave the country," reasoned Ellen, "why would he risk another run-in with Benton? I can't believe he'd come back to the League just to have it out with him, much less to kill him."

Fitz decided to be blunt. "Revenge, that's why. Don't look shocked, it happens all the time. When people get angry or frightened they do things you'd never expect. From what you say, your friend Bill was both. I've been on the force for thirty years, and I know it all too well. So does Nita, don't you, honey?"

"Fitz is right, Ellen. No matter how close you are to Bill, you have no idea what he might be capable of under the circumstances. Think about it. He's already feeling desperate, then Benton calls him a homosexual in front of everybody in the lunchroom and gives every indication that he's going to have him arrested for a federal crime. It takes him a few days to arrange the trip to Canada, then when he's ready to leave he takes his revenge on Benton and gets the hell across the border. It's only a day's train ride to Montreal, so he's probably there by now."

Ellen looked so dejected that TJ couldn't resist putting his arm around her shoulders. Since his parents were there, it clearly wasn't a come-on, and she accepted it as a genuine gesture of comfort. She leaned into him. Fortunately she didn't look up or she would have seen his face flush.

He wanted to follow up with reassurance, but what could he say? Don't worry? Totally lame. It's probably all a mistake? Equally dumb. He can take care of himself? Not helpful. We'll find him? How?

Fitz came to his rescue. "Tell you what. In the morning I'll call over to Midtown North and speak to Jake Kaminsky. Find out if they're after Millstein, or if he's in custody. He's in trouble for burning the draft card anyway, so there's probably a warrant out if they don't have him already."

Ellen sighed, and a tear ran down one cheek. She quickly wiped it away. "Thank you, Mr. Fitzgerald," she said weakly. "I guess that's all you can do. Don't think I'm not grateful, but I hate to think of him in jail." She straightened up, and TJ discreetly removed his arm. She looked Fitz in the eye. "And I don't care what you and Mrs. Fitzgerald think. I know he didn't kill Mr. Benton."

Nita smiled. She reached across the table, took Ellen's hand, and said, "Then we'll just have to find out who did."

TJ kicked himself mentally. *Shit,* he thought, *that's exactly what I should have said.*

Twenty-Four

When Hector Morales's popular Forensic Psychology class, "Inside the Criminal Mind," let out at noon, TJ stayed behind.

"Professor Morales," he began, but Morales stopped him before he could say another word. A beaming smile accompanied his admonition to the young man he'd known since his protégée Juanita Diaz Fitzgerald gave birth to him nineteen years earlier.

"I'm off duty, Juanito, so Tío Hector will be just fine."

TJ returned the smile. "Okay, Tío Hector, I've got a question for you. It has to do with the Thomas Hart Benton killing, I'm sure you've heard about it. Do you have time now?"

"I have another class at one. Let's grab some lunch, and we can talk in the dining hall. No one will overhear us." John Jay College shared the Police Academy's military-style cafeteria, where the raucous crowd and resonant acoustics made it difficult, if not impossible, to eavesdrop on adjacent tables.

It being Friday, the dining hall was relatively quiet, and they managed to find a table to themselves, out of earshot of others. Not that TJ's queries were all that private, but they were personal, and he preferred not to broadcast his close relationship with Morales in case his fellow students thought he had an inside track on good grades.

Such favoritism never would have occurred to Morales, whose reputation for rectitude had earned him the nickname Spic and Span four decades ago, when he was a lowly patrolman in his East Harlem neighborhood. He had worn the offensive sobriquet as a badge of honor, joking that he was the only clean cop in the Twenty-Third Precinct, though he was relieved when it was replaced by El Zorro— the fox—a label he proudly accepted as a testament to his investigative prowess. He was renowned for his ability to collect and evaluate evidence, and his reputation as an interrogator was legendary.

Once they had their food and were settled at the table, TJ outlined the Benton case, at least as much as he knew. Morales listened with interest, especially as he described Ellen. When he confessed that he was smitten with her, Morales came back with "¡Bien hecho, Juanito! It's about time you stopped fooling around and got yourself a steady girlfriend."

After TJ finished blushing, he told Morales about their encounters with the abrasive artist, and about Breinin's public outburst when the body was being removed. Then he got around to Bill's predicament, and what he had heard about his run-in with Benton in the League cafeteria.

"Of course that's only hearsay," he added, well aware that such evidence is questionable at best. "But if it's true, then what happened to Benton points the finger at Bill, and he's made himself look even worse by running away. But that may have nothing to do with Benton. He's on the run from the draft board."

"That's certainly a complication," said Morales. "Also, from what you tell me, he knew the place like the back of his hand. He knew where the knife was kept. He probably would have been able to enter the building, commit the crime, and leave without being noticed. So what's your question?"

"Why would he do it? If he's on the run, why would he make himself even more of a wanted man? Now it's not only for draft dodging, but for murder, too. No way he wouldn't be suspect number one."

"Did you talk this over with Nita?" TJ said he had. "What does she think?"

"Actually it was Dad who said he could have done it for revenge, and Mom backed him up. He said it was such a strong motivation that people sometimes do stupid, irrational things. If what Ellen told me is true—and she got it secondhand—Benton called Bill a coward, a homo, and a kike. Bill tried to stab him there and then, but his buddies stopped him. So then he cools down, he has to work on the getaway to Canada, why wouldn't he just cross it off? Why would he have waited until he was ready to run and then settle the score?"

"Because he wanted revenge, like Fitz said. He and I have both had cases where the most mild-mannered, unassuming people turned into cold-blooded killers when sufficiently provoked. And often it's not a spur-of-the-moment thing. They plan it out. I'm not talking about a professional criminal organizing a hit, like the sort of cases we're analyzing in class. These are ordinary people who get pushed over the edge but can't retaliate immediately, so they figure a way to get even later on. Sometimes they never go through with it because they don't get the opportunity. Maybe their target goes away, or dies. Sometimes they think better of it, for fear of the consequences, and live with the anger and humiliation. That often happens when it's a wife or girlfriend with kids—she swallows it for their sake. But a guy like Bill, who's getting ready to disappear, maybe he figured he's got nothing to lose."

"Por Dios, Tío Hector, you're painting a pretty damning picture. I was hoping you'd say he's not the type to do such a thing, but you're telling me that anybody could, even a sweet, gentle guy like Bill."

"Sí, Juanito, I'm afraid that's just what I am telling you."

———

When Fitz finally rolled in around seven, he found TJ waiting anxiously for a report.

"Hold your horses, buddy," he said as TJ pressed him, "let me get my coat off, for Pete's sake. And I'd kill for a beer—well, maybe I wouldn't go quite that far. Anyway, let's get a couple, and I'll tell you what I found out."

Fitz's call to Kaminsky had yielded significant details that were not public knowledge. Before he relayed them to TJ, he made his son promise not to share them with anyone, even Ellen.

"I don't want this getting around the school," he said sternly. "What Jake told me is confidential information related to an open investigation. I'm sharing it with you because I trust you, and I think you can use what you know to mitigate Ellen's fears without giving anything away. Will you agree?"

"Of course, Dad. You know I won't let anything slip, promise."

"All right, then. Jake told me that there are a few suspects, not only Bill, though he's the prime one because he's done a bunk. There are others who had motive and opportunity."

"Can you tell me who?"

"You probably already know they're looking at the Russian guy, Breinin, because he freely expressed his hatred of Benton. What you don't know is that the knife they found in Benton's chest belongs to Breinin. It's an antique dagger, called a kinzhal, that the Cossacks carried back in the nine-teenth century. He used it as a still life prop. It was either right there in the studio prop cabinet, or Breinin had it on him. Thing is, he has an alibi, says he was home with his family when Benton bought it. They're trying to check that out, find people other than the wife and kid who can corroborate his story."

Fitz took a swig of beer. "They haven't ruled out Christopher Gray, the guy who found the body. It's kind of a long shot, but there's a theory that Benton might have been against him becoming a professional muralist, so Gray got into a fight with him, knocked him out, and he died as a result. Then Gray tries to make it look like somebody else killed him with the kinzhal. But it's pretty tenuous. Why wouldn't he just leave the body for someone else to find? They don't much like him for it, but he's still on the list."

"I've met Chris," said TJ. "He's the one who told me about Bill's boyfriend in Nam and the fight in the cafeteria, though he didn't go into detail about the nasty names Benton called Bill. It'd take a lot of evidence to make me believe he'd get physical with a guy Benton's age. The old lush probably had a bad heart, and God knows what his liver looks like, maybe Swiss cheese."

Fitz chuckled. "Dr. Helpern is probably slicing it up right now. Anyway, there's more." He took another swallow of his Schaefer.

"Turns out the League isn't the only place Benton made trouble. Couple of years ago he had a run-in with the head of the American Academy, Lewis Mumford. He took exception to Mumford's political views, tried to assault him in public, and resigned his Academy membership. Then he gets himself reinstated over Mumford's objections. Mumford's furious, so he quits in protest."

"I know about that," TJ interjected. "Benton actually bragged about it when he came to our class, though he didn't mention the guy's name."

"No love lost there," Fitz continued, "and maybe resentment deep enough to inspire a lethal payback, so they're checking on Mumford's whereabouts on Wednesday evening. And that's not all. A couple of weeks ago, Benton got into a shouting match at the Whitney with Andy Warhol and that bunch of weirdos who hang around with him. Jake tells me his source said it got pretty rough. One of the weirdos threatened Benton quite explicitly. Called him a scumbag, and said she'd exterminate him with a six-inch blade, which is actually what killed him."

"A woman?" said TJ.

"Hard to tell with the Warhol crowd, but Jake says he was assured it was in fact someone of the female persuasion. So he's following up, sending a detective to Warhol's place to nose around, see if he can find out who it was gave Benton the death threat. I wish the sorry bastard luck!"

Twenty-Five

After his phone conversation with Fitz, Kaminsky looked over the duty roster and picked the sorry bastard.

At twenty-nine, Angelo Valentino was the youngest detective in the precinct. With the movie-star looks and suave manner of his namesake, he'd been dubbed Sheik by his fellow cops. Kaminsky figured he should be able to penetrate Warhol's headquarters, known as the Factory, without attracting any negative attention. He hit the intercom buzzer.

"Sheik in the squad room?" he asked the desk sergeant. "Good, I got a job for him. Send him in."

Casually dressed in a sports jacket, open-necked shirt, and slacks, Valentino looked like an NYU grad student—which in fact he was, putting himself through law school at night. His apparent informality disguised a formidable talent for evidence gathering, backed up by remarkable intuitive powers of deduction. *If he graduates from law school and becomes a prosecuting attorney,* thought Kaminsky, *defendants beware.*

"Detective Valentino front and center," he said, coming to what passed for attention and shooting Kaminsky a saucy salute. "What's up, Jake?"

"Take a load off, Sheik," said the inspector, pointing to a chair. "I got a case I think will interest you." Valentino raised his eyebrows and lowered his body onto the offered seat. He crossed his legs, leaned back, and listened attentively as Kaminsky ran through the case history.

"We gotta check out this Warhol business," he said, "and that's where you come in. I want you to go over to the Factory and nose around, see if you can get an account of what went down at the Whitney. Ever been there?"

"The Whitney, or the Factory?"

"Either or both."

"Matter of fact, I've been to the Whitney and seen the Benton show. I took my kid there to see the toy circus by Alexander Calder, the guy who makes the mobiles. They told her about it in school, and she nagged me until I gave in. Actually it's a really clever thing, all handmade. They got a TV monitor with a film of Calder playing with it, so you can see how it works, and we both thought it was fun. Since we were there we had a look around the museum and kinda stumbled onto the Benton show. Angie, that's my girl, she liked Benton's pictures but I didn't go for 'em. Anyway, that's the first time I been in the new building, which I also wasn't crazy about. You been there?"

"No, not yet, but I've seen it from the outside. Not very inviting, is it?"

"All the charm of a bunker, outside and in."

"Been to the Factory?"

"Nope, but I've heard plenty about what goes on there. They're making porno films and trying to pass them off as art, for Chrissake. Add the drugs, and you got a heavy scene, man. The boys in the Seventeenth have raided it a few times."

"See if you can find out who threatened Benton. Supposed to be a woman, but could be a tranny. It helps that you've actually seen the show. Maybe you can get them talking about it."

The young detective stood. "Give it my best shot," he said, and headed out.

———

The fifth-floor loft in a seedy commercial building at 231 East Forty-Seventh Street had been Warhol's headquarters since 1963, when he was transitioning from a lucrative career in commercial illustration to fine art, with no guarantee of financial or critical success. For a man who wanted to be rich and famous, it was a risky proposition, but by the time Sheik took the freight elevator up to Warhol's workshop, the gamble had paid off. Leo Castelli, one of the top dealers in contemporary art, was shrewdly marketing Warhol's paintings, and his place in the Pop pantheon was secure.

Sheik had heard about the Factory from his buddies at Seventeen, so he stopped off at home to change into a turtleneck sweater, black Levi's, and harness boots, topped off with his black leather motorcycle jacket. They had told him what to expect, so he wasn't surprised to find the whole place, including the elevator, covered in silver paint, tinfoil, and cracked mirrors. Warhol had a reputation as an onlooker who instigated activity and then, distant and detached, watched it through his camera lens. A fully reflective environment seemed perfectly suited to his passive voyeuristic persona.

Raucous music was audible even before Sheik reached the top floor. As he stepped out of the elevator, he saw a large open space. At one end of the loft, a band was practicing. At the other end, a spaced-out couple was lounging on a large red sofa. Apart from a few rickety wooden chairs and a table holding a Bell & Howell movie projector, the couch seemed to be the only significant piece of furniture. A few people were fooling around with camera equipment and silkscreens, and a man was styling the bleached blond hair of a kimono-clad woman seated in front of one of the fractured mirrors.

No one paid any attention to him. People wandered in and out all day long, regulars and strangers came and went— the place was Liberty Hall. He assumed Warhol must be around somewhere, and sure enough he spotted a guy who fit his description talking on what looked like a pay phone on the back wall. When he got closer he could see that the coin box was missing, so the artist had evidently rigged it to a conventional phone line. Just one of the many playful touches that distinguished Warhol's world from the real one.

When he saw Sheik, Warhol cut short his conversation and went to greet the handsome newcomer.

"Hi," he said amiably, "can you give me a hand over here?" He turned and walked the unidentified visitor to where two young men were manipulating a large silkscreen onto a sheet of canvas laid on the floor. He pointed to one end of the canvas.

"Grab hold of that end and pull it straight, will you?" he asked. "I don't mind folds, but I can't stand wrinkles."

Sheik crouched down and did as instructed, and the screen was positioned on the flattened canvas. He and Warhol stood back and watched as one of the assistants poured black ink onto the screen and another fetched a squeegee. With one man on each side, they pulled the tool over the surface and forced ink through the screen.

"Now hold that end again, please," said Warhol, and Sheik grabbed the canvas as the assistants raised the screen to reveal a portrait of the art dealer Sidney Janis, another of the prescient engineers who drove the Pop Art Express. His 1962 *New Realists* exhibition, which included Warhol's *200 Campbell's Soup Cans*, had helped launch the movement.

The assistants tacked the canvas on the wall to dry, and Warhol studied it approvingly.

"Wow, that's great," he said. "Let's do another one, on a different background." He turned to Sheik. "What's your favorite color?"

"What's yours?" he countered.

"Green, like money," was Warhol's reply.

"Okay," said Sheik, "let's do green." A new canvas was laid down, and one of the assistants applied a coat of bright green acrylic paint.

"Give it half an hour to dry," Warhol advised. "How about some Coke while we wait?"

Sheik wasn't sure if he meant a liquid or a powder, but he went along. "Sure," he said. Warhol led his helpers to an elderly fridge in one corner and fished out four bottles of Coca-Cola. The band was also taking a break for refreshments. Not soft drinks.

Warhol made use of an antique wall-mounted opener and handed the bottles around. They pulled up some chairs and toasted the new portrait.

"I think Sidney will love it," Warhol remarked. "Don't you think he has a nice face? I want to do a whole series of him."

Sheik had no idea who Sidney was, but he figured, knowing Warhol's preoccupation with celebrities, that he must be someone important. He decided to use Sidney as an opening line to what he hoped would be an informative conversation about the Benton incident.

"I think I recognize him," he lied. "Wasn't he at the preview reception for the Thomas Hart Benton show at the Whitney?"

"I don't know, he could have been," said Warhol, "I wasn't

there. I think I got an invitation, but I get so many I can't keep track. But Rodney and I and some of the gang went to see it a couple of weeks ago."

"What did you think of it?" prompted Sheik.

"Oh, my God!" chimed in Rodney, one of the two assistants, "it was a fiasco!"

"Really? What was wrong with it?"

"Actually, we hardly got to see the paintings, because no sooner did we go in than we ran into Benton himself, and he made a scene in the gallery. Everybody got freaked out, and we had to leave."

Sheik pretended to look startled. "Was that you guys? I heard about that from a friend of mine who's a guard there. What happened to set him off?"

"Well, confidentially, it was all Candy's fault," said Rodney, not so confidentially, directing his remarks to the room in general. "Andy was admiring a painting of a nude woman, and Candy announced, rather too loudly, that she had a much better body than that slut and that she'd pose naked for Benton any time he liked. And give him a blow job if he wanted one. Of course Candy didn't know he was standing right there!"

Thinking this might be the woman who threatened Benton, Sheik asked, "Who's Candy?"

"*Me*, that's who!" came a voice from across the room, where the party in question was having her elaborate coif expertly styled by Billy Name, the hairdresser and studio manager who was responsible for the Factory's silver lining.

Candy Darling rose from the chair in a huff of offended dignity and marched over, powder-puff mules clacking, to confront them, hands on hips. "He really was *very* impolite to me, you know. Instead of insulting me, he should take me up on *both* offers." Apparently news of Benton's death hadn't reached the Factory. "Just think, if he paints *me* in the nude he'll have a whole new career."

She shrugged off her kimono to reveal herself in all her manly glory. From the neck down, she was a he. And a quite well-endowed one at that.

It was all Sheik could do to keep a straight face as Candy struck a few cheesecake poses. Andy, however, had no such inhibitions. He giggled and applauded, as did Rodney and their companion, who said, "Bring it over here, sugar Candy, and we'll see just how sweet you are."

Candy wagged a scarlet-tipped finger at him. "Look but don't touch, you naughty boy. I'm saving myself for a hot date tonight, *not* with you, Ondine. Billy's giving me a special do for the occasion." She collected her robe and put it back on with theatrical flair.

"Anyway," she continued, "it wasn't me who got the old goat so riled up. It was Valerie who really made him pop his cork. She's the one who called him a scumbag. But then *every* man's a scumbag to her, so he shouldn't have taken it personally." She flounced back to Billy's hairdressing station.

Sheik jumped right into that opening. "I'd love to hear Valerie's side of the story. Is she around?"

"I haven't seen her in a while," said Warhol. "She usually

comes around when we're filming, looking for a part—and a handout. She's been in a couple of my movies. She wants me to produce her play, but it's not too interesting." With that he lost interest in Valerie. "Let's see if the green paint is dry."

It wasn't until they were positioning the silkscreen that Rodney thought to ask, "Who are you, man? Haven't seen you here before."

"I'm Sheik," answered Valentino truthfully, but Rodney misunderstood.

"You don't look chic to me, fella. In fact you're fuckin' butch, so that's what I'll call you."

"Butch is fine with me," he said with a grin, "or Fuckin', if you want to be on a first-name basis."

Twenty-Six

With other cases demanding his attention, Inspector Kaminsky had had a distracting morning. The previous evening's call from Rouses Point had told him the border patrol had failed to identify anyone fitting Millstein's description on the New York Central train that arrived at five after four. There had been a few young men traveling with families, but their documents were in order, and some male college students, also with valid IDs, who didn't look anything like Millstein. Today he'd received similar reports from the other border stations with vehicular crossings. Either Millstein had changed his appearance and obtained convincingly forged identity papers, or he hadn't crossed into Canada the day before.

Falucci's interview reports were on Kaminsky's desk when he returned from the scene of an armed robbery.

The Millstein one was inconclusive, and it made for discouraging reading. It stated that the detective visited the family's apartment at four p.m. on Thursday, November second, 1967, and found Mrs. Anna Millstein, age forty-three, at home. She identified herself as the mother of William Millstein, age twenty-one, her only child. Neither her son nor her husband, Samuel Millstein, age forty-five, were at home.

As Kaminsky scanned the report, it was clear that Anna Millstein had no intention of cooperating with the investigation. Falucci had not told her the nature of the inquiry, only that he wanted to interview William in connection with an incident at the Art Students League. She gave no indication that she knew about Benton's death and seemed more stubborn than nervous. When Falucci asked where he was, he got the same answer she'd given on the phone: out of town. All her answers were equally terse and unhelpful. When did he leave? A few days ago. Where did he go? He didn't say. When will he be back? I don't know. Do you have a photograph of him? No.

Falucci had left his card, with instructions to contact him when William returned. He put the card on the hallstand by the door, and Anna Millstein glanced at it contemptuously as she let him out. He was certain she tore it up as soon as he left.

Outside the building, however, he had better luck. He

had spotted a couple of the neighborhood hoodlums loitering on a stoop and asked if they knew where he could find Bill. They were about to blow him off when he flashed his shield and said he was interested only in talking to Bill, not in the reefers they were no doubt carrying. They both said they hadn't seen him around lately, and one of them told him to ask at Rudy's, a bar and grill a few blocks down on Ninth Avenue. He said Bill worked there weekends as a busboy.

Many legends surrounded Rudy's, a classic watering hole that was rumored to have received the city's first liquor license when Prohibition was repealed in December 1933. Earlier, it was said, the place was a speakeasy where Al Capone bent his elbow before he moved to Chicago. Adjacent to the theater district, it was a favorite haunt of the literati and glitterati. It was also where the Mets baseball team, New York's "lovable losers," habitually drowned their sorrows. From its vintage neon sign to its original mahogany bar, almost nothing had changed in decades except the prices, though the hot dogs were still free.

Falucci knew Rudy's well from the periodic brawls and noise complaints to which Midtown North responded. In the lull between the lunchtime rush and the evening influx, the place was relatively quiet. He found the owner, Helen Rudy, tallying receipts in a booth in the rear. Lying next to the booth, her two large German shepherds eyed him suspiciously and emitted low warning noises as he approached, ready to see him off if he made a wrong move toward Helen or her money.

"Shut up, boys," she commanded, "here comes the law. Better behave, or it's the hoosegow for you." The dogs quieted down, and Helen greeted Falucci with a genial wave. "C'mon over, Tony, and park it here. What'll ya have?" She motioned to the waiter.

"Good to see you, Helen. I'll have a ginger ale, thanks," he said as he slid into the booth, and the waiter took his order to the bar. "How's business?"

"Always slow between Halloween and Thanksgiving," she answered, though the pile of bills she was counting looked substantial, especially for a midweek take. Falucci had never known a bar owner to say business was booming, except during the World Series.

"I'm told you have a busboy working here named Bill Millstein," he began, but she interrupted him.

"Had, Tony, past tense. The faggot ran out on me, no notice, nothin'. And he better not come back, 'cause if he does, Prince here'll have him for lunch, won't ya, boy?" She glanced down at the dog, which replied with a growl. Falucci took that for "with pleasure" in Alsatian.

"I guess that means you don't know where he is. I've already talked to his mother, but she's clammed up. I may go back and see the father when he gets home from work, but I don't think I'll get anywhere with him, either."

The ginger ale arrived, and Helen toasted Falucci with the Guinness she was nursing. "Here's to crime, Tony, so's you can earn your pension."

He smiled as he returned her toast, then got serious.

"I'll be back on the beat if I don't make some headway on this case. Problem is, I think the guy may have skipped the country."

"What'd he do, rob a bank or something?"

He told her about Bill's induction notice, and that he'd burned his draft card and said he was going to Canada, but nothing about any other reason for wanting to find him. That was reason enough.

Helen was sympathetic. "I guess that explains it, but he could have told me. I'm no snitch, I'd never have turned him in." More than once she'd let locals wanted for smuggling arms to the Irish Republican Army hide out in one of the upstairs rooms, and as far as her sympathies for the war effort were concerned, she was vehemently opposed to Lyndon Johnson and his policies. In her opinion he was a villain who might well have engineered the Kennedy assassination so he could take over the presidency.

"You called him a faggot," said Falucci. "Are you saying he's queer, or is that just what you call any guy you're mad at?"

"I shouldna said that, but he got my Irish up. Left me shorthanded last weekend, and I'm scramblin' to cover for him, so I was pissed off at him, still am. In fact he is queer, not that it's obvious, far from it. Personally I don't give a flying fuck what people do in private, as long as they don't cause trouble in here. Bill never brought his sex life into the bar, never flirted or came on to anybody. Just a really nice kid, good at his job, too. That's another reason why I'm mad at him for leavin' me in the lurch. He'll be hard to replace."

"Then how do you know he's queer?"

"Because he told me, only he said gay, not queer. He needed somebody to talk to, and he knew I wouldn't judge him. He couldn't go to his parents, he was afraid his old man would kick him out."

"What was the problem?"

"His boyfriend, Vinnie, got drafted. He was real upset about it, with good reason. This was about a year ago. I'd met the guy a couple of times, when he came in to meet Bill after work. An Italian kid from the neighborhood, also seemed straight, so I assumed they were just, you know, good buddies. I think they'd known each other since high school. They were both deep in the closet, used to double-date with girls to keep it looking kosher, never said a peep to the draft board when they registered, but now they were goin' down to the West Village together on the sly. Hangin' out with others like 'em, where they could express their feelin's openly. Bill told me it wasn't just about gettin' laid, said him and Vinnie are really in love. On Christopher Street, they could finally be themselves."

"Think I can get a line on Bill down there?"

Helen laughed out loud, and the dogs jerked their heads at the guttural sound.

"Fat chance! They got a network that helps draft dodgers, like an underground railroad for runaway queers. Ever heard of fairy dusting? That's what they call it when one of 'em disappears over the border. If they dusted him, he's gone."

———

The Breinin report was more promising. Falucci had arrived at the Bethune Street apartment at five thirty and met Mrs. Patricia Breinin on the way in. He identified himself, explained his reason for visiting, and told her he had some questions for her and her daughter. "I'm sure Susan is here," she said as she admitted him.

The entrance hall led to a back parlor on the right that doubled as a dining room. To the left, the north-facing front parlor had been adapted as Breinin's studio. That door was closed, but Falucci could hear music inside, from either a radio or a phonograph.

"Do you want to speak to Ray as well?" asked Patricia. "I don't like to disturb him when he's working, but I will if you need him." Falucci said not to bother him—in fact he didn't want her husband to be present, but didn't say that to Patricia. So she showed the detective into the back parlor, where Susan Breinin was doing her homework at the dining room table. A pretty teenager, she had inherited her father's coal-black hair and piercing dark-brown eyes, but not his bombastic manner.

"Hi, Mom," she greeted her mother cheerfully, then looked expectantly at their visitor.

Patricia introduced him. "Susie, this is Detective Falucci from the police. He's investigating the Benton killing, and he needs to ask us some questions." She offered Falucci a chair and took one herself.

"Gosh, isn't it terrible?" said the girl. "Papa said somebody stuck his knife—Papa's, I mean—in Mr. Benton. I
hope you find out who did such an awful thing."

Falucci took out his notebook and jotted down some
preliminaries. Susan gave her age as fifteen and said she was
a sophomore at the High School of Music and Art on West
135th Street, to which she commuted by subway. She was
usually home around four, unless she had glee club practice
or some other after-school activity. On Wednesday she
came straight home. She and her father had tea together in
the kitchen—she'd made it in the antique Russian samovar
that was a Breinin family heirloom.

"I'll make some for you, if you'd like," she offered, but
he declined politely. "Maybe when we're done. I won't
be much longer." He was hoping to finish before Breinin
appeared.

"What did you do after tea?" he asked. She said she'd
settled down to work on an essay for English class, and her
father had gone back to his studio. He closed the dining
room door behind him, and she heard the studio door open
and the radio playing classical music on WQXR, as usual.
She wasn't sure of the time, but she thought it must have
been around four thirty Breinin had put it somewhat later,
closer to five.

Falucci then turned to Patricia, who said she was thirty-
seven—some twenty years younger than her husband,
noted the detective without comment. Maybe a second
wife, he speculated. She said she worked as a salesclerk at the

S. Klein department store on Union Square. Her shift ended at five, and she walked home across town—unless it was raining or snowing, in which case she took the Fourteenth Street subway to Eighth Avenue. Sometimes she stayed a few minutes to chat with her coworkers, but she was usually home by five thirty.

On Wednesday, however, they were stock taking in her department, and she didn't leave until five forty-five, arriving home around six-fifteen. Her husband was still in the studio—she heard his radio playing—but he came out right after she got in, and they all had dinner. Knowing she'd be late, she'd made a stew the day before, so all she had to do was heat it up.

Falucci silently noted the time discrepancy, and confirmed that Breinin had left for the League at seven, his usual time. He then thanked Mrs. Breinin and her daughter and left without encountering the artist. It was six p.m.

He walked to the IND subway station at Fourteenth Street and Eighth Avenue, took the uptown E train five stops to Seventh Avenue, and walked four blocks north and half a block east to the League. That took him thirty minutes, including a five-minute wait for the train. He then went up to the fifth-floor studio, taking the stairs instead of the elevator. He chatted with the cop on duty, looked around the room, and killed time until half an hour had passed. Then he repeated the route in reverse. He was back at the door of 31 Bethune Street by seven thirty. The whole operation took ninety minutes.

By his calculation, based on the times given by Patricia and Susan, Breinin could have left the apartment at four thirty, gone to the League, killed Benton and returned home by six, with neither of them aware that he'd been out.

Twenty-Seven

When TJ walked Ellen home on Thursday night, he'd made a date to meet at the Up 'n' Down the next evening. At the time he didn't have anything to offer but sympathy. But now that Friday was here, he had a plan. True to his word, he wouldn't tell her where his information came from, but he was determined to go where Nita had pointed.

Seated in one of the twin armchairs, with two open cans of Schaefer on the little table between them, he laid it out for Ellen, who occupied the other chair.

"Let's forget Bill for now. We can't help him anyway. I'm gonna do what Mom suggested, find out who really did kill Benton. I heard that a woman threatened him at the Whitney, said she was going to, what was the word? Oh, yeah, exterminate him. Maybe she did. I need to find her."

Of course Ellen was curious. "How do you know that?"

"I'm in a building full of cops all day, and they're a fount of information," he said cryptically. "Word is, she's one of Andy Warhol's gang. They hang out at a place they call the Factory. I'm going over there and check it out. Once I identify her, the police can take it from there."

Ellen was immediately enthusiastic. "Let's go right now!" She jumped up and headed for her coat, then stopped and turned. "Wait a minute, where is the Factory?"

"Hold on," he said, raising his hand in a cautionary gesture. "I said I'm going, not we. They're a bunch of degenerates and druggies. It's no place for a nice girl like you."

She rounded on him, her eyes cold as blue ice. "Don't you dare patronize me! I'm the one who started this, and I'll see it through, with or without you. I can find the Factory on my own, thank you." She marched to where her coat hung on a hook on the back of the apartment door. She grabbed her coat off the hook, put it on, shoved her keys and wallet into the pockets, took a woolen muffler off another hook and wrapped it around her neck.

TJ stood immobilized and silent as she prepared to leave. *Jesus, what an idiot I am,* he thought ruefully. Once again he searched for the right thing to say and came up empty.

Ellen opened the door. "Are you coming? If not, you can wait here for me. Michele won't be home from The Bitter End 'til after one, so you'll have the place to yourself. There's more beer in the icebox. Help yourself."

Her little speech had given him time to think. She was standing very straight, her head held high with indignation, as he approached her. Thinking he was after his jacket, she closed the door. But that was not his objective.

Since words failed him, he chose action. He wrapped his arms around her and kissed her on the mouth, not lustfully, but fervently. Two words suddenly dawned on him. Still embracing her, he bent his lips to her ear and whispered, "You're wonderful."

Ellen sighed and leaned back in his arms, relaxing now, but still alert. A Cheshire cat smile lit up her face. "And you're exasperating!" She reached up, took his face in her hands, and returned his kiss in equal measure.

Both a bit dazed, they stood for a few moments, just taking each other in. Then they laughed and hugged and laughed some more—at themselves, at each other, and at the situation.

TJ's next hug turned into an embrace. One hand cradled Ellen's head as he kissed her again, more deeply this time. She responded, and he twisted slightly so that his free hand could find its way inside her coat, along her back and, with growing urgency, to her breast, sending spasms of desire through her body. As he drew her closer, she could feel his shallow breathing, his thumping heart, and his erection pressing against her groin.

He hesitated. The next move, she knew, was hers.

Slowly, so as not to make him think she was pushing him away, she stepped back, shrugged off her coat, unwound the muffler, and hung them up again. She took his hand, and led him into the bedroom she shared with Michele. The light was off, and she left it that way, sensing he was unsure of himself and guessing, correctly, that he had never gone all the way before. She had, with her high school sweetheart. They had consummated their relationship in late March, when he was home on spring break from college in Chicago, not long after she'd moved into the Up 'n' Down.

After a romantic reunion dinner, they'd returned to the apartment to find that Michele had discreetly gone to the movies. As their usual necking and petting escalated, they decided that making it was the perfect way to celebrate her independence. As it turned out, he'd come prepared with a condom. Before he went back to Chicago they'd run through a few more.

In anticipation of his return in the summer, she had invested in a diaphragm. Then in June she got the letter telling her that he had a summer job on campus and wouldn't be coming back. Reading between the lines, she assumed he was also working on a new girlfriend, probably a classmate who had more in common with him now than she did. So she dried her tears, put the cap in the drawer and, with typical pragmatism, decided to chalk it up to experience and be thankful for her erotic adventure—lessons she was about to put to good use.

———

She sat on her bed and urged TJ down beside her. She kissed him lightly, drew back, and looked into his eyes, steadying herself for her revelation.

"I want you to know," she said softly, "that I don't sleep around. In fact I've only had one other lover, and we broke up months ago." She paused, letting him absorb this information.

He averted his eyes. What was he thinking? She couldn't read him, couldn't gauge his reaction, and began to second-guess herself. *Maybe I shouldn't have told him. Maybe he won't want me now that he knows I'm not a virgin. But I had to be truthful, I couldn't bear to deceive him, because I love him. Please, God, don't let him reject me.*

Actually he was grateful that she was so forthright, and that she had taken the initiative. He didn't resent her previous relationship. On the contrary, he was surprisingly relieved that he didn't have to be the one to deflower her. He found the prospect intimidating, since he was uninitiated himself. But she had removed that stumbling block.

In the face of his silence, Ellen pressed on. "I'm serious about you, TJ, really serious, or I wouldn't go all the way with you. I think you feel the same, at least I hope you do. But if you don't, please tell me. I'll still go through with it, 'cause I'm not a tease, but then I won't see you again."

He thought his brain would burst, it was so full of emotion. Suddenly the words were there, gushing out. "Serious? My God, Ellen, I'm in love with you! Head over heels. What a stupid cliché, but I don't know how else to put it. I just can't tell you, I can't think straight."

Gently, she pushed him down onto the bed, her long hair cascading over him as she kissed him deeply, then whispered, "You don't need to think, just feel." His arousal was immediate and obvious. She pressed her hand against his crotch, and he groaned with pleasure.

"I need to do something first, for protection," she told him. Another lingering kiss that left him aching for her, and she was gone. But not for long.

When she returned, she was wearing the diaphragm, a bathrobe, and nothing else. He had kicked off his shoes, but had remained fully clothed, not knowing what the etiquette was. He was not completely inexperienced, but this was just what he had only dreamed about, and he was fearful of doing something wrong and spoiling it.

Don't rush, don't push it, let it happen naturally, he told himself. And sure enough, when she was lying beside him, unbuttoning his shirt while he caressed her nubile body, his nervousness evaporated. Somehow his clothing vanished in the most miraculous way, his hands gravitated to her responsive places seemingly on their own, and his lips found just the right spots to kiss and lick and suck. And she seemed to know exactly what to do to him and for how long.

Assuming he would climax as soon as he entered her, she wanted to match him if possible. That was the ideal, but it usually took some practice. He had already given her one orgasm with his tongue and was working on a manual follow-up as he knelt between her legs. She signaled her readiness by wrapping them around his waist. He slid inside her, and remarkably they came together on the first try.

———

Delighting in the afterglow, they lay in each other's arms, resting quietly between whispered endearments. But it wasn't long before they remembered the cause of the emotional outpouring that had brought them to bed.

Wanting to protect Ellen, but knowing she wouldn't allow herself to be left out of his plans, TJ decided to change tactics.

"I'm having second thoughts about the Factory," he said, as she nestled her head against his shoulder. "If we just walk in and start asking questions, they'll get suspicious right away and we'll never get anywhere."

Ellen sighed. "You're right. But what's the alternative? We've got to find out who she is."

Suddenly she raised herself on one elbow and looked at him eagerly. "Listen, I have an idea. Michele sometimes goes to a club called Max's Kansas City, and she says Warhol's gang is in there practically every night. It's just a couple of blocks from here. Michele's friendly with the bartender, kind of sweet on him, actually. I bet she could get us in, and we wouldn't stick out like nosey parkers. Let's go ask her."

"Honey, you're not only wonderful and beautiful, you're brilliant!" TJ reached up and pulled her close. Immediately they were hot again, and their new plan was put on hold for the next half hour.

After an awkward shower in the apartment's ancient bathtub, struggling to keep their footing, and failing to keep straight faces as they soaped each other and jockeyed for position to rinse off under the faltering spray, they dressed and headed to The Bitter End.

It was about nine, and the place was jumping. Paul Butterfield Blues Band were on stage, belting out their highly amplified rock versions of Chicago-style classics like "Shake Your Moneymaker" and "Got My Mojo Working," as well as their own compositions.

Butterfield was one of the few white lead singers who could carry it off, and the crowd was eating it up.

The bouncer recognized Ellen and waved her and TJ in. They spotted Michele, tray in hand, shuttling between the kitchen and the pews. The only empty seats were at the musicians' table, so they worked their way to the back, where Paul Colby occupied the manager's booth, and waited politely until the band finished its number and took a break.

"Hey, Ellen, baby, whatcha doin' here on a Friday night?" asked Colby. "You want to go to work? Tie on an apron and give Michele a hand. Five an hour plus tips, how about it?"

"Tempting, Paul, but I've got a date." She introduced TJ to Colby, who replied with a quick handshake and a perfunctory "Glad to meet ya," and got an equally terse "Likewise" in reply.

"We're only here for a few minutes," said Ellen. "I have to talk to Michele, just a quick word. When's her break?"

Colby checked his watch. "Soon as the second set starts, maybe ten minutes. You want to wait here?" He gestured toward the opposite side of the booth, and they slid in.

"I gotta talk to the band, ask 'em to turn down the volume a bit. This place is too small for that much amp," he said, and rose. "If I bump into Michele I'll tell her you're here."

She had already spotted them and detoured in their direction on her way back to the kitchen with a load of empty plates and glasses.

"Well, well, what's this? A bona fide date, or are you two just slumming?" She set the tray on the table and plopped down in the booth. "Ooh, that feels good. I've been on my feet for three hours. The other waitress called in sick, so I haven't had a minute off."

"Won't Paul be mad if he sees you goofing off?" asked TJ.

"What's he gonna do, fire me? I'm the only one on tonight, so he'd have to take my place!" She laughed out loud at the thought. "Anyway, nobody's going to starve in five minutes, and the busboy can fill in. So what brings you to this dump instead of some more romantic club?"

"Believe it or not," said Ellen, "we're here to see you, and it's a club we want to ask you about. Max's Kansas City. You've been there, right?"

"Sure," she replied, "but if it's an intimate bistro you're looking for, Max's is definitely not it. It's usually a madhouse."

"It's not for a date," said TJ. "Isn't it where the Warhol crowd hangs out? We're looking for somebody who may have something to do with the Benton murder, and we think she's one of Warhol's cronies."

"I'll be damned," said Michele, astonished. "What the hell are you two cooking up? You don't want to get mixed up with that bunch, they're all either crazy or stoned, or both. Why not let the cops handle it?"

"We want to clear Bill Millstein," TJ explained. "Right now he's the prime suspect. If we can identify and locate this woman we will put the police on to her, but we have to find her first."

Michele shook her curls and got up from the booth. "You're the crazy ones. Okay, I'll fill you in on Max's, but not now, it'll take too long. I won't be home until late, and I'll be wrecked, so let's do it tomorrow."

TJ told her he got off from work at Brother's Candy & Grocery on East Fourteenth Street at four p.m. and could get to the Up 'n' Down by a quarter past.

"Don't rush," she said, "Ellen and I will be waiting for you. I don't have to leave for work 'til half past five. We'll have plenty of time, and maybe I can talk you out of it."

Ellen looked at TJ, and back at Michele. "Don't count on it," she said.

Twenty-Eight

F amous Artist Murdered," thundered the headline in the
New York Daily News, and the *New York Post*'s menacing
banner read "Artist's Killer at Large." As usual, *The New
York Times* was more reserved, leading with "Thomas Hart
Benton's Killer Sought," subhead "Artist's Death a Homicide,
Say Police."

The postmortem report had been released. The autopsy,
personally conducted by Dr. Helpern, determined that
Benton had been struck on the back of the head and rendered unconscious before being stabbed in the heart. He
noted that the blade had punctured the right ventricle,
resulting in pericardial tamponade. The sac around the
heart filled with blood, preventing it from pumping and

causing cardiac arrest. Death, he concluded, occurred within moments of the blow.

Beyond the fatal internal hemorrhage caused by the knife, Benton's heart showed minimal scarring from the myocardial infarction he had suffered in 1966. His lungs were dark and mottled from six decades of smoking, which had probably contributed to the heart attack. Remarkably, there was no evidence of lung cancer, and though his liver was steatotic, the condition had not progressed to cirrhosis.

"Constitution of an ox," was Helpern's unofficial diagnosis. As he said to his aide during cleanup, "If Benton hadn't been murdered at age seventy-eight, he could have expected to live well into his eighties."

———

No sooner had the morning papers hit the stands than Stewart Klonis's phone began to ring. As predicted, his private number had been discovered by enterprising reporters with friends at New York Telephone, so both his line and the League's main number were flooded. His secretary, Rosina Florio, was fielding calls from students, instructors, and models wanting to know whether classes were canceled. She was also getting inquiries from out-of-town newsmen in places like Chicago, Indianapolis, and Benton's home state of Missouri. Those calls were routed to Klonis.

All the reporters asked variations of the same question: was the killer someone who attended or worked at the League? Klonis gave them all the same answers: "I am not aware of any charges against anyone connected to the League. The investigation is under way, and all inquiries should be directed to the Eighteenth Precinct. Yes, the school is open and functioning as normally as possible under the circumstances. I have every confidence that the police will apprehend the killer. Please contact them for further information."

The Midtown North switchboard was also busy. Inspector Kaminsky had prepared a statement that was equally vague, since none of his leads had yielded results, at least not yet. He simply said, truthfully but without elaboration, that several avenues of inquiry were being pursued.

A thorough search of Studio Nine had turned up no further evidence, so the police had unsealed the room. Since there were no mural sketches in Chris Gray's locker, the idea that Benton had gone up there to look at his efforts and panned them—tenuous at best—was out the window. As far as anyone they interviewed knew, Gray had never had an argument with Benton, so they crossed him off the suspects list.

There was no sign of a William Millstein at the Canadian border crossings. Either he was effectively disguised, or he had crossed before the warrant was issued. Falucci's report on Breinin called his alibi into question, so Kaminsky had ordered an officer to check with the Wednesday afternoon instructors and students in case anyone had seen him in the building.

Sheik hadn't yet tracked down Valerie, last name unknown, and hadn't wanted to ask more direct questions about her at the Factory for fear of tipping his hand. After he left there, he had headed to the Seventeenth and talked to one of the cops who'd raided the place. The Warhol file included a list of those present during the raids, but there was no Valerie on it.

The uniform told him that, when the creeps weren't at the Factory screwing each other for the camera and shooting up speed and smack, they hung out at Max's Kansas City, a restaurant and nightclub on Park Avenue South, at the northern end of Union Square. He decided to stop by there and sniff around. If Valerie was a regular with Warhol's crowd, maybe the bouncer knew her. Or he could ask inside if anyone had seen her. He could pretend to be interested in producing her play.

There were advantages and disadvantages to tackling Max's on a Saturday night. On the upside, everyone who was anyone was bound to be there—that was also the downside. The place would be mobbed.

Twenty-Nine

When TJ arrived at the Up 'n' Down at four thirty, he was greeted with a passionate kiss from Ellen, which he returned, and a knowing smile from Michele.

"Yes, I told her," said Ellen, snaking her arm around his waist as she led him to sit with her at the dining table. Michele perched on the arm of one of the easy chairs and regarded them with approval.

"Okay, lovebirds, let me fill you in on Max's Kansas City. It's a real phenomenon in a neighborhood that's dead after hours. The owner is a guy named Mickey Ruskin, who used to own joints in the Village that catered to the art crowd, and they followed him across town. Some of them already had a hangout around here, the Cedar Tavern, down on University Place, but it closed a few years ago. When it reopened a couple of blocks away, it was all gussied up, too ritzy for them. So now they argue about what, in the art world, passes for life-and-death issues at Max's. You'll hear them going at it tonight. A bunch of macho windbags, but they're pretty harmless.

"Anyway, when Andy found out that the bona fide artists hung out there, he decided rubbing elbows with them would lend him credibility. But I can tell you, it didn't work. They think he and his gang are freaks, and they don't make a secret of it. When they come in, the guys at the bar either snub them or taunt them—they call him Wendy Airhole. So he goes straight to the back room and takes it over. There's a big round table back there, and that's his headquarters."

"Do you go to the back room?" asked TJ, amazed at her familiarity with the scene at Max's.

"I did, a couple of times, but frankly it was boring. All bitchy gossip and in-jokes, obviously intended to make outsiders feel excluded. Drag queens primping and dishing, and everybody stoned out of their gourds. The waitresses hate them because they're doing speed and acid, and when they're tripping they ain't tipping. Not my thing at all. I prefer the front room, where the art banter can be entertaining, and some of the guys are pretty cute. At least you know they're straight."

Michele turned her attention to preparations for the evening's scouting expedition. "You both look a little on the square side," she declared. "Once I get you into some hipper clothes you'll fit right in at Max's." She went to the closet and brought out a Mexican black lace minidress that she'd bought at Fred Leighton on MacDougal Street.

Ellen regarded it with alarm. "I can't wear that, it's see-through! I'd die of embarrassment. Besides, I'm sure it's way too big for me."

Michele brushed off her concerns. "It's too small for me, that's why I never wear it, and it's meant to be loose. If you're so modest, put on a leotard and tights underneath."

Ellen rummaged in her dresser drawer, found the dance outfit, and headed to the bathroom to change. When she emerged, both Michele and TJ agreed the new look was way cool.

Michele handed her a pair of large pendant earrings and a silver lamé scarf. "Wrap this around your neck," she advised, "and wear your sexy black boots. You'll need some makeup, too."

Under protest, Ellen let her apply frosted eye shadow, heavy eyeliner, and a pair of false eyelashes. The finishing touch was bright pink lipstick. When she turned to show TJ, he couldn't help but laugh.

"It's not the you I love," he said, "but I have to admit it's kind of glamorous, in a theatrical sort of way."

"Max's is full of theatrical characters," said Michele. "Believe me, she won't be out of place. Now for you, TJ." She stepped back and appraised him thoughtfully.

"The jeans and sneakers are okay, but you need something more, shall we say, decorative on top." Back to the closet she went, this time emerging with the flowered blouse she was wearing when they first met. "Take off your shirt, undershirt, too, and try this on," she told him.

He stared at the garment in horror. "You've got to be kidding. A girl's blouse? They'll think I'm a fag."

"Exactly right. Especially since you'll be wearing the same shade of lipstick as Ellen. Hmm, maybe a bit of eye makeup, too."

TJ's response was emphatic. "No way!"

"Come on, scaredy-cat," Ellen teased. "We need to find Benton's killer, and it could be that woman from Warhol's gang. We have to find out if she's with him at Max's, so we're going to have to look and act like we belong there."

"Look, it's a freak show," said Michele. "You'll just be like one of the gang."

TJ decided to compromise. "Okay, I'll do the blouse, but you can forget the makeup. What if some of the guys from John Jay, or worse, the Police Academy, are in there? Lots of them are from around here. I'd never live it down."

"Tell them you're working undercover—on-the-job-training for detective or something."

"With eye shadow and lipstick? Maybe if it was the Stonewall, but you wouldn't catch me dead in that place."

"All right, have it your way," Michele conceded. "See how the blouse fits, and I'll give you some beads to dress it up. Lots of straight guys wear beads these days." Reluctantly, TJ stripped off his shirt and T-shirt and slipped on the blouse gingerly, as if it were either ice cold or burning hot. It fit surprisingly well.

"Damn," he said, "how do you button this thing?" The buttons were on the left side instead of the right, and he fumbled to find them.

"Don't button it all the way. Leave a couple open, to show off your manly chest. Let's top off the beefcake with some icing." Michele draped a few strings of colorful plastic and glass beads around his neck, then stepped back to admire her creation.

"You'll do nicely," she said with a satisfied nod. "I'd say you're both ready to rock and roll. Of course it's way too early. Andy and his gang won't make an appearance before nine, but we'll walk over there now and I'll introduce you to the bouncer, that's Fudge, and my buddy Frank, the bartender. That way you won't have any trouble getting in later."

Thirty

It had rained that afternoon, and reflections from the streetlights glistened on the pavement. The trio turned up their coat collars against the cool, damp breeze and headed north on Park Avenue South, while Michele gave Ellen and TJ a bit more background on their destination.

Why, they asked, was it called Max's Kansas City? She said that, according to Ruskin, after owning bars and coffeehouses in the Village for several years, in 1965 he'd wanted to open a steakhouse-style restaurant.

"When I was a kid," he explained to a curious reporter, "all the steakhouses had Kansas City on the menu because the best steak was Kansas City cut, so I thought it should be 'something Kansas City.'" His friend, the poet Joel Oppenheimer, suggested "Max's" as the something, and the name was born.

Ruskin got his artist friends to do the décor, including a laser-beam projection from Frosty Myers's studio two blocks north, through the plate-glass window and onto the back wall, bouncing off mirrors along the way. A crushed-car sculpture by John Chamberlain was a traffic hazard in the narrow passageway leading to the back room, where Dan Flavin's corner piece of red fluorescent tubes cast a rosy glow over the Warhol entourage.

The art-world establishment congregated up front by the bar, where they continued the booze-fueled debates that had begun at the Cedar Tavern in Abstract Expressionism's heyday. But by the mid-'60s, the Cedar was history and a new wave of movements—Pop art, Op art, minimalism, conceptualism, Happenings—offered a virtual smorgasbord of artistic activity that crossed genre boundaries and invaded the worlds of dance, theater, film, music, and fashion.

This was the dynamic milieu that defined Max's appeal. No lesser authority than William S. Burroughs, the Beat Generation iconoclast, declared that the place was "at the intersection of everything." The mix of old guard and avant-garde attracted the jet-setters and pop-culture celebrities, as well as the hipsters, wannabes, and young hopefuls who congregated nightly under the sign announcing the house specialties: steak, lobster, and chickpeas.

TJ was curious about Michele's friendship with the bartender. "How do you know this guy Frank?"

"Believe it or not, he's a folk music fan. Tuesday is his day off, and he came to The Bitter End hoot one Tuesday night a couple of months ago. You remember him, Ellen, he's the tall Italian stud with the cute moustache. He sat with us after we finished our set and flirted with me, said I was one groovy chick. He told me he liked a woman he could look in the eye."

"Oh, yeah, him," replied Ellen with a smirk. "You didn't fall for that line, did you?"

"You know me better than that, girl. But he gave me his number, and he said to come to Max's any evening as his date, which I've done a few times. Meanwhile, as I recall, you weren't paying much attention to us, since you had an admirer of your own putting the make on you."

TJ bristled with mock indignation. "Do I have a rival? Show him to me, and I'll knock his block off." He stopped, crouched, and raised his dukes. That prompted a playful punch in the gut from Ellen, followed by a gentle headlock from her opponent. The match was decided by a kiss.

"Break it up, you two," scolded Michele, "we're here." The restaurant's awning was only a few feet ahead. With a wave and a friendly greeting to Fudge, who gave her a nod of approval, she led them inside.

Behind the bar, Frank DiBenedetto was polishing glasses and chatting to a few early birds. He was every bit as studly as Michele had said. When he saw her, his face lit up and he came out to greet her with an enthusiastic hug.

"Hey, beautiful, long time no see. It's been at least two weeks. You throw me over for one of those long-haired folkies? Tell me no or you'll break my heart."

"Listen to this guy," said Michele to her companions. "As if I were the love of his life. The reason his eyes are brown is that he's full of shit."

Frank was deeply offended. "No shit, baby. Of the dozens of foxy ladies in my life, you're the only one I truly adore."

"Before I throw up," replied Michele, "I want you to meet a couple of real lovers, my roomie, Ellen, and her boyfriend, Tim." They had decided to use his first name instead of his nickname. "These two are doing a little private detective work. They're on the lookout for a woman who hangs out with Andy. Probably a lesbian."

"More than one of those," observed Frank. "What's her name?"

"We don't know," said TJ, "but we're hoping to get into the back room and keep our ears open, see if we can figure out who she is."

"Mind if I ask why you want to find her?"

Ellen gave him a brief synopsis of the Benton case. "Oh, right, I read about that in today's paper," he said.

She explained their desire to clear their missing friend. "We know he didn't kill Benton, and we think this woman may be the real killer. We need to identify her and tell the police who she is. The feds will still be after Bill as a draft dodger, but at least he won't have a murder charge looming over him."

"If I ever get in trouble with the law, I hope I'll have friends like you to go to bat for me," said Frank, impressed. "Here's what you do. Come back around eight thirty, go to the back room and sit at the small table next to the big round table, have some dinner, on the house. I'll tell the waitress you're my guests, and she'll put a reserved sign on the table, so you'll be there when Andy and company arrive. He always takes the big round table, it's unofficially reserved for him. That way you can eavesdrop, and if you're not getting anything you can start talking about Benton and see if they pick up on it."

TJ liked the plan. "It's sure worth a try." He shook Frank's hand gratefully. "Thanks for doing this, man. We really appreciate your help."

"Anything to please my darlin' Michele," he said as he hugged her again and planted a wet kiss on her grinning lips.

"You can please me by letting me go, you big ape," she countered, her smile turned upside down in feigned disapproval. "It's half past five, and I've got to get over to The Bitter End by six."

Frank clutched his heart and turned his eyes toward the ceiling. "Oh, no, she's leaving me again! I just can't compete with those guitar-strumming country boys who never take a bath. What have they got that I haven't got, besides BO?"

"My paycheck," was Michele's concise answer, and he couldn't argue with that.

Thirty-One

After walking with Michele down to Union Square, they parted company. TJ and Ellen returned to the Up 'n' Down, where they found plenty to occupy them for the next couple of hours. Their activities did not involve listening to records or guitar practice for Ellen. What they did practice was variations on the previous evening's sexercises, with care not to disturb Ellen's elaborate eye makeup. This also caused complications in the postcoital shower. She had to wear two shower caps, one for her hair and another for her face. When TJ saw her shields in place, he discreetly left her to bathe alone. He knew he'd be laughing too hard if he got in there with her.

By the time they'd cleaned up and put on their mod costumes again it was past eight o'clock, time to head back to Max's. A crowd was already gathering on the sidewalk out front, and Fudge was screening admissions. Those he judged to be under the legal drinking age of eighteen or mere gawkers and celebrity-spotters were turned away. He'd been alerted to expect TJ and Ellen, and he waved them through. Even this early, the place was packed with a raucous crowd of art-world denizens, mostly men and a few women, already several drinks in.

Behind the bar, Frank spotted them and beckoned them over.

"Better grab your table before someone else decides to ignore the sign," he advised. "What are you drinking?" They ordered draft beers, and Frank drew them as he signaled to a waitress. "Hey, Debbie, over here." An adorable, petite bottle blond with a pert smile and striking green eyes approached them.

"These are my guests, Ellen and Tim," he told her. "They're the ones for the table in back." He put their beers on a tray with a bowl of toasted chickpeas. "Enjoy," he said, as Debbie picked up their order and led them to the table.

"Watch that hunk of junk on the wall, it's got claws," she cautioned as they made their way down the passage. She'd bumped into the sharp corners of Chamberlain's *Miss Lucy Pink* too many times to be a fan of his sculpture. She much preferred the Flavin in the back corner, with its fluorescent tubes, well above contact height, that bathed the room in eerie red light.

Luckily their table was still unoccupied. Debbie served their beers, took away the reserved sign, and handed them menus.

"Since this is on Frank, why don't you go for the ship 'n' shore special?" she suggested. "You get a nice broiled lobster tail and a club steak. It comes with salad and fries or baked potato. If you're really hungry, start with the onion soup or the shrimp cocktail. Think about it, and I'll be back in a few."

———

An hour later, having followed Debbie's recommendations and cleaned their plates, they were still anticipating Warhol's arrival. Fringe members of his circle now occupied most of the booths and tables, but the big round table where he and his inner clique stationed themselves remained empty and waiting.

TJ pushed back his chair. "I'm going up front to get a couple more beers," he said as he stood.

"Debbie will bring them," said Ellen.

"I want to pay for them," he replied. "I don't like taking too much advantage of Frank's generosity. We've already had two on the house and eaten almost thirty dollars' worth of food, so I'm feeling a bit guilty. I won't be long." He bent down and gave her a kiss on the cheek.

She turned her face and gave him one back, on the lips. "I'll be counting the minutes," she murmured in his ear, which gave him a thrilling rush. *Boy,* he thought as he worked his way forward, *love sure makes you goofy.*

The front room was noisy, smoky, and much more crowded than when they'd arrived. It took a while for TJ to get near Frank, who was talking to a strikingly handsome man seated at the bar, also Italian by the look of him, in a black motorcycle jacket. TJ squeezed in next to him as he was saying "—looking for Valerie. Bouncer says she's not here, but you might know where I can find her."

Frank, who was drawing a beer for the customer, snickered. "I haven't seen Miss Scumbag around lately. Sometimes prayers are answered."

TJ's ears pricked up. Scumbag. That's what Fitz said the woman at the Whitney had called Benton.

"Does Miss Scumbag have a real last name?" asked Sheik.

"Solanas," said Frank with disdain, "Valerie Solanas, a crazy dyke. The founder and only member of the Society for Cutting Up Men, acronym SCUM, complete with a manifesto she hawks around the Village. She tried selling it in here once, but Fudge threw her out. She was raving that all men are scumbags, swearing to eliminate males altogether and set up a female utopia. A real nutjob. She hangs around Andy, but she's a misfit even in his creepy crowd."

Just then Frank noticed TJ and remembered his mission. "Hey, Tim, aren't you looking for a dyke who hangs out with Andy? Maybe it's Valerie."

Sheik turned and regarded the young redhead's blouse and beads. "In spite of your girlie outfit, I doubt she's your type," he said dryly.

TJ felt his face redden and struggled to cover his tracks. "No. I mean yes, you're right. I'm not, you know, looking

to date her or anything. I just want to talk to her about…
um…something I'm working on."

"Thinking of starting a Society for Cutting Up Dykes?"
quipped Sheik. "That would be SCUD, like the Soviet
missile, our secret weapon in the war against murderous
lesbians. Eliminate them before they eliminate us."

That prospect tickled Frank's funny bone, and he chuckled as he served another customer while Sheik and TJ waited
impatiently for him to return. When he did, TJ put a five
on the bar and ordered two more beers. Not wanting to
embarrass him, Frank took the money, drew the beers, and
gave them to him with two dollars change. Sheik drained
his glass and ordered another beer as well.

"Listen," Frank told them both, "you don't have to wait
here for Solanas, she's not hard to find. She lives in the
Chelsea Hotel. Just hang around the lobby, and she'll find
you. She turns tricks there. She calls herself a writer, but she's
actually a hooker—makes her living balling guys. Funny
profession for a man-hating lesbo."

"What does she look like?" Sheik asked him.

"Medium height, scruffy brown hair, big chin, scowls
a lot. Nasty, pinch-faced bitch. If you're after some mean
pussy, she's just the ticket."

"No thanks," said Sheik emphatically, "I'm only interested in her play. Andy told me she offered it to him, but
he turned her down. I'm starting an experimental theater
company, and I'm looking for new material. Guess I'll head
over to the Chelsea and see if she's around."

"Why don't you go along, Tim?" suggested Frank.

Much to Sheik's relief, TJ demurred. "I can't, I have to take Ellen home. I can find Valerie another time, now that I know where to look."

In fact he didn't need to find her at all. He had the information he needed—her full name, a description, and her likely whereabouts—to give the police a solid lead to the woman he believed must be Benton's killer.

Returning to the back room with the drinks, TJ could see that Ellen was annoyed. She frowned as he approached their table. "What took you so long?" she demanded. Her expression changed as she saw the excitement he'd struggled to conceal out front.

"Listen, I'm really sorry, but it was worth the wait." He sat, moved in close, and lowered his voice. "I found her!"

"No kidding! Is she here?" Ellen whispered eagerly.

"No, but now I know who she is, and where she lives. Another guy was asking about her at the bar. Nothing to do with Benton, he wants to produce a play she wrote. Just a coincidence that I overheard what he said, but from what Frank told him about her it has to be the same woman, a lesbian who hangs out with Warhol. He called her Miss Scumbag, because that's what she calls all men, and Dad told me the woman we're looking for called Benton a scumbag."

Ellen picked up on that immediately. Her heavily penciled brows furrowed, and her mascara-rimmed eyes narrowed. "So you got this inside info from your father? You said it was from somebody at college."

Idiot, I put my foot in it again, he winced inwardly, and tried to make a course correction. "I didn't exactly say that, not in so many words. But you're right, I did imply it. I promised Dad I wouldn't tell anyone, even you, so if you're there when he asks how I found her, please pretend you didn't know anything about why we were here or who we were looking for."

Her frown melted away, replaced by a nod and a grin. "Okay, supersleuth, I'll play dumb. Now, for Pete's sake, don't keep me in suspense. Tell me who she is!"

Keeping his voice low, which was hardly necessary given the surrounding chatter, TJ described his conversation at the bar, though he omitted the jokes at his expense.

"Her name is Valerie Solanas, and she lives in the Chelsea Hotel. So we don't have to wait around here for her to maybe show up. From what Frank said, Fudge probably wouldn't let her in anyway."

"Thank God we can split," said Ellen. "I want to go home and wash my face. These eyelashes are driving me cuckoo!"

TJ helped her on with her coat. "I'll call the police first thing tomorrow morning. I have all the information they'll need."

He left a generous tip for Debbie, and he and Ellen elbowed their way to the bar, where he expressed his appreciation to Frank.

"Thanks for the great dinner and the information, man. You really came through for us."

But, like Frank, TJ was unaware that the handsome guy in the motorcycle jacket was an undercover detective who now had the same information.

Thirty-Two

O ver breakfast, Nita and Fitz listened with a combination of amusement and appreciation as TJ recounted the events of last night's adventure at Max's.

"I guess your time at John Jay isn't being wasted," observed his mother. "Tío Hector is training you well."

"You'll probably become the youngest detective on the force," said his father, clearly pleased by the young man's initiative and hopeful that it would inspire him to make more of a commitment to police work.

Happy as he was to have his parents' approval, TJ reminded them that he was still uncertain about his choice of career. Nor could he claim to have done any sophisticated sleuthing in the quest for his quarry's identity.

"I was just in the right place at the right time," he said modestly, to which Nita replied that it was his deductive reasoning that had put him there.

"Honestly, I can't even take credit for that," he told her. "It was Ellen's idea to go to Max's. She knew it's the Warhol gang's hangout. She thought we could be less conspicuous there than if we tried nosing around at the Factory, and she was right." Her cleverness and pluck brought a proud smile to his lips.

"You should have seen her, Mom, all dolled up like one of Warhol's groupies, with big dangly earrings and a ton of eye makeup. She's so natural and unaffected, it made her really uncomfortable, but it was the perfect outfit for Max's. I won't tell you what I looked like, it's too embarrassing."

Nita beamed at him as she cleared the table. "You two going steady?"

TJ rolled his eyes. "Oh, Mom, people don't 'go steady' anymore. We're just seeing each other in class and hanging out together, that's all, nothing formal. We've only known each other a few weeks."

The voice in his head admonished him. *Liar,* it said, *you wouldn't dream of dating anyone else. You're nuts about Ellen, and she says she feels the same way about you. How much more steady could it be?*

———

Before he left for work at Brother's, TJ phoned Midtown North to make his report, but his information about Valerie Solanas was redundant.

"Thanks for the tip," said the desk sergeant politely, "but we've already got officers on the way to pick her up."

Guess I just lost bragging rights, said TJ to himself. He wanted to ask how the police had identified her, but he knew the cop wouldn't answer that question.

Still, he could congratulate himself that he'd managed to track down Solanas all by himself, even if it was a stroke of good luck that gave him the vital clues. And if she turned out to be the killer, the NYPD would no longer be interested in Bill. He'd still be wanted for the federal crime of evading conscription, but if he'd made it to Canada the government's welcoming policy meant he didn't need to worry about extradition—as long as he stayed in the closet.

When the fairy dusters gave Bill his fake papers and instructions on transitioning to life in Canada, they had warned him that the Canadian Immigration Act prohibited the admission of homosexuals. He would have to continue to pretend to be straight, and so would Vinnie if he decided to move to Canada and reunite with Bill after his discharge. The dusters would tell him how to contact his lover. They'd know how to find Bill, even if Uncle Sam didn't.

———

With elaborate wrought-iron balconies on its north-facing façade and an art-filled interior accessed by an ornate twelve-story winding staircase, the Chelsea Hotel, at 222 West Twenty-Third Street, had been home to generations of residential and transient eccentrics since 1885. Among the lengthy Who's Who of notable writers, artists, and musicians who roomed there at one time or another were several members of the Warhol circle, including Edie Sedgwick, René Ricard, Nico, and Viva, as well as Valerie Solanas—one of those who didn't appear in Warhol's 1966 film, *Chelsea Girls*, which was shot on location inside the hotel.

Officers Gomez and Fisher arrived at the hotel at nine a.m. and spoke to the desk clerk, who informed them that Solanas was out.

"Haven't seen her in a few days, and never again would be too soon. We have a lotta loony toons in here, most of 'em benign, but she's one I wouldn't turn my back on without protection. I always keep the desk between me and her."

"Why's that?" asked Gomez.

"Take a look at this," said the clerk. He reached under the counter and pulled out a water-stained mimeographed tract, titled *SCUM Manifesto*. "She peddles this piece of crap on the street. Charges women a buck and men two bucks for it. As if any guy in his right mind would buy it."

"Why not?" said Fisher.

"Look right here on the first page and you'll see why not." The clerk pointed to the opening declaration of intent, which called on women to overthrow the government, eliminate the money system, institute complete automation, and eliminate the male sex.

"It's one long list of grievances against men. She says they've turned the world into a shit pile, and the remedy is for women to exterminate them," he continued. "And look what she says here, toward the end." He flipped the pages and read, "If SCUM ever marches, it will be over the President's stupid, sickening face; if SCUM ever strikes, it will be in the dark with a six-inch blade."

Fisher and Gomez looked at each other, and Fisher asked, "Can we take that?"

"Keep it," said the clerk, tossing the document on the counter dismissively. "It was too messed up to sell, so she left it here for my enlightenment. It enlightened me, all right. I learned that she's one dangerous dyke."

While Gomez collected the manifesto, Fisher handed her card to the clerk. "Call me when she comes in," she told him. "I don't need to tell you not to let on that she's wanted for questioning."

"Mind telling me what for?"

"Yes, I do mind. Just let me know when she's in the building."

Thirty-Three

The League cafeteria was exceptionally quiet between classes when instructors Robert Brackman, who taught painting, and Robert Beverly Hale, the anatomy teacher, both of whom had morning and afternoon sessions, took their lunch break. Joining them were Dagmar Freuchen, whose popular fashion illustration class had finished at half past twelve, and Edward Laning, whose class started at one.

"I guess it's no surprise that only about half my students showed up this morning," said Hale, "and I expect the same will be true for this afternoon's class. And some of the ones who did come are a bit nervous, to say the least. Can't say I blame them, with Benton's killer still at large."

Freuchen was not so sympathetic. "What nonsense,"

she countered. "You'd think a homicidal maniac was on the loose. Benton was a sexist blowhard who finally got his comeuppance. Whoever killed him did us all a favor. Now we can have our lunch in peace!"

Laning shook his head. "You're a cold one, Dagmar. Must be that icy Nordic blood in your veins. You may be glad he's out of your hair, and frankly I won't miss him, either, but you can't deny it's disconcerting to the students. Under the circumstances, it's likely that one of them, or one of us for that matter, is a murderer."

"It's not only the students," said Brackman, "the models are spooked, too. Larl Beecham, who poses for me in the mornings and Charlie Alston in the afternoons, called in sick on Friday and hasn't been back since. I don't think there's anything wrong with him, except maybe cold feet." Both his and Alston's life drawing, painting, and composition classes were held in Studio Nine, the crime scene, which had been reopened on Saturday.

"I hope Priscilla Watkins shows up for me this afternoon," said Hale, "She was bit skittish at the end of last week. I'm in the middle of a series of anatomy lectures, and I really don't want to start over with a different model."

"Wally Green is taking it stoically," observed Laning, "even thought he'd gotten pretty friendly with Tom. I saw them in here together more than once. I think Tom went out of his way to be nice to him after embarrassing him in my evening class. But whatever Wally's feeling, he isn't showing it. He's just carrying on as usual, steady as ever, no nerves or anything."

"Probably because he's a World War Two veteran," said Brackman. "He saw plenty of action in the marines, Pacific theater. If that didn't harden him to violent death, I don't know what would."

"That could account for it, all right," said Hale, and the others agreed.

"I may not have mentioned it before, but I knew Wally as a youngster, back in '34, the year I started here," Brackman told them. "His last name was Gruen then. His father was an artist, Johann Gruen, who taught a watercolor class on Saturdays, when I was teaching drawing. Little Walter used to come in with him. Sometimes he'd sit in on his dad's class, and sometimes come to mine. Good-looking kid, quiet bordering on shy, and pretty talented. I thought he had the makings, but then Gruen lost his job and Wally didn't come back to the League until a couple of years ago, when he started modeling. Hadn't laid eyes on him in thirty years, but I recognized him. I suppose, being a portrait painter, I could see that he still has the same facial structure and the same shy, guarded expression."

"Do you know why he changed his name?" asked Hale.

"He told me it wasn't his doing. His mother changed it when the U.S. declared war on Germany, and people with German names were shunned, sworn at, even attacked. He was sixteen at the time. His parents were divorced by then, and she didn't want Wally to carry the stigma."

"I know what that's like," said Freuchen with feeling. "I'm Jewish—my maiden name is Cohn—so you can imagine the irony when Peter and I were ostracized by ignorant people who assumed the Freuchens were German. And that was while our native Denmark was occupied by the Nazis, and the resistance was fighting to protect Jews from arrest and deportation to the death camps!"

"Anyway," Brackman resumed, "Gruen was a popular instructor, and he moved up to a weekday slot in '35. But he was there less than a year, and then he was out. I don't remember the circumstances, but I don't think it was voluntary. Fortunately he got on the WPA right away, so he didn't need to teach in order to support the family."

"What a godsend that was, for so many artists, me included," said Laning. "During those years things were so bad the League nearly went under. I bet half the people teaching here now were able to get through the Depression because of the WPA's Federal Art Project. That's what paid for me to do the library murals, and the ones I did on Ellis Island, too. Imagine, a weekly paycheck from the government, just for doing your own work. The way I see it, Gruen was actually better off, don't you think?"

"Sure he was," replied Brackman, "while it lasted. But, as you know, when we got into the war the project ended."

The art project actually limped along for a couple of years after Pearl Harbor, restructured as a war services program making posters and window displays, but it was impossible to justify spending government money on art when the military needed planes and tanks and battleships, as well as people to build them and soldiers and sailors to use them. With unemployment no longer a problem, the WPA got its so-called honorable discharge early in 1943.

Brackman skipped over the rest of Gruen's story, which he'd been told in confidence.

When Wally was hired, Brackman had reintroduced himself and asked how his father was doing. Wally said he'd passed away many years ago, which didn't surprise Brackman, since he hadn't heard about Gruen or seen his work in any shows since the late '30s.

Once Wally had gotten to know Brackman and felt comfortable confiding in him, he told him what had caused his father's death.

After Gruen left the League, in spite of landing a steady WPA job he became increasingly depressed and withdrawn. His work and his health suffered, and in 1940 he was kicked off the project for repeated absence due to alcoholism, which Wally said was also what caused his parents' marriage to fail. Gruen committed suicide three years later.

Respecting Wally's privacy, Brackman kept those details to himself.

"Sadly," he continued, "in 1943, Gruen died suddenly. Wally had just turned eighteen, and rather than waiting to be drafted he enlisted in the marines. That's where he learned to play football. After the war he stayed in, played for the Quantico team for fifteen years, then coached for two and retired from the service in '63.

"Like so many career military men, he had a hard time adjusting to civilian life. He's never married, and he was rootless. He tried playing semipro ball, but he was nearly forty and couldn't get into the starting lineup. After warming the bench for a couple of years, he gave up and gravitated back here."

"Lucky for us he did," said Laning. "He's one of the best models we've ever had, if not the best."

Thirty-Four

In his afternoon Forensic Analysis class, TJ raised a question that had been bothering him.

"If a murder weapon with no fingerprints or other trace evidence belongs to someone who has a grudge against the victim, but other people had easy access to it, how do you determine which one used it?"

"An excellent question," replied Professor Morales, who knew why TJ was asking it. "The same three basic criteria—motive, means, and opportunity—apply whether you're dealing with a single suspect or several. Let's say, for the sake of argument, that this is a premeditated killing, and five people have reasons to want the victim dead." He chalked the numbers from one to five vertically on the blackboard, and made three columns, one for each criterion.

"Let's look at motive first. What are things that would

motivate someone to kill?" he asked the class. Several hands went up. Jealousy was the number one choice, followed by deception, rivalry, greed, and revenge.

Morales filled in each row under the motive column. "Suspect number one is someone whose spouse or lover was caught cheating: jealousy. Suspect number two has been swindled out of money or property: deception. Suspect number three wants to eliminate someone standing in the way: rivalry. Suspect number four has something to gain by the victim's death: greed. Suspect number five has a score to settle: revenge." He turned to the class. "Which is the hardest to determine?"

A young woman's hand went up. "I think five is the hardest. The other four could well be known to the killer's family and friends, but five might depend on finding out something that only the killer knows."

"Yes, a deep-seated personal grievance is the least evident motive," said Morales. "It often doesn't come out until the suspect is confronted with witness testimony or overwhelming forensic evidence, or decides to confess out of remorse. But sometimes others besides the killer do know the motive, even if they don't remember until it's acted on. For example, a boy was bullied in school, then meets up with his tormenter years later, and the buried hatred surfaces. His schoolmates knew how much he hated the bully, but it's not until the bully's murdered that they make the connection."

TJ was thinking that there were plenty of people with well-known grievances against Benton, from those like

Breinin whose animosity went back decades to those he'd offended recently. His talent for making enemies was legendary, even more widely acknowledged than his artistic ability.

Morales returned to the blackboard and checked all five rows under the means column. "In our hypothetical case, according to Mr. Fitzgerald, all the suspects had access to the murder weapon. The owner is top of the list, but just because someone owns a lethal weapon doesn't mean he or she is the one who used it. If you found your mother's kitchen knife sticking out of your next-door neighbor's back, you wouldn't assume your mom killed him, would you?" That got chuckles from the students, one of whom remarked, "If it was my mom, you would."

"With blades and blunt instruments," continued Morales, "when we have the weapon we look for fingerprints, which Mr. Fitzgerald says are not present. It was either wiped clean, or gloves were worn. However, there may be blood on the killer's skin or clothes, and with ligatures, some fiber may be transferred, but you have to get these traces right away. With firearms there's usually gunshot residue, but again, if the killer has time to clean up and dispose of the clothing before being tested, the physical evidence is lost."

Morales addressed the third column. "Since all of our five potential suspects have both the motive and the means, the deciding factor is opportunity. You need to establish, not who could have done it, but who couldn't have. In other words, which of the suspects would not have been in a position to kill the victim.

"As everyone knows, the term for this type of vindication is alibi, a Latin word meaning 'elsewhere.' A true alibi proves conclusively that an accused person was in another place when the crime was committed. A false alibi is a smoke screen, intended to cover the criminal's tracks or to deflect the investigation away from a suspect who has something else to hide. If the suspect actually was elsewhere, but was committing a different crime or cheating on a spouse, he or she might invent a story to conceal that information."

"So," Morales concluded, "in the absence of a clear motive and singular means, the investigator's job is to eliminate those who have valid alibis, not always a straightforward process. Corroborating witnesses, especially family members, may lie, willingly or under duress, to protect a suspect, and outsiders can be unreliable—they think they saw him at the races that afternoon at three, when the victim was shot, but they aren't sure. They pass over him in a lineup and pick out a plainclothes police officer. Then we have to find out where *he* was when the murder was committed." That prompted another laugh from the class.

"Who can tell me what's likely to be an ironclad alibi? Give me some examples."

"You were already in jail," suggested one student, "or in the hospital, someplace you couldn't leave on your own."

"You were out of the country," said another, "and your passport stamps prove it."

"You were in another city, and people who know you saw you there," was another possibility.

"You could even be near the crime scene, but with plenty of neutral witnesses who could swear you were with them," offered TJ. "Like everybody in this class knows I'm here now, and it happens that somebody's getting strangled in the next room. Even if I hated the victim, and maybe even threatened him, there's no way I could be killing him."

"Opportunity obviously depends on proximity," noted Morales, "but as Mr. Fitzgerald points out, it isn't necessarily decisive. In other words, being nearby doesn't make you guilty, but it does call your alibi into question unless you can muster reliable corroboration. Clearly the other three examples—incarceration or hospitalization from Miss Bertram, and being overseas, across the border or out of town from Mr. Ramsey and Mr. Gordon—are easier to verify. Frankly, I'd say being behind bars is as good as it gets."

———

As the classroom emptied, Morales motioned to TJ to stay behind. "A word, Mr. Fitzgerald," he said offhandedly, keeping his tone impersonal. Once they were alone, however, he reverted to familiar mode and pulled up a chair next to his desk for TJ.

"Well, Juanito, did our discussion contribute anything to your private investigation?"

"Sí, Tío Hector. Dad got an update from Inspector Kaminsky this morning, and he says they eliminated two of the suspects for reasons the class mentioned."

He told Morales about going under cover with Ellen to Max's Kansas City in an effort to identify the woman who publicly threatened to kill Benton.

"I found out who she is, but when I called Midtown North to report it, they were already on to her. They sent cops to the Chelsea Hotel—that's where she lives—to pick her up yesterday, but she wasn't there. When they contacted the Tenth Precinct to ask the beat cops to be on the lookout for her, they were told she'd been busted for soliciting and sent to the Women's House of Detention. She's been there awaiting arraignment since last Monday, two days before Benton was killed. So she has Carol Bertram's number one ironclad alibi."

Morales nodded in agreement. "¡Ella lo hace! But you said two suspects were cleared. Who's the other one?"

"Lewis Mumford, the former president of the American Academy. Benton was a member, and two years ago they had a very public falling-out. They disagreed about America's involvement in Vietnam—Mumford denounced it, Benton protested, almost got into a fistfight with him and then resigned when Mumford wouldn't back down. But a year or so later, without consulting Mumford, the academy voted him back in. Mumford went apeshit and stormed out himself. There was going to be a reinstatement ceremony for Benton this week, so that could have been the spark that set Mumford off."

"Okay, vengeance was his motive," agreed Morales, "but I take it there was a lack of means or opportunity?"

"Both," said TJ. "It's the alibi Jim Gordon said, being in another city. Last Wednesday at six p.m. Mumford was giving an anti-war speech at a conference in Chicago. He has two hundred eyewitnesses."

"So you're left with Breinin, the mad Russian, and your gay friend Bill, both of whom fit the profile of suspect number five on our list." Morales gestured at the blackboard. "We know they each had a motive and the means—access to the murder weapon—but did they have the opportunity?"

"According to what Kaminsky told Dad, Breinin's alibi is shaky. Not only is the timing of his whereabouts way off, but when the cops questioned the people who were in the League around the right time on Wednesday, a couple of folks on their way upstairs from the cafeteria said they saw a man in a red velvet jacket in the stairwell at around five. Breinin wears a jacket like that all the time; it's practically his uniform. Unfortunately they can't make a positive ID 'cause they didn't see the guy's face. He had on a wide-brimmed hat and a scarf, and he was already below them, going down fast, when they came out on the third-floor landing."

"Jake's certainly sharing a lot of inside information," observed Morales. "Isn't he curious why Fitz would be so interested in this case? It's pretty unusual for a deputy chief to monitor a precinct investigation, even of a homicide."

"Oh, he knows why," said TJ. "Dad told him right up front that his son was a student at the school where it happened, so it's only to be expected that he'd want to be kept informed."

Morales aimed his foxiest grin at TJ. "And do Jake and Fitz know that you're on the case, too?"

"I don't think Dad let on to the inspector, but he and Mom know I went searching for Solanas and succeeded in identifying her. I told them all about it. They were kinda pleased that I took the initiative. Mom says you're teaching me well."

"Nita was my star pupil," said Morales, "and her outstanding detective work is still making me proud. Thanks to her, and other Spanish-speaking officers from the community, the Twenty-Third has one of the department's best clearance rates."

Morales stood, and TJ followed him to the door. "Nita's always called herself the precinct's chief snoop," he remarked as they headed out, "but her deductive skills are much more subtle than that, certainly as good as mine ever were, if not better. As I've told her, if I'm El Zorro, she's La Raposa, the vixen—a worthy successor to this old fox, whose hunting days are over."

Thirty-Five

Solanas was a wild-goose chase," said TJ as he walked Ellen home from the subway. Now it was dark when she left the Automat at half past five, and his protective instinct was working overtime. Despite her objections, he had insisted on meeting her when she emerged from the Union Square station and escorting her to the Up 'n' Down every weekday except Thursday, when they would travel home from the League together.

He also committed to accompanying her and Michele to and from The Bitter End on Tuesday nights, homework be damned. He'd just have to spend lunch hours in the John Jay library instead of the cafeteria and sneak study time at Brother's on the weekends. At least he'd be getting a crash course in folk music appreciation, with no homework, quizzes, or term papers.

Today was the first day of their new routine, and Ellen was still not convinced that she needed such coddling.

"Really, I can take care of myself," she had argued, but TJ was adamant.

"Union Square is full of unsavory characters. It's not safe after dark," he pointed out, and she couldn't disagree. There had been several recent muggings and purse-snatchings, though it wouldn't be long before the cold weather would deter the prowling juvenile delinquents and drive most of the vagrants to shelters.

"You know how much I love you," he said as he took her in his arms. "I'd never forgive myself if something bad happened to you. For my sake, let me keep an eye on you, just to be on the safe side."

It was such a reasonable request, so heartfelt, how could she refuse?

Walking hand in hand with Ellen through the square, TJ told her that Solanas was in jail when Benton was killed.

"We were discussing alibis in class today," he said, "and Tío Hector calls that an ironclad one. Obviously you can't be out there killing someone if you're already locked up."

Ellen's frustration was just as obvious. "So now what? With her eliminated, Bill is still the prime suspect, goddammit." She kicked at an empty soda can, sending it skidding across the pavement and under a bench.

Suddenly TJ remembered the first time they had walked through the square together, when they passed the anti-war rally.

"I wonder," he said, half to himself, "yes, maybe I could find out from them."

"Find out what? From who? What are you talking about?"

"From the group that had the speaker here, back in September. They were burning draft cards, remember? What was it called? The guy was standing in front of a banner with the name on it." He stood still and closed his eyes, trying to recall the scene. *Observation, the first rule of detective work. That's what Mom always says.* He saw the scene in his mind's eye—the shouting man in fatigues, the bullhorn raised to his mouth, his figure framed against the banner—and the words came into focus.

"Got it! Vietnam Veterans Against the War! Maybe they're the ones who helped Bill get to Canada, or maybe Mexico. He may have been long gone when Benton was killed. If I can find out when he left it could clear him."

Ellen agreed, and her mood brightened. "You're right. The last time anyone at the League saw him was a week before, when they had the fight in the cafeteria. Suppose he went straight to that group and told them he'd burned his draft card and wanted out. How long would it take to arrange that? Probably not long, I bet they do it every day. Oh, TJ, what a great idea!" She gave him a big hug and a kiss on the cheek.

"I have to figure out how to find them. Maybe the guys that hang around at Brother's know." The candy store was a mecca for the neighborhood youths, many of them registered for the draft and not all eager to serve. "Let me take you home and I'll run over there now, see what I can find out."

———

Brother's Candy & Grocery, an all-night convenience store at 542 East Fourteenth Street, served as Stuyvesant Town's unofficial social center. Having worked there on weekends since high school, TJ was on a first-name basis with many of the regulars. When he arrived, not long after six, the place was packed with people picking up a quart of milk or a dozen eggs on the way home from work, kids killing time between school and dinner, flirting teenagers, and elderly widows with no one to cook for buying sandwiches and gossiping. Even on a chilly November evening, guys smoking and shooting the breeze spilled onto the sidewalk outside both the Fourteenth Street and Avenue B entrances. Lately the war had become topic number one among the draft-age men who gathered there nightly.

TJ recognized two young men in conversation. One he knew was a veteran, but was he in favor of the war, or had he turned against it?

He approached them with a friendly greeting. "Hiya, guys. What's goin' on, Dick?" He saluted the vet. "How ya doin', Ralph?"

"Jesus Christ, TJ," said Ralph, "can't you stay away from this place? Ain't it your day off?"

"Yeah, I'm just picking up some stuff for my mom. Don't let me interrupt."

"No sweat, man. I was about to start lecturing Dickie boy over here." He hooked his thumb at his pal. "He's headed to Nam. I was gettin' ready to talk him out of it."

"Hey, you can't say for sure they'll send me over there," Dick countered. "I could get posted stateside, or land a cushy desk job in Saigon, like you did." Ralph had spent his hitch in the administrative office of General William C. Westmoreland, commander of the U.S. Military Assistance Command.

He came back with, "Fat fucking chance. I only lucked out 'cause I got clerical skills. You got nothin' but brawn, no brains at all. They're not gonna let you sit it out stateside. They'll take one look at you and hand you over to Westmoreland. And he'll feed you to the Viet Cong."

Dick smirked. "So what am I supposed to do, go to induction in a dress?"

"No, dickhead, you don't go to induction at all."

"Right, I just sit home and wait for the MPs to pick me up. It don't take much brains to know that wouldn't be a real good idea."

"Not only no brains, but no imagination, either," said Ralph in disgust. "No, you don't sit home and wait, you scram north, across the border."

Dick was appalled. "Are you out of your fucking mind? My old man would kill me. He fought in the good one, infantry. He thinks we should nuke the gooks."

"Don't tell him."

"You think Ma wouldn't know I wasn't packing for boot camp? And what would I do with myself in Canada, jerk off until the war's over? Then what? You think I could just waltz back home, all is forgiven? No fucking way." He flicked his cigarette into the gutter and marched off.

"There goes dead meat," muttered Ralph, ready to drop the matter, but TJ had the opening he was looking for.

"So let's say he has a change of heart. Where would he go to arrange it? Vietnam Veterans Against the War?"

"They're sort of a subgroup of the War Resisters League, they're the ones who'd fix him up. They got an office just off Union Square. Don't remember the address, but I bet they're in the phone book. Hey, your number's not up, is it?"

TJ was quick to reassure him. "No, my student deferment's still good. But I got a friend who's looking for an escape hatch. You think this War Resisters League would help him?"

"Count on it," said Ralph.

TJ headed to the phone booth at the back of the store and consulted the battered directory chained to the shelf. Under W he found the listing, at 17 East Seventeenth Street.

———

The War Resisters League, founded in 1923 as a secular pacifist association, was the first organized peace group to call for the Unites States to withdraw from Vietnam. It had inspired the April fifteenth Spring Mobilization to End the War, a rally that brought tens of thousands of protesters into the Manhattan streets and led to the formation of the veterans' group. The WRL office was the headquarters for a range of anti-war activities, including demonstrations, parades, sit-ins, and mass draft card burnings. Working with the Greenwich Village Peace Center, it was also an embarkation point for fleeing draft resisters.

There were lights on in the fourth-floor windows when TJ arrived. Evidently the WRL kept evening hours. He rang the buzzer and walked up to a shabby, crowded office. The walls were covered in posters, and a large bulletin board was studded with fliers, news clippings, and photographs. Several men and a couple of women were busy mimeographing leaflets, typing articles for the organization's monthly bulletin, *Win*, and talking on the telephone.

An amiable, middle-aged staffer greeted him. "Hi, son. I'm Karl. What can I do for you?"

Assuming that TJ was a resister, a conscientious objector, or a spy, Karl Bissinger invited him to a chair by his cluttered desk and prepared to quiz him about his motive for visiting the WRL. The military had been known to send in ringers who pretended to want help getting out of the country, so he had learned to be wary of even the most earnest plea for passage on the reincarnated underground railroad.

Instead, TJ told him about the Benton case and Bill's situation.

"So you see," he said, "if Bill was already out of the country he'll be cleared. Can you help me find out?"

Bissinger was taken aback. "You're not going to believe this, but I was at the Art Students League in the '30s, when Benton taught there. I wanted to be a painter, but to make a living I started doing commercial work and then got into photography. That's my day job, taking pictures of fashion models for the glossy magazines.

"Anyway, I read about Benton's murder, and I can't say I was either surprised or sorry. He was a homophobic bully. Why, when I was there he hounded out one of the other instructors, the man I was studying with, just because he was gay. Went to the board and got him fired."

"Would they really fire someone just because he was queer? Sorry, I mean gay."

"Maybe not now, but back then they would, especially if a big shot like Benton demanded it. The son of a bitch had just been on the cover of *Time*—the first artist ever, for Chrissake. What Benton wanted, Benton got."

Bissinger leaned over the desk and took TJ's measure. "Listen, son, I think you're leveling with me, but I have to be careful. The army's not very sympathetic to us. How do I know you won't turn Bill in if I tell you where he is?"

TJ's eyes widened. "Do you know?"

"Answer my question," said Bissinger sternly, his eyes fixed on TJ's.

"I don't need to know where he is. I just want to find out when he got out. He did get out, didn't he?"

Bissinger leaned back, satisfied. "If he did, it was probably handled by the Greenwich Village Peace Center, down at the Methodist church off Washington Square. I work closely with them, especially the fairy dusters."

"Who are they?"

"They specialize in shipping out gays. They trust me to send them bona fide resisters because I'm gay."

No wonder he's so against Benton, thought TJ. A question crept into his mind. *Could Bissinger have heard that Benton was in town and decided to get back at him? Maybe that's too far-fetched, but Dad said these old grievances sometimes wait years to surface.*

While TJ was speculating to himself, Bissinger picked up the phone and dialed.

"Hi, this is Karl. Doing fine, Alex, and you? Listen, I want to find out if you dusted a fella named Bill Millstein. Would have come to you late last month. Yeah, I'll hold." He put his hand over the mouthpiece and nodded to TJ. "He's checking."

When Alex came back on the line, he told Bissinger that Millstein, traveling by train from New York City under an assumed name with a false New York State driver's license as identification, crossed the Canadian border at Rouses Point on Monday, October thirtieth. The Committee to Aid American War Objectors had confirmed his safe arrival in Montreal that evening.

"Thanks, Alex. Glad to know he made it safely. Keep the faith." He rang off. "Remind me what day Benton was killed."

"Last Wednesday, November first."

Bissinger smiled. "By then your friend Bill had already celebrated Halloween in another country."

———

Eager to relay this information to Ellen, TJ thanked Bissinger for his help, wished him luck with his anti-war efforts, and headed across Union Square to the Up 'n' Down. There he found the roommates rehearsing for their Bitter End hoot. Ellen had put down her guitar to let him in, and as she embraced him she could sense that he had news. Seated with her instrument, Michele glanced up expectantly as they entered the living room.

"Hey, you look like the cat that swallowed the canary," she observed. "What gives?"

"We don't have to worry about Bill," he told them. "I found out he was long gone when Benton was murdered."

Ellen literally jumped for joy. "TJ, you're fantastic!" She threw her arms around him and kissed him with gusto. "But how on earth did you find out, and so quickly?"

"It runs in the family. My mom's a detective, remember?" he teased, then gave an account of his conversation with Ralph and his visit to the WRL office. The girls listened attentively, smiling and nodding at each turn of events.

"It's incredible," he concluded, "but this guy Karl actually was at the League back in Benton's day. Said Benton got his teacher kicked out because he was gay. That made me wonder if Karl might have wanted to get even. Then, when I was walking over here I thought, wait a minute, it's more likely to be the guy who got fired. Maybe he's still around and still carrying a grudge, like Breinin. Could be he's the one who settled an old score."

Michele asked the obvious question. "Well, yeah, maybe, but who is he?"

TJ kicked himself mentally, this time out loud. "Oh, shit! I was so focused on learning about Bill, it didn't occur to me to ask. Have you got a phone book?"

Michele pointed to a shelf under the coffee table, on which sat a turquoise Princess phone—the latest touchtone model. The girls' mothers had insisted on their having one and chipped in to pay for it, ostensibly for security but really so they could check in on their children regularly.

TJ looked up the number and punched it in. "Cute phone," he said as the call rang.

"War Resisters League, Dave speaking."

"Hi, I'm Tim Fitzgerald. I was just there, talking to Karl. Yeah, that's me. Is Karl still around? Would you put him on, please? Thanks."

When Bissinger came on the line, TJ asked him Michele's question. "The guy you told me about, the one who Benton got fired. Who was he? Do you remember his name?"

Bissinger hesitated. In his line of work, unconsidered answers to seemingly innocent questions could have unfortunate consequences. "Of course I do. Why do you want to know?"

TJ didn't want to tell him the real reason, so he made one up. "I just wondered if maybe he came back to the League later on, after Benton left. Maybe he could even be teaching there now."

"Not likely," said Bissinger, "he's long dead. Killed himself back in the '40s. His name was Johann Gruen."

Thirty-Six

Nettled by his morning call from an unrelenting Rita Benton demanding action, as well as pressure from Klonis and Goodrich, daily inquiries from the press, and the curious scrutiny of Deputy Chief Fitzgerald, Inspector Kaminsky was increasingly frustrated by the lack of progress on the Benton investigation. He called a meeting of his team and, gathered in front of a blackboard in the Midtown North conference room, they went over the leads one by one. It was not a happy occasion.

"Okay," said Kaminsky gruffly, "here's what we've got. Millstein, suspect number one, is still at large, whereabouts unknown. Suspect number two, Raymond Breinin, hasn't got an airtight alibi. A few other possibles, Chris Gray,

Valerie Solanas, and Lewis Mumford, have been eliminated. So where are we? It's almost a week since Benton was offed, and we're running out of leads."

"I'm bringing Breinin back for more questioning this afternoon," said Falucci, "but I'm not sold on him, even with that red-jacket sighting in the stairwell. Sure, there are plenty of points against him. He's made no secret of his history of bad feeling toward Benton. The timing of his whereabouts is unclear, plus his knife is the murder weapon. It's just too cut and dried."

In spite of his foul mood, Kaminsky hadn't entirely lost his sense of humor. "You get the bad pun award for that cutting remark, but I take your point. Pun intended." There were appreciative snickers from the team.

"All right, let's get serious. We have to find Millstein. But that doesn't mean giving up on Breinin. It's a process of elimination. They both had motive. As far as we know, they both had opportunity. And they both had easy access to the means. Eliminate one, and the other's our man."

He turned to Sheik. "Find out who helped Millstein get away." He pointed to a note on the blackboard. "Helen Rudy told Tony that there's a pipeline especially for queers. Fairy dusters, she called them. Go downtown and see if you can nose 'em out. We need to know if he's gone or still around, and if he's gone, when he left town and where he went. If he's in Canada, the government won't cooperate on the draft-dodging charge, but they'll let us extradite him on the murder warrant."

"I'll talk to the boys down at the Sixth," said Sheik. "That's their territory, I bet they know every queer in the neighborhood."

———

At the breakfast table, once again TJ had news of the Benton case to share with his parents. Actually, he needed their advice. He had uncovered vital information regarding Bill's whereabouts, but how to relay it to the police without compromising the source?

"They won't just take my word for it," he reasoned. "They'll need confirmation that he was already gone. What Karl told me he got from some guy named Alex at the Peace Center. He told Karl 'cause they trust him, and if I pass it to the cops they won't trust him anymore. But this information clears Bill."

"You'd better believe they're working hard on this one," said Fitz. "They may be on to the same source, getting the same dope as you did. Like with Solanas. They're not sitting still waiting for the information to fall in their laps, not with Jake in charge." As a deputy chief who knew the strengths and weaknesses of every precinct in all five boroughs, his faith in Kaminsky was well founded.

With her detective's cunning, Nita proposed another approach. "Let's look at it a different way. Let's assume the other country Karl mentioned is Canada. Much more likely than Mexico, splitting from New York. Benton's murder is all over the papers here, but it may not have made it to the Canadian papers. Bill may not even know Benton is dead. And if he did read about it, he'd realize it happened after he left, so he'd probably just mentally thank whoever killed him and forget about it."

"You're right, Mom" said TJ. "He'd know he wasn't involved, so he wouldn't expect the cops to come after him."

"Bill knows it, and now you know it, but you can't tell the cops without blowing the network. What they're doing isn't illegal, as long as they aren't forging papers—anyone can cross the border with proper ID—but if they gave Bill a fake identity, that would be a criminal offense. We don't know for sure they did that, and, frankly, we don't want to know, not when our priority is clearing Bill."

"You're not talking about shielding lawbreakers, are you?" said Fitz, slightly shocked by her devious turn of mind.

"Not shielding, honey, just not digging too deeply. Not, let's say, turning over any unnecessary rocks. And certainly not siccing the pigs on the peaceniks."

"Then what?" blurted TJ, clearly frustrated by the impasse she had outlined.

"Think about it," she replied patiently. "Who would the police be most likely to believe? Not you, obviously. Not Karl or Alex, even if you did rat them out."

TJ thought about it, and the answer came to him. "Why, whoever took Bill in, of course."

"Exactly. What you need to do is go to the Peace Center, explain the situation, persuade them to contact Bill and get him to verify his arrival in Canada. Do it from his end, not theirs. That way the peaceniks are off the hook."

"You think they'll listen to me?"

Nita gave him an encouraging smile. "One way to find out."

———

Eager to follow his mother's advice, TJ cut his morning class and walked down to the Washington Square Methodist Episcopal Church at 135 West Fourth Street, an elaborate marble confection dating from 1860. Behind a bright red side door, the scene in the Peace Center was similar to the WRL headquarters. The walls were plastered with posters, the phone was ringing, typewriters were clacking away, and the mimeo machine was going full blast. He asked a bearded young man, wearing a T-shirt with the slogan *MAKE LOVE NOT WAR*, if he could see Alex and was directed to a desk just as cluttered as Bissinger's.

"What's happening, man?" said Alexander Clifford. Rail-thin, in his late thirties, he was known as the fairy godmother, since he specialized in helping his fellow gays. Like Bissinger, he assumed this was another potential client for the underground railroad, though apparently this time it was a straight one.

There was a folding chair next to the desk, and TJ sat in it. All during his walk he'd been formulating the best way to put his case without setting off alarm bells. He had decided that honesty, but not complete disclosure, was the best approach.

"Recently a friend of mine was looking for a way to avoid conscription," he began, "and I think he may have come to you."

"Why would you think that?"

"Because he's gay, and he got drafted. I heard that your organization can help guys like him."

"Where did you hear that?"

"Look," said TJ, "Let's not beat around the bush. I believe you did help him, and I want to help him, too. The reason I'm here is that there's a warrant out for his arrest. He's wanted for murder."

"You're shitting me," said Alex, alarmed. That could bring the law down on the center and disrupt the whole operation.

"No shit, man. I'm talking about the Benton killing at the Art Students League last week. My friend was a student there, and he had a run-in with Benton that looks like a strong motive for murder."

Alex stood, and fixed a hostile gaze on TJ. "Get the fuck out of here. If you think I'm gonna finger him, you've got another think coming."

TJ realized Alex took him for a snitch. "No, listen, it's not like that. Please hear me out."

Still standing, his hostility softening to skepticism, Alex leaned on the desk. "Well, I'm listening."

"I don't want any information, I swear to God. But you can contact him. The New York cops don't care about the draft dodging, but for sure they'll go after him for murder. Just let him know about the charge so he can clear himself."

Alex considered the alternative. "Suppose he's guilty, and we helped him get away? That would make us accessories."

"He's not guilty."

"How do you know?" The obvious question, which TJ answered evasively.

"I just don't believe he could have done it. I think the cops are on the wrong trail."

Alex's next question was equally obvious. "What's his name?" TJ told him.

I'll be damned, said Alex to himself, *that's the second time someone's asked about Millstein. Karl must have found out about the murder rap. Why didn't he tell me to warn Bill? Maybe he got in touch with the committee people himself—I told him they confirmed Bill's safe arrival.*

"Okay," he said, "here's what I'll do. I'm not telling you I know anything about your friend Bill, or that anyone here at the Peace Center helped him, but if he went to Canada I have a contact in Montreal who should know where he is. They can get in touch with the cops. Who should they call?"

"Inspector Jacob Kaminsky at the Eighteenth Precinct is in charge of the investigation," TJ told him. "He'll want verification, something to prove Bill was across the border before Benton was killed."

This guy knows a lot about this case, thought Alex. *I don't trust him, but what he says makes sense.*

"If he was across—and I'm not saying he was—they'll have proof."

Thirty-Seven

When her break came, after the lunchtime rush, Ellen joined a couple of League students who had opted for the Automat instead of the cafeteria. Having polished off two helpings of macaroni and cheese each, plus Boston cream pie for dessert, they were lingering over their coffee, not too eager to return.

"How is it across the street?" Ellen asked. "I haven't been back since last Thursday, when everybody was still in shock."

"Not good," said Dan Forsberg, the full-time student who'd almost come to blows with Benton. "The classes are only half full, and the cops are in and out, poking around, questioning people they've already questioned before. Fortunately for me, since I was involved in that cafeteria dustup, I have several witnesses who saw me in there between classes on Wednesday afternoon. I was there from five until the place closed at seven."

"You shoulda been working on your mural project for Laning, like I was, you lazy bastard," said Chris Gray. "If you'd been down in Studio Sixteen with me, we could have vouched for each other. I'm not sure the cops believed me when I told them I was there when Benton was getting done in, 'cause nobody saw me."

"Have they questioned you again?"

"No. Actually I think they figured I wouldn't have reported finding the body if I was the one who killed him. Besides, they think it was Bill."

Ellen chose this moment to drop her bomb. "But it wasn't, you know."

"I don't know," said Chris, "not for sure. I don't want to believe he could have done it, but I can't be absolutely certain he didn't."

"I can."

"Listen, Ellen, I know how much you care for Bill, and your belief in him is admirable, but—"

She cut him off. "Thanks to TJ's detective work, Bill is in the clear." She told them what TJ had learned from Karl.

Dan was the first to react. "Holy shit! Being over three hundred miles away is as good as an alibi gets. But can he prove it?"

"TJ called me this morning to say he was going to see the people who helped Bill get away and tell them that he's wanted for murder. They can warn him to get the proof."

"Won't that give him away?"

"Not necessarily. He doesn't have to tell the cops where he is now, only when he got across the border, which was two days before Benton was killed."

"What kind of proof would be enough to get him off the hook?"

"I don't know, maybe some sort of affidavit from the group that took him in. Anyway, TJ and I know he's innocent, and now you do, too."

"Well then," said Chris, "who's guilty?"

This question prompted a new round of speculation.

"Remember that guy from the Academy Benton was bragging about giving the shaft to? He could've been angry enough," said Ellen, prompting quizzical looks from the guys. "Oh, no, that's right, you weren't at our Thursday night class when Benton came in. Bill was the monitor then."

"You mean Lewis Mumford?" said Dan.

"Yes, that's him. Benton didn't mention his name, but TJ found out who it was. How do you know?"

"Because Klonis said he was cleared. I heard him talking to Peter Blume in the hall. He's a member of the Academy, so Klonis thought he'd like to know. Told him Mumford was in Chicago when Benton was killed."

"Even farther away than Bill was," observed Chris.

Ellen described the hunt for the mysterious woman who had threatened Benton at the Whitney, her adventure with TJ at Max's Kansas City, and the blind alley down which it had led. Chris said he'd heard that somebody had seen a man in a red jacket hurrying downstairs at about the right time, and the rumor was it was Breinin, who had told the cops he was home with his family. Since nobody else had as strong a motive—except maybe Bill, who was out of the picture—it looked like Breinin had moved to the top of the suspect list.

"I just don't see it," said Dan, shaking his head. "Using his own knife, then leaving it in the body? That's outright stupid, and whatever else Breinin is, he's not stupid. Sure, he's a hothead. I could see him punching Benton, even strangling him, but knocking him out and then stabbing him in such a calculated way, that just doesn't seem like his style."

"So you think whoever did it deliberately framed Breinin?" asked Ellen.

"Now that makes sense. Everybody knew he had it in for Benton. All the killer has to do is get a red jacket like Breinin's, lure Benton up to Studio Nine, incriminate Breinin by using his knife, then keep his head low and scram down the stairs. Not many people use the front staircase, especially during the break between classes. If anyone saw him, they'd assume it was the Russian."

"What happens when he gets to the lobby? Wouldn't he be pretty obvious?"

"Maybe he didn't go all the way down," suggested Chris. "He could have stripped off the jacket, stuffed it in a bag, and gone out on a lower floor. Or he could have gone out the side entrance and into the street, or into the basement and changed there. Then he could just leave, or come back upstairs and blend in as usual, with no one the wiser."

"Jesus," said Dan, "that means it's got to be a League insider, someone who knows the building and the schedule, when the coast was likely to be clear, where to find the knife."

"That was assumed from the beginning," Chris reminded him. "If it's not Bill, and not Breinin, and it's neither of us, then it's somebody who hasn't been suspected yet."

"Don't be too hasty," said Ellen. "It could be an old enemy from Benton's teaching days. Someone who found out he was hanging around the League and saw his chance to finally get even."

Suddenly she glanced at the wall clock and jumped up from the table. "Oh, wow, look at the time! My break was over five minutes ago. Cindy's going to give me hell." The girl who came out from the kitchen to fill in for her didn't like to spend one second more than necessary in the nickel-thrower's booth.

With a sheepish apology, ungraciously accepted by a frowning Cindy, Ellen resumed her station, slipped on the rubber finger guards that helped her make change more efficiently, and adopted the regulation friendly smile required of Automat cashiers. But there wasn't much demand for her nickels during the midafternoon lull, and her mind wandered, lost in the haze of half-formed conjecture.

Gazing out over the dining room, she saw that Dan and Chris were still at their table, deep in conversation. *I guess they don't have afternoon classes today,* she mused.

Presently they rose and made for the exit, still talking earnestly. She wondered what they were on about. Certainly something to do with the Benton case.

I'm going over there when I get off, she decided. *I bet they have another idea, and I want to find out what it is. Michele and I don't have to be at The Bitter End until eight. I'll have plenty of time.*

———

True to his promise, TJ was waiting downstairs by the token booth when Ellen came through the turnstile at the Union Square subway station, only half an hour late.

"Where were you? I was worried," he scolded, but not too angrily. *Goddammit, I bet I sound like her father,* he thought, annoyed at his overprotectiveness. Fortunately she brushed aside his concern.

"Sorry, but I had to run across to the League after work, to see Chris. He and Dan came into the Automat this afternoon, and we talked during my break. I told them about Bill, I hope you don't mind."

"No, I'm glad you did. But why did you go to the League?"

"I had a hunch they were on to someone else, and I was right. Someone nobody even thought of, because he hasn't been around in decades. They were just grasping at straws, but I think they hit on something."

"Okay, are you gonna tell me, or do I have to guess?"

"Of course I'll tell you, silly. Come on, let's walk. I have to get changed for tonight's hoot." She linked arms with him, and they headed across the square.

"Remember the guy Karl told you about, the one Benton got fired? You said his name was Johann Gruen, right?"

"Yeah, Benton had it in for him because he was gay. But it can't be him, because he's dead."

"They didn't know that. It was Chris who got the name, and he only heard part of the story."

She had found Chris in Studio Sixteen, at work on his mural project. She had pulled up a bench easel next to his and, in her usual forthright way, asked him what he and Dan were discussing so earnestly after she left the table. He told her that they had picked up on something she said.

"I had lunch in the cafeteria yesterday, and there was a group of instructors at the next table. They were talking about, what else, the Benton business, and I overheard Bob Brackman mention a guy with a German name, Johann Gruen, who taught here years ago."

"You mean back in Benton's day?"

"Exactly. Brackman said Gruen left under a cloud, not voluntarily. What you said made me wonder if Benton had something to do with it. I didn't hear the whole story because I had to get up to Studio Nine to prepare for Alston's afternoon class. But the most interesting part of what I did hear is that Gruen's son is at the League now."

"You mean a student?"

"No, not a student."

"Is there another instructor named Gruen?"

Chris had led her along. "There are two Fogartys, father and son, but not two Gruens."

"Come on, Chris, out with it!"

"Okay, okay. It's Wally Green, the model."

For a few moments Ellen had been uncharacteristically speechless. She had gazed quizzically at Chris for clarification, which he'd provided.

"His last name got changed when we were at war with Germany. Anyway, when you said it might be somebody from Benton's past, I started thinking that maybe Wally told his father that his old enemy was back, and Gruen finally took his revenge. Of course that's just guessing, but Dan thinks it's plausible, and that maybe we should tell the police to question Gruen and check his whereabouts at the time."

Ellen finished her account of this conversation and looked at TJ, who had stopped walking when she dropped Wally Green's name.

"Are you thinking what I'm thinking?" she asked him.

TJ nodded. "If what Karl Bissinger told me is true, Benton did get Gruen kicked out, because he was a homosexual. What Karl didn't mention is that he was married, and had a son. A son who carries his dead father's grudge. A son who, after all these years, sees a chance to settle the score, and takes it."

Thirty-Eight

A s they entered the Up 'n' Down, Michele's jovial greeting quickly dissipated. "You two look serious," she observed. "What's the problem?"

"We have to do some thinking," said TJ. "There's a whole new angle to the Benton case, and we need to decide what to do about it." He took Ellen's coat, removed his own, and hung them on the door.

Ellen plopped into one of the armchairs. "Gosh, Michele, I don't know about tonight's hoot. My mind is really someplace else. Would you mind going solo?"

"No way. We're a duo act, remember? It's Ellen and Michele or no one. I'm sure they won't care if we skip a week."

She headed to the kitchen. "What we need is a beer. Better to think over a drink," she quipped as she took three bottles out of the fridge, poured the beer into glasses and returned with them to the living room. TJ perched on the arm of Ellen's chair, Michele took the other armchair, and they put on their thinking caps.

At first their strategy session was pretty scattershot. After filling Michele in on what they'd learned, they couldn't decide what to do with the information, or how to follow where it led.

"A lot of this is just hearsay or gossip, nothing substantial," TJ reminded the girls. "How do we know Karl's story is true? Chris catches part of a conversation and jumps to a conclusion. If he and Dan go to the cops, they'll find out Gruen is dead—if he really is dead, that is."

"Why would Karl lie about that?" asked Michele.

"Oh, I don't think he was lying. Maybe he just made an assumption, or heard it from somebody else who got it wrong. Like I said, it's only gossip."

"I guess there are a couple of ways to check it," offered Ellen. "We could go to the library and look up the obituaries in back issues of the newspaper, but that would be very time-consuming. We don't know when he might have died, except that Karl said it was long ago."

"Don't they have an index for obituaries?"

"I don't know, I never looked for one before. Anyhow, there's a much quicker and easier way to find out."

"You mean, ask Wally?" said TJ.

"Well, yes, I suppose so, but that's not what I had in mind. Why would he tell us? If his father is alive and possibly implicated, he'd lie to protect him. If he's dead, he'd lie to protect himself, because that would make him the top suspect."

TJ looked thoughtful. "You're right. Either way he'd have no reason to level with us, and it would just put him on his guard. So what did you have in mind?"

"Apart from Karl, who's the source of this secondhand information? Chris overheard it from Mr. Brackman. Let's ask him."

TJ leaned over and planted a kiss on Ellen's forehead. "That's why I love you, honey," he announced. "Inside this beautiful head there's a real brain! You've got it all in one gorgeous package."

She swatted him away playfully and stood. "Listen to this guy. Almost as bad as your bartender boyfriend," she said to Michele, "only his eyes aren't quite as brown." She finished her beer and took the glasses to the kitchen.

"You know," she said as she returned to the living room, "I think we have a plan. Let's find out when Mr. Brackman is there." She went to the bookshelf and found the Art Students League 1967–1968 class schedule. It listed Robert Brackman as the instructor for both morning and afternoon classes in life drawing, painting, portraiture, and composition, Mondays through Fridays, as well as two evenings a week, Mondays and Tuesdays.

"Jesus," said TJ, "the guy practically lives there. He should be there right now. Let's go." He headed for the coats.

"No, wait," Michele called after him. "Look here," she

pointed to a qualifying note. "It says 'instructors present one evening only,' so maybe tonight's not his night. You're better off waiting 'til tomorrow anyway. That gives you time to decide how to approach him. You can't just go up to him and say, Hi, you don't know us but we're investigating Benton's murder, and we think Johann Gruen did it—that is, if he's still alive. Can you tell us, please?"

"No, you're right," admitted TJ. "Besides, it would be good to know what Chris and Dan are planning to do."

"I don't think Chris is in tonight," said Ellen. "He has the Alston night class on Mondays, Breinin's on Wednesdays, and now he's doing our class on Thursdays instead of Bill. Dan's only a day student." Unfortunately, Ellen's workday started at nine, which was when the League opened. Waiting until the morning meant she'd have to leave it up to TJ.

"Tell you what," he said. "My first class on Wednesday isn't until eleven. I'll head over there first thing and talk to them both, then see you at the Automat before I do anything else. You can sell me some nickels while I fill you in."

———

The day had been a productive one for Sheik, though it didn't produce the result he wanted. Before heading downtown he had telephoned the Sixth Precinct and spoken to Detective Michael Flynn.

"Listen, Mickey, I'm trying to get a line on a murder

suspect, a queer named William Millstein. Does he happen to be on your blotter?"

"Don't sound familiar, but I can check. Does he live around here?"

"No, he's from Hell's Kitchen, but word is he hangs out at the gay bars on your patch. What I really want to know is who would help him if he wanted to disappear. In addition to the murder rap, he's a draft dodger."

"You want the fairy dusters," Flynn said. "They got a network that handles all the arrangements. We've never been able to prove that they're actually breaking the law, but we're pretty sure they're faking IDs for deserters and guys who've been denied conchie status. The volume's going up every week, so we'll catch 'em sooner or later."

He gave Sheik the address of the Greenwich Village Peace Center, and told him to ask for Alex. "I bet you come up empty. Those boys are experts at protecting their own."

The southbound Eighth Avenue E train took Sheik to West Fourth Street, and a short walk from the station led to the church. A small sign on the red side door identified the Peace Center, where he was directed to Alex's desk. On the ride downtown he had decided to make it official, so he pulled out his shield and identified himself.

Alex, who was used to regular visits from the authorities, looked at the detective's badge with disinterest, folded his arms, leaned back in his chair, raised his eyebrows and said, "Well?" He did not invite his visitor to sit.

"I'm looking for a runaway, one William Millstein," said

Sheik. "I believe you may have helped him get out of the country."

"I'm a nonbeliever myself," answered Alex tersely, thinking, *What took them so long? That kid who was in here earlier was way ahead of them.*

"Believe this," said Sheik, his eyes locked on Alex's. "He's wanted by the New York City Police Department for murder. If you shipped him out to avoid conscription, that's a federal matter, and the feds can pursue it if they want to. But by aiding a murder suspect, whether you knew it or not, you and your organization are accomplices after the fact, which lands you in deep shit, man. I could get a search warrant, close this place down in a heartbeat, ransack your files, haul everyone in for questioning, really spoil your day."

He leaned across the desk. "Am I going to do that, or are you going to cooperate?"

Still wearing his impassive expression, Alex weighed his options. If he dug in his heels, a search warrant would yield information he'd rather the police didn't have and lead them to Millstein anyway. On the other hand, he couldn't admit responsibility for Millstein's escape without incriminating himself. He decided on an evasive maneuver.

"I think I can save us both a lot of trouble. As you no doubt know, the Peace Center provides helpful advice to people seeking to emigrate from the United States, all perfectly legal. We don't inquire as to their motives."

Like hell, you don't, thought Sheik. *But let's hear the rest of your horseshit.*

"Of course, being pacifists, as our name indicates, we assume that many of those who come to us are against the war in Vietnam. It's their right to express that opposition by leaving the country. And we're not the only group helping them. If they choose to go to Canada, we refer them to organizations there that can facilitate the process."

Sheik was tiring of Alex's monologue. "Get to the point."

"What I'm saying is that I can get in touch with those organizations and find out if your suspect—what did you say his name was?"

Jesus fucking Christ, as if you didn't know, said Sheik to himself. "William Millstein. Want me to spell it?"

"No, that's all right, I think I have it," said Alex, jotting down the name in a pantomime of accommodation. "As I was saying, I can find out if they've had contact with him and let you know. It shouldn't take long. Give me a number where I can reach you."

Sheik would not accept stalling tactics. "How about right now?" He pulled up the folding chair and sat by the desk. "I'll wait."

Fortunately Alex had put through a call to Montreal as soon as TJ left his office, so the committee people knew the story and were no doubt already working on verifying Millstein's alibi.

"Very well," he conceded, "have it your way. I'll try Montreal first, they're the closest." He reached for his Rolodex, pretended to look up a number he knew by heart, and dialed. When the call was answered, he kept his tone impersonal, even though it was a familiar voice at the other end of the line.

"Hello, this is Alexander Clifford. I'm calling from the Greenwich Village Peace Center in New York. To whom am I speaking? Hello, Mr. MacDonald. I wonder if you can help me. I have a police detective here in my office who's looking for a man who may have emigrated from here to Canada recently."

At the other end of the line, Ian MacDonald got the message loud and clear. The cop was right there and might even be listening in on an extension.

"Certainly, Mr. Clifford. Let me have the man's name, and I'll see what I can do." Alex gave him the name, the one he expected.

"Any idea when he might have crossed?" MacDonald asked.

Alex looked up from the receiver and spoke to Sheik. "He wants to know when." That alerted MacDonald that only one phone was being used, but he still assumed the cop might be able to hear him.

"Last Thursday, November second," said Sheik. Alex relayed the information to MacDonald, who said he'd look into it and call him back. Alex went through the motions of giving him his telephone number.

"It's a criminal complaint, not an immigration matter," he explained, as if MacDonald didn't know. "I'm sure you understand we want to give the police our full cooperation. So if you have no record, will you check with Toronto for me? Thank you very much, Mr. MacDonald. I look forward to hearing from you as soon as possible. Goodbye."

This elaborate formality was making Sheik gag. *What a charade. I suppose he has to cover himself, but give me a break. He probably talks to this Canadian asshole two or three times a week.*

Alex replaced the receiver and folded his hands. "So there it is. I've done what I can do. Believe me, I don't want the kind of trouble you described so graphically, so I'll be in touch with you as soon as I have any information at all."

Sheik rose and handed over his card. "If I don't hear from you within an hour, I'll be back with that warrant, and you'll wish you'd never been born."

"Message received, and understood," said Alex, his voice as restrained as his manner. As he watched Sheik leave, he silently cursed the God he didn't believe in for wasting such good looks on such a ball-breaker, and a straight one at that.

———

By the time Sheik got back to Midtown North there was a message waiting for him from a Mr. Clifford, with a return number. He thanked the desk sergeant, took the slip to his office, and put the call through.

"Clifford? Valentino here. What have you got for me?"

"Ian MacDonald called me back to inform me that your man did enter Canada and pass through Montreal. He arrived there on October thirtieth. From the little you told me, I inferred that the murder took place after that date, am I right?"

Cursing silently, Sheik was not going to admit his disappointment, nor was he going to take Alex's word for it. "I'm sure you realize I need proof of that."

"Of course. All those who are processed by the Committee to Aid American War Objectors are registered on arrival with the Canadian Immigration Service. That's a government agency. Millstein was taken to their office the morning after he arrived and officially logged in on October thirty-first. MacDonald is mailing me a photostat of the record. Should arrive in a couple of days. I'll personally deliver it to you. There'll be a log number on it, so if you want to, you can contact the CIS for verification."

Sheik clenched his teeth. *Shit, there goes the most likely one down the drain.* "Does Millstein know about the murder charge?"

Alex was enjoying this. If Sheik could have seen him, he'd have resented the smile the peacenik wore as he spoke. "I couldn't say. I don't know his present whereabouts. They don't tell us, you see, for security reasons. I'm sure you understand. But I'd guess they'll get a message to him, just to let him know the charge has no merit. I assume you'll rescind the warrant? Under the circumstances, the Canadians are unlikely to honor it."

"Not until we have the proof and get it verified," said Sheik coldly, eager to end his conversation with this patronizing pansy. "Notify me as soon as you have the document."

"Certainly. Always happy to help law enforcement. Peace, brother." He hung up, a self-satisfied smirk still on his face.

———

Sheik decided to share the news of this setback with Falucci, whose office was next door. The door was ajar, and he found his fellow detective deep into a pile of paperwork. The Benton murder was not their only open case.

"Hey, Tony, got a minute?"

"Do me a favor and interrupt me," said Falucci, glancing up as he slammed a bulging folder shut, "though you don't look like you're gonna be very good company."

Sheik slumped into a chair and offered Falucci a cigarette. The two men lit up, and Sheik expelled a deep lungful of smoke, as if he could breathe out his frustration with the tobacco fumes.

Falucci regarded him with sympathy. "Okay, pal, what's the beef?"

Sheik recounted his visit to the Peace Center and his telephone call from Alex Clifford. "If that prissy turd is telling the truth—and you better believe I'm gonna check that document real carefully—Millstein is out of the picture. So much for suspect number one. Now Breinin moves to the top of the list. In fact he's the only one left on it. Have you had him back in yet?"

"I sent Jenkins down to pick him up. They're not back yet, should be any time."

"You gonna tell him about the red jacket sighting?"

"Yeah, sure. One more nail in his coffin. Might just make him realize we've got the goods on him. I've thought all along that him being so vocal about hating Benton made him too obvious, but like you said, with Millstein eliminated he's all we got now."

Thirty-Nine

TJ was waiting outside Ellen's building when she came down at half past eight. They walked together to the subway, caught the local, and arrived outside the Automat twenty minutes later. Across the street, several students were already waiting for the League's doors to open for the nine o'clock classes.

"Don't worry," he reassured her, "I'll be back here as soon as I find out what Chris and Dan are up to. You go on in now, you don't want to be late for work."

"Five more minutes won't matter," she said, and wrapped her arms around him. He returned her embrace, they kissed, and like lovers everywhere lost track of time as they immersed themselves in each other. Only when they heard the loud squeak of the hinges on the League's iron grillwork gates did they snap out of it.

"One more kiss for luck," said TJ, as he bent down again, and she rose on tiptoe to meet his lips. She waved him off as he jaywalked to the opposite side of Fifty-Seventh Street and entered the League.

Inside the lobby he spotted Chris heading toward the twin studios at the far end of the main hallway and followed him to Studio Fifteen. When he entered, he found Chris wiping down the bench easels and Dan removing his sketch pad from his locker. *Lucky I got them both at once,* he thought. *That last kiss worked like a charm.*

Chris saw him first. "Hi, TJ, this is a surprise. You haven't quit John Jay and signed up full-time here, have you?"

"I'm not ready to take that leap yet," he replied, "not as long as the war lasts, for sure. My student deferment is too precious to lose."

Dan heard their exchange and joined them. "So what brings you here so early?"

"I need to talk to you both," said TJ, and motioned them into the side hallway that flanked the studio, where they could speak privately.

"Ellen told me what you found out about Wally Green's father. Are you planning to tell the police?"

"We thought we ought to wait until we got more information," said Chris. "I didn't hear the whole story. We don't know that Gruen's leaving had anything to do with Benton, and we don't want to make trouble for Wally or his dad for no reason."

Dan chimed in. "We thought about going back to Brackman to get the rest of the story, but Chris said he mentioned that he didn't know the details. So we're thinking maybe we should ask Klonis. He was here then, and he was on the Board of Control, so he should be able to tell us what happened."

"That's a great idea," said TJ, "if he's willing to tell us."

"Let's find out," said Chris.

———

As usual, Stuart Klonis was at his desk. The past week's chaos had left him little time to reflect on the long-term consequences of Benton's murder, but he realized that the longer it took to solve the case the worse it was for the League. Repeated calls to Inspector Kaminsky had yielded nothing of consequence, except that one of his most prominent instructors was still under suspicion. As long as Breinin hadn't been charged, Klonis felt it was his duty to give him the benefit of the doubt, but he was hearing rumors that some of the students, and even one or two of the other instructors, were not being so fair-minded. So when Rosina Florio buzzed him to announce that a student delegation wished to see him, he feared there would be a demand to fire Breinin on suspicion. Reluctantly, he told his secretary to send them in.

Klonis recognized Chris Gray as the winner of the coveted Abbey Scholarship, vaguely remembered Dan Forsberg as a full-time student, but couldn't place the redheaded youth who accompanied them. So as not to embarrass him, Chris introduced himself and his companions and explained their mission.

"We hope you won't think we're out of line, sir, but we think there may be another angle to the Benton case, and we're hoping you can help us."

This was not what Klonis was expecting to hear. Immediately relieved, as well as curious, he invited them to pull up chairs and tell him what was on their minds.

Chris told him what he'd overheard in the cafeteria. "I wasn't eavesdropping, sir, it wasn't, like, a private conversation. But what Mr. Brackman said made me wonder if there was a connection between what happened to Mr. Gruen and, ah, what happened to Mr. Benton."

Klonis saw what he was getting at, albeit indirectly. "You mean, you think Gruen murdered Benton? Why would he do that?"

"Well, if it was Benton who got him fired, that would be a motive," suggested TJ, who believed Gruen was no longer capable of exacting vengeance.

"It all happened more than thirty years ago," Klonis reminded them, "A long time to harbor resentment strong enough to motivate someone to kill. Mind you, I wouldn't have ruled it out, given the circumstances, except that Gruen is no longer living. A very sad situation, one I've always felt a bit guilty about." He shook his head at the memory.

"What circumstances?" asked Dan.

Klonis leaned his chin on his hands and reflected. "You have to remember how influential Tom Benton was in those days. He was arguably the most prominent artist in the country, and his presence added luster to the League. He attracted students at a time when we were in dire financial straits. He knew what an asset he was, and he used that leverage to get Gruen fired. To the board's discredit, we capitulated, and it was the beginning of the end for Gruen. He left in disgrace, and ironically, within a few months Tom was gone, too—off to Kansas City with no fond farewells."

Once again Dan picked up on Klonis's remark. "How do you mean, disgrace?"

Klonis sighed. "Oh, well, they're both dead, so I guess I might as well tell you. Tom had taken a shine to Gruen, became a mentor to him. As with other younger men he took under his wing, he invited him to his home, socialized with him, so the relationship was personal as well as professional. It was no secret that Gruen looked up to Tom, idolized him, really. They had the same humanistic philosophy about the social function of art, and I'm sure Gruen thought that associating with Tom would help his career.

"Unfortunately Gruen's feelings went deeper than Tom realized. One night after evening class they were alone in the men's room, and Gruen locked the door. Tom said Gruen told him he'd fallen in love with him and recognized him as a kindred spirit—a closeted homosexual whose machismo and marriage disguised his true nature, just as Gruen's wife and son were his cover."

The trio exchanged looks. They had decided to keep Wally's relationship to Gruen to themselves if Klonis didn't mention it. Perhaps he didn't know, in which case they weren't going to tell him.

Klonis continued, "As you know, Tom was not a large man, and Gruen was big and powerful. According to Tom, Gruen forced himself on him, they struggled, and Tom broke free and came straight here in an absolute rage. Lynn Fausett, a fellow muralist who was president at the time, and I happened to be working late, trying to balance the books. Tom stormed in, shouting that Gruen was a homosexual—though that's not the word he used—who had accosted him in the men's room, groped him, and tried to rape him. He threatened to call the police and charge him with assault. Of course that would have exposed Gruen's homosexuality, which he'd been disguising his whole life.

"We calmed Tom down as best we could and promised to deal with the situation internally. The only thing that would satisfy him was Gruen's immediate expulsion, so that's what we did. We didn't even have the guts to face him and hear his side. We sent a letter. Just fired him, no reason given, but it was obvious to him who was responsible. If we'd held our ground, called Tom's bluff and mediated some sort of compromise, perhaps an apology, Gruen might not have... well, let's just say he might still be alive."

Forty

After thanking Klonis for his time, Chris and Dan headed back to the studio and TJ said he had to report to Ellen before heading to John Jay.

"Looks like Wally's a top suspect, all right," said Chris, "but I hate to point the finger at him without more to go on."

TJ was looking pensive. "Hang on," he said, "I have an idea. Is there a schedule for the models anywhere handy?"

"Sure," said Chris, "It's posted on the bulletin board by the registration desk." They went back to the outer office and consulted the class listing, which had suffered several revisions in the past week. In the models column they found Green scheduled to fill in for the missing Beecham in Breinin's Wednesday evening class in Studio Nine.

"Man, that's kinda creepy," said Dan. "If he's the one who did Benton in, he'll be posing on the very spot."

Once again Chris was circumspect. "Don't jump to conclusions, buddy. We don't know that he had anything to do with it, but I have a hunch our young sleuth here is planning to find out." He cast a quizzical glance at TJ, who nodded and spoke in a low voice.

"I'm gonna come back here tonight and follow him home. If I can find out where he lives I can snoop around, maybe get something on him."

"What're you gonna do, just knock on his door and ask politely to look in his closet for a red jacket and a fedora? Maybe suggest he write out a confession?"

TJ didn't appreciate Chris's sarcasm, though he had to admit he couldn't do anything without access to Wally's place. But he had an ace up his sleeve that he wasn't about to reveal.

"Stop kidding," he told Chris. "I have a plan. I hope he'll go straight home tonight, and if he does I'll know the next step."

"Okay, keep it to yourself," said Dan, "but remember, if Wally is the killer he'll be on his guard. You watch your step with him. He's an ex-marine. Guys like him eat guys like you for breakfast, and there ain't no leftovers."

———

Over at the Automat, Ellen's face lit up as TJ entered and made straight for the cashier's booth, blind to everything but her. Ignoring the glass between them, he bent forward to kiss her and bumped his forehead. Not to embarrass him further, she suppressed a laugh.

Rubbing his brow and feeling very foolish, he spoke to her through the circular window. "I have to run to class, but I have a plan that may help us get to the bottom of this case. It'll have to wait until tonight. I'll tell you all about it when I pick you up at the subway."

"What did you find out from Chris and Dan?" She was impatient for some news, however meager.

"They're not going to the cops just yet, they're waiting for me to try something. That's all I can tell you now." He scooted around to the back of the booth and leaned over the gate. With no glass in the way, she gave him a proper goodbye kiss, much to the delight of the morning coffee club at a nearby table.

———

By the time Ellen rushed through the Union Square turnstile and into TJ's arms that evening, she'd been on tenterhooks all day.

"What happened at the League this morning? What's the plan? Do you really think you can solve the case? Tell me!" She was nearly hopping with anticipation.

"Easy does it, honey, one thing at a time. First, there's a whole new angle." He told her about the meeting with Klonis, and his revelation about why Gruen was fired.

"If Gruen were still alive, Benton's showing up again

after all these years might have rekindled the old hatred and pushed him over the edge. But what if it had that effect on his son? Maybe he thinks Benton is responsible for his old man's suicide. Suddenly, out of the blue, Benton appears, and Wally sees his chance to take revenge."

Ellen nodded in agreement. "Remember the reaction he had when Benton touched him? I thought he just didn't like being pawed like that, but maybe there was more to it."

"I'm going to follow him home tonight," TJ told her. "He's modeling for Breinin's evening class that lets out at ten."

"What's the point of that?" Like Chris, Ellen didn't see what good it would do to find out where he lived. "Why don't you just tell the police you suspect him, and they'll question him, maybe search his apartment if they think they have something on him."

"We decided we don't want to finger him unless there's a reasonable suspicion. Right now all we have is speculation, and it would be terrible if he was hauled in for no reason, like it would have been with Bill. No, we need more to go on, and I think I know how to get it—or at least find out if he's implicated."

"I still don't see the point."

"Let's just say I know what I'm doing. I'll tell you if it pans out."

Ellen punched him on the arm. "I've said it before, and I'll say it again. You are exasperating!"

Forty-One

As Chris prepared Studio Nine for Breinin's evening class, he wondered how many students would turn up. This was the first time the Russian had been back since Benton was killed, and many of them believed he was the killer. Would that put them off, or maybe encourage them to come out of morbid curiosity? Not a very charitable thought.

Mulling over these matters, he jumped when he heard a voice behind him.

"Hi, Chris. I guess it's time for a new pose. Show me what you did last month with Larl."

"Jeez, Wally, you startled me. You're quiet as a cat."

"Got nine lives, too, though I used up a few of 'em on Iwo Jima. Ancient history. You're a vet, right?"

"Yeah, but I had a soft hitch, never left New York. The

worst action I saw was the hookers and pushers hustling me on Fort Hamilton Parkway."

"Lucky bastard. Take it from me, combat sucks cock." Wally turned away as students started arriving. It looked like most of them were showing up. "Better get changed." He ducked behind the curtain to disrobe.

Not knowing what to expect, the class was slow to settle down. Chris opened his locker and retrieved his newsprint pad. When Wally emerged, he showed him the drawing. It was a seated pose, right leg tucked under the left thigh, the torso twisted to the left, right arm resting on the chair back, left hand on the seat behind the left buttock. Not an easy position to hold without cramping, but Beecham, a modern dancer with the Katherine Dunham Company, was a pro.

So was Wally, who took direction from Chris. They decided on a standing pose, one leg up on a chair. Wally leaned forward to rest his arm on his thigh and tucked his other arm behind his back, relieving the students of the challenge of rendering both hands to Breinin's satisfaction.

Breinin showed up at seven thirty, just as everyone had gotten down to work. He always arrived with a flourish, and not surprisingly he was extra animated tonight.

"So," he bellowed, as he flung his hat and scarf on a chair and focused on the new model, "where is Beecham? Is he afraid I will stick kinzhal in him?" He made a hooking motion with his right arm, which brought gasps from a few of the already intimidated students.

"He was switched to the Laning anatomy class," Chris

told him. Beecham—who, like many of the students, was understandably reluctant to return to the scene of the crime—had asked for the reassignment. All week the classes in Studio Nine had been sparsely attended. Tonight was the exception, and Chris decided that his cynicism was well founded after all.

"Don't worry, little ones," said Breinin in his most patronizing tone, "murder weapon is still with police. If you anger me, I have to kill with bare hands." Grinning menacingly, he held them up and clenched his fingers, as if throttling someone's neck, causing more gasps from the class.

Breinin's laughter filled the studio. "You will pardon my little joke. I let off steam like boiling samovar, or else I explode. Ridiculous police take me to their ugly station yesterday afternoon and tell me someone sees me on the stairs when Benton dies. I tell them is bullshit, I am not there. Then they ask me same questions I already answer. When are you home? When do you leave? Who can vouch? I tell stupid detective same things again. Let them try to prove different. They will fail."

That wasn't exactly a denial of guilt, but of course Breinin had already insisted he didn't kill Benton, much as he might have wanted to.

———

As ten o'clock approached, the studio door opened a crack. There was a rule against entering when the model was posing, nor did TJ want to be visible to Wally, so he stood outside and tried to get Chris's attention. Fortunately his easel was toward the rear, near the door. TJ beckoned to him, and he stepped into the hall.

"Just want to let you know I'm ready to go. I'm going to wait outside on the street until he comes down. I don't want him to see me here on a night I'm not supposed to be here."

"He doesn't know you're only here one night a week," said Chris. "Besides, he probably wouldn't recognize you. There are a lot of students coming and going."

"Yeah, but not many with bright red hair like mine. That's why I'm wearing a knit cap pulled down around my ears. At least I won't send a signal like a traffic light."

"That's a smart precaution," Chris had to admit. "I hope he doesn't lead you to some bar or his girlfriend's place instead of his apartment." He checked his watch. "Better get downstairs, we're about to break up." He shook hands with TJ and wished him good hunting.

It was a mild, clear night, with plenty of people about on Fifty-Seventh Street, so TJ easily remained inconspicuous as he hung around near the League entrance. At about ten-fifteen he saw Wally emerge from the building and head west. TJ had no trouble keeping his tall, athletic figure in sight as he turned down Seventh Avenue and entered the subway station at Fifty-Third Street on the downtown side. TJ did the same, but went in the other direction on the platform.

After the E train pulled in and TJ saw his quarry get on,

he did so as well, and quickly moved from car to car until he saw through the windowed door that Wally was seated in the next one, reading the evening paper and paying no attention to anyone around him. As they neared the Fourteenth Street station, Wally rose, folded his paper, and stood by the doors. The doors opened, and TJ hung back for a moment as Wally got off and walked toward the exit. Then, as the doors were about to close, he hopped off and continued his pursuit. *So far, so good,* he congratulated himself. *I'm sure he hasn't noticed me.*

From a safe distance, he followed Wally as he crossed to the stairs that took him to the east side of Eighth Avenue. From there it was a short walk to 240 West Fourteenth Street, a five-story converted brownstone with an Italian restaurant, The Piedmonte, on the garden floor. For a moment TJ was afraid Wally was headed there for a late supper, but as he got closer he could see that the restaurant was closed for the night.

Wally climbed the tall stoop and entered the residential door, which had a *ROOMS FOR RENT* sign taped to the glass. After he was safely inside, TJ went up the steps and checked the doorbells. There were eight of them, one for the fortune-teller on the parlor floor front, one for the apartment at the rear, and six above. The name Green was in the slot next to number four.

Satisfied that he had the information he needed, TJ decided to walk across to Stuyvesant Town. On the way home, he considered his next move.

Forty-Two

When he was a kid, TJ used to play with his mother's set of locksmith tools. Handsomely packaged in a leather case, it included torsion wrenches, various picks, short and medium hooks, a saw rake and a snake rake, as well as a set of skeleton keys—everything a detective needed to get doors, cabinets, and drawers to open without their owners' consent.

Nita was an expert lockpicker, and she used to enjoy watching TJ struggle to find the right tool to use on the apartment's security fixtures. But he had a deft touch and excellent hearing, and it wasn't long before he got the hang of it. He could even open the tiny, delicate lock on her jewelry case without leaving so much as a scratch on the keyhole.

"All you need is a black outfit, a ski mask, and rubber-soled shoes, and you'd make a great cat burglar," she had teased him. "You definitely have the knack."

"I'd sure know better than to break into anyplace in East Harlem," he'd countered, acknowledging Nita's stellar reputation. "If you were on the case, you'd have me nailed before I left the scene with the loot."

Neither he nor Nita had used the pick set in years, but he knew she kept it in the bottom drawer of her dresser. After breakfast, he waited until his parents had left and checked the drawer. He found the leather case under some summer blouses, clothes Nita wouldn't be wearing for several months. She certainly wasn't going to want the set today, or she would have taken it with her, and he only needed it tonight. He was sure he could slip it back in place tomorrow morning without her knowing it had been gone.

When he scouted Wally's building he had identified the outside and inside door locks as standard tumbler models, similar to his own front door. So he practiced on the lock at home and quickly regained his old finesse. Satisfied that he hadn't lost his touch, he left the set in the hallstand drawer and headed off to John Jay. He planned to retrieve it on his way out that evening, while his folks were still finishing dinner.

He would meet Ellen at the subway, walk her to the Up 'n' Down and wait while she changed, then together they'd take the subway to the League. Only he wasn't going to Laning's class tonight.

It all went according to plan. He grabbed a quick bite, explained that he had to rush to meet up with Ellen, and called goodbye from the hall as he retrieved the pick set and shoved it into his jacket pocket. With Ellen's advent, Nita and Fitz had gotten used to seeing very little of their smitten son, so they smiled at each other across the dinner table as they heard him hurrying out.

"He's got it bad," observed Fitz. "Reminds me of a guy I used to know, an Irish cop who fell head over heels for a Cuban cop."

"Remember what you called us back then?" said Nita. "The mick and the spic. Equally offensive to both, I'll give you that."

Fitz chuckled. "Since when were you ever sensitive, baby? You heard much worse on the beat, and look what Hector had to put up with. From your own people, too."

"The Irish have no shortage of insults for their own kind," she retorted. "I've heard your family call each other names I wouldn't use in public. Some of them I can't even pronounce. Paddy's probably the least objectionable."

"You don't know what disrespect is until you've been cursed at by an Irishman. Get over here, you bean álainn."

"If that's a curse, it's a very pretty one," said Nita as she slid onto Fitz's lap, kissed his ear, and whispered, "say it again."

"Bean álainn," he sighed. "My beauty. May I have you for dessert?"

"With whipped cream on top," she purred.

———

As he and Ellen rode uptown, TJ laid out his plan.

"I'm going to Wally's apartment and see if I can find anything that ties him to the killing," he told her, and again she questioned what good it would do him to prowl around West Fourteenth Street.

"I'm going inside," he confided.

Ellen was incredulous. "What? How can you do that? Apart from its being illegal, you need a key."

He pulled the pick set from his pocket and showed it to her, carefully shielding the contents from the view of other subway riders. "I have everything I need right here."

"You're going to break in? I don't believe it."

"Really, it's easy when you know how. I'm gonna make sure Wally's posing tonight and then go down to his place, check it out, and be in class within an hour. I'll just be late for once, come in at the eight o'clock break. No one except you will know what held me up."

"I think you're crazy. Suppose someone sees you?"

"It's a rooming house, with a fortune-teller on the second floor. People go in and out all the time. I may not even have to pick the outside locks, just hang around until somebody rings the fortune-teller's bell and gets buzzed in. Anyway, I know what kind of locks they are, so it won't take me much longer than a guy fumbling for his keys."

———

When they got to the League, TJ walked Ellen to Studio Fifteen, kissed her, and slipped into the side corridor, where a break in the partition allowed him to see into the studio. It was nearly seven, and most of the students had taken their places. Wally emerged from behind the screen and settled into his pose. Satisfied, TJ walked back down the hall, out onto the street, and west to the Eighth Avenue subway.

Getting into Wally's building was every bit as easy as he'd imagined—easier, in fact. For the convenience of the fortune-teller's clients, the outer door had been left off the latch. Opening the inside lock was a quick job, and once in he climbed the stairs to the third floor, where he found two numbered doors, with number four at the rear. Like the outside locks, the one that secured Wally's apartment was an old tumbler model, no challenge to TJ. Within a few moments he was inside.

It was a single, fairly large studio with a kitchenette to the right of the door. An odd arrangement, but this had originally been one of two bedrooms of a residential brownstone, now converted to separate studio apartments that shared a bathroom at the end of the hall.

The room was as orderly as one would expect from a former military man's living quarters. It was sparsely furnished with a double bed, neatly made up as if ready for inspection, a chest of drawers and, under a window looking out over a garden that had been glassed in for The Piedmonte's extra seating, an oak desk with a brass reading lamp on top. A Formica breakfast table with two chairs occupied the nook next to the kitchenette. TJ glanced in and found it clean and tidy.

The only apparent extravagance was a handsome Philco radio-phonograph console, next to a record rack. Apparently Wally was a music lover. TJ resisted the urge to look through the albums and turned his attention to the desk. It was old but serviceable, with three drawers along the right side and a shallow lockable drawer under the top. The desk, and the wooden chair on rollers that went with it, probably belonged to the furnished room.

Careful not to disorganize the contents, TJ checked the side drawers. The top one was empty except for a small rectangular box, in which he found Wally's impressive collection of Marine Corps decorations: a Bronze Star, a Good Conduct Medal, an Asiatic Pacific Campaign Medal, and two Purple Hearts. He stood looking at them for a few moments, taking in their significance, then he closed the box and replaced it in the same position. He found nothing of interest in the other two drawers.

The shallow drawer was locked, but it was a simple device and he had it open in no time. What he found inside convinced him he was on the right track.

Partially hidden by assorted papers, he could see what he recognized as a blackjack—a short sap that could easily be carried in a pocket and hidden in the palm of a large hand. The flexible grip had a leather strap to keep it from slipping when deployed, and the slightly bulbous business end was probably filled with buckshot or sand. The weapon—highly effective for rendering people unconscious—was popular with criminals and law enforcement officers alike, and there was a collection of various models, some dating back to the nineteenth century, on display at the Police Academy.

Aware that someone as fastidious as Wally would know if anything was out of place, TJ gingerly examined the papers without moving them from their positions. There was a takeout menu from a Chinese restaurant on Eighth Avenue, a checkbook and statement from Chase Manhattan Bank, a rent receipt, a West Side YMCA membership card, and a New York Jets season ticket.

Peeking out from under the bank statement was a sales slip from S. Klein, the department store on Union Square. TJ cautiously peeled back the statement, and his eyes widened as he saw that the receipt, dated October 28, was for one jacket, one hat, and one scarf, total $41.85 plus 84¢ sales tax. "Bingo!" he said under his breath.

Easy does it, he told himself as he checked that the contents looked undisturbed, closed the drawer, and relocked it. Beside the bed was a closet, where TJ hoped he would find the red velvet jacket, paisley scarf, and fedora that he now believed Wally had used to disguise himself as Breinin. Though TJ didn't know it, the Russian's family bought all their clothes at S. Klein. Breinin often bragged that, even on the pittance he was paid by the League, they could afford the best quality because his wife worked there and got the employee discount.

TJ opened the closet door to reveal Wally's modest

wardrobe—a topcoat, two sports jackets, slacks and a few shirts, plus a zippered clothing bag that contained his military uniform. There were a couple of pairs of shoes and a pair of boots on the floor. No red jacket or paisley scarf. He sighed with disappointment.

He saw a box on the shelf that looked like it might contain a hat and was about to reach for it when he heard a voice in the hall and a key being fitted into the lock.

Oh, my God, he's coming home! How can that be? TJ had been sure he'd have plenty of time to search the apartment. He couldn't have been there for more than fifteen minutes. What the hell had gone wrong?

All he could think to do was duck into the closet and pull the door shut just as the outer door opened and someone entered.

Oh, man, if he finds me my goose is cooked.

He held his breath as footsteps advanced into the room. *Christ, he's going to hang his coat in the closet.*

Quietly, careful not to trip over the footwear, he shrank back as far as he could, putting the topcoat and the zippered bag between himself and the closet door. Thankfully there was no light inside, so he just might go unnoticed.

But how would he get out? The thought of hiding there until Wally left in the morning made him wish devoutly that he'd never decided to play detective.

The footsteps stopped outside the closet, but the door remained closed. He heard some rustling and a couple of thumps—it sounded like Wally was getting into the bed.

Maybe if he goes to sleep right away I can slip out. I hope he snores, so I'll know when the coast is clear.

But doesn't he need to get undressed, put on his pajamas, and hang up his clothes? Shit, I'm done for.

He suddenly felt light-headed, and realized he was still holding his breath. He opened his mouth, exhaled slowly, breathed in deeply but silently, steadied himself against the closet wall, and prepared for the worst.

Then he heard footsteps again, walking away from his hiding place. A door opened and closed. The kitchenette? No, that door had been open when he came in.

Wally must have gone out, probably to the bathroom in the hall.

Assuming he had only a few minutes to make his escape, he emerged from the closet ready to bolt for the exit.

But as he shut the closet door he glanced at the bed and did a double take. It had been stripped, and a pile of clean sheets, pillowcases, and towels had been left on the mattress. The footsteps had been those of the landlady bringing in the week's supply of fresh linens. Thoughtfully, so as not to disturb her tenants, she always did it when she knew they'd be out.

TJ collapsed onto the bed with a heartfelt sigh of relief. Immediately his inner voice admonished him, *Pull yourself together, idiot, and get the hell out of here.*

Wisely, he did as he was told.

Forty-Three

TJ entered the League's lobby just as Laning's class took its eight o'clock break. As he approached Studio Fifteen he was startled to see Wally walking toward him, on his way to the men's room. In spite of himself—the model couldn't possibly know where he'd been—TJ felt his color rising, so he coughed as an excuse to cover his face with his hand.

"You're late tonight, son," said Wally as he passed. "Maybe you should have stayed home. Sounds like you're coming down with something."

"Thanks, I'm okay," he replied, his hand still masking his embarrassment. "It's just a tickle." He hurried on, afraid he might somehow give himself away. But that was ridiculous. It's not like he was wearing a sign saying, "I just broke into your apartment and searched it."

As soon as she saw him enter the studio, Ellen jumped up from her bench and ran to meet him. He signaled to Chris, and the three of them adjourned to the side corridor.

"Well?" said Ellen anxiously, "what did you find out?"

Chris was in the dark, so TJ summarized what he'd been up to, leaving out a recap of his close call.

"Ellen's the only one I let in on my plan," he said, "so she wouldn't wonder why I wasn't going with her to class at seven. I see she didn't give the game away." He put his arm around her and gave her a serious hug, which helped dispel his pent-up nervous energy.

"Man, you took a chance and a half," said Chris, impressed, "but it looks like you got the goods—" He checked himself as he spotted Wally reentering the studio.

"Let's meet after class and decide what to do," suggested TJ, and it was agreed. So in they went, followed by Laning, ready to do the rounds.

"Feeling better about your work, Fitzgerald?" he asked, to which TJ replied, "Yes sir, I sure am," not in reference to his drawing.

———

Over coffee at the Carnegie Deli, which stayed open until eleven, Chris, Ellen, and TJ put their heads together. Chris wanted to examine the pick set, but TJ discreetly declined to display it in the restaurant.

"Let's get serious. What I found is suggestive, but not

conclusive. It's not illegal to own a blackjack. He might carry it for protection, in case somebody tries to mug him."

"Then why was it in the drawer? Why didn't he have it on him?" wondered Ellen.

"I don't know, but anyway it doesn't prove anything. Just because he has one doesn't mean he used it on Benton."

"What about the receipt from S. Klein?" asked Chris. "That's where Breinin buys all his clothes. Kind of coincidental, don't you think?"

"Yeah, but nothing in Wally's wardrobe matched Breinin's outfit—at least not the jacket. There was a greenish tweed one and a brown plaid one, nothing even close to red and certainly not velvet. I didn't check the box on the shelf, which I suppose might have the hat and scarf in it. I should have, when I knew it wasn't him who came in, but I just wanted to get out while the going was good."

"The point is," offered Chris, "if he did disguise himself as Breinin he would have dumped the clothes, not kept them in his closet. The receipt is the important thing. Okay, it isn't proof, but it's pretty damn interesting, don't you think?"

TJ didn't answer. He sipped his coffee in silence for a few moments before he spoke. The thrill of his adventure had given way to remorse as the full realization of the consequences hit home.

"Why am I so reluctant to take the next step? Contact Inspector Kaminsky and tip him off to investigate Wally. I don't have to tell him what I did or what I found. I can just say I know what happened to Gruen, who was actually

Wally's father, that it was Benton's fault, and maybe that gives Wally a motive. The cops would follow up on it."

"Well, that was your plan, once your suspicion was confirmed, wasn't it?" Ellen reminded him. Chris nodded in agreement.

TJ looked at them both, his conflict evident on his face.

"You should have seen his medals. He's a genuine war hero. He put his life on the line for his country, our country. I know it was before I was born, but I feel like we owe him, goddammit. And if you ask me, Benton got what he deserved." He brought his coffee cup down hard on the saucer, causing heads at nearby tables to turn.

"Take it easy, man," said Chris sympathetically, as Ellen covered TJ's free hand with hers. "I hear what you're saying. You didn't find what you were looking for, but more than you bargained for. Maybe you should step back, and let me take it from here. After all, I'm the one who told you about Gruen, so it makes sense for me to go to the police."

He stood up and put a dollar bill on the table. "Coffee's on me," he said. "Come on, let's go home and get some sleep, decide what to do in the morning. Arlene will be wondering what kept me so late, probably thinks the cops hauled me in again. Maybe I'd better call her." He headed to the pay phone next to the restrooms, while Ellen and TJ put on their coats.

"You know he's right," she said, and he nodded reflectively. "Tell him he should contact the police first thing tomorrow morning." So when Chris came back and they walked out onto Seventh Avenue, that's what TJ did.

Forty-Four

At nine a.m., Chris presented himself at Midtown North, asked to speak to Inspector Kaminsky, and was directed to his office. When he had interviewed Chris on the night of the murder, Kaminsky had pegged him as level-headed and cooperative, but far from comfortable being questioned. Now he was curious to know why the young man was returning voluntarily to the place he'd been so eager to leave.

With that curiosity masked by a neutral tone perfected by decades of practice, Kaminsky greeted Chris and offered him a chair.

"What's on your mind, son?"

Before Chris could speak, the intercom on Kaminsky's

desk buzzed and the clerk told him that Mrs. Benton was calling.

Kaminsky couldn't suppress a sigh. "Tell her I'm in a meeting, and I'll call her back in a few minutes," he instructed, anxious to delay yet another fruitless conversation, filled with invective on her part and evasion on his. He had nothing new to report.

"Sorry for the interruption," he said. "Mrs. Benton is understandably frustrated by our lack of progress on the case."

"That's why I'm here, sir. I think I may have another lead for you."

"Really?" Kaminsky wondered if this was an effort to deflect the investigation from Breinin, whom he knew was one of Chris's mentors.

Chris shifted in the hard chair, his discomfort evident. He had worked out an approach that avoided any mention of the evidence TJ had found, yet was suggestive enough to warrant police action, and was not fully confident that he could keep the story straight. He settled down and plunged ahead.

"Your men have been all over the League for the past week, so I'm sure you know that there's plenty of guesswork about who's responsible. Lots of people are betting on Breinin because of his history with Benton, but I found out that somebody else also has a grudge that goes back decades."

He told Kaminsky that Benton had gotten a fellow instructor named Johann Gruen fired from the League, and that Gruen never got over it. He said that Gruen's son, Walter Green, was now working there as a model and blamed Benton for ruining his father's career, which had led to Gruen's suicide.

Kaminsky wanted to know where Chris got this information.

"I overheard something in the cafeteria that got me wondering," he said, truthfully. "One of the instructors was talking about Wally and mentioned that his father taught there back in the '30s, when Benton was there. That made me think that maybe Gruen heard Benton was in town and decided to settle an old score, but I found out later that Gruen killed himself years ago, so then I thought his son might want revenge."

The inspector was not content with such generalities.

"Why did Benton want to get rid of this Gruen guy? And how do you know his son has a grudge against Benton? Maybe somebody, or something, else was responsible for his old man's suicide."

Trying not to sound defensive or evasive, Chris told Kaminsky what he'd learned in the meeting with Stewart Klonis. "Benton hated queers with a passion, so when Gruen came on to him, he didn't just reject him, he got rid of him. According to Mr. Klonis, that was the beginning of the end for Gruen."

"I've spoken at length to Mr. Klonis," said Kaminsky, "and he never mentioned Walter Green as someone who might have wanted Benton dead."

"He doesn't know that Wally is Gruen's son," Chris explained. "When his parents got divorced, his mother changed their last name to Green so people wouldn't think they were German. He never told Mr. Klonis about the connection."

"I see," said Kaminsky, who was beginning to wonder if there might be something to Chris's theory. "I suppose you know about the sighting on the staircase, another reason why we're concentrating on Breinin. How does that square with what you're telling me?"

Chris had a ready answer. "Everybody knows how Breinin loves his red jacket, but it's not custom made. They sell them at S. Klein."

Kaminsky grinned. "So you've been doing a little detective work on your own."

Not me, thought Chris, *and not at the department store, but it's fine if that's what he believes.*

"Well," he said, "I didn't want to come to you with nothing more than hearsay. I wanted to satisfy myself that Breinin isn't the only man in a red jacket who might have been on that staircase."

"Sure you're not just trying to steer us away from Breinin?"

"Of course not," Chris insisted, "and I'm not trying to implicate Wally," which was in fact what he was trying to do. "I just thought you should know what I found out about his background. He's a really nice guy, sweet and even-tempered. It's hard to believe he'd be capable of murder."

That sounded pretty foolish to him, especially considering that Wally was a former marine who'd no doubt done his share of killing in the war. But Kaminsky would find that out soon enough. No need to embellish his incriminating story.

Kaminsky rose from his chair, signaling an end to the interview.

"Thank you for coming in, Mr. Gray. I appreciate your sharing this information with me, and I assure you we'll look into it."

———

A call to the League's registrar confirmed that Walter Green was scheduled to model for Robert Brackman's morning class in Studio Fifteen, which ended at twelve thirty. Kaminsky scheduled Detective Valentino to pay him a visit, and reluctantly asked the clerk to telephone Rita Benton, who was staying with Joe and Maria Kron in Mattituck. At least—assuming he could get a word in—he could tell her they had a new lead in the case.

Sheik arrived at the League a few minutes early and located Studio Fifteen at the end of the ground-floor hallway. As the door opened and students began to file out, he saw the model step behind the privacy screen to change. He noted the man's powerful physique, still trim and muscular in early middle age, not that of a former athlete gone to seed.

This guy keeps himself in shape, he said to himself, *not that you'd need to be all that strong to knock out an old man*

like Benton. Even a woman could do it. Hit him in the right
spot with a pipe or a piece of wood and he'd go out like a light.

They'd found nothing like that at the scene, but there
were plenty of potential weapons all over the building. The
place was a junk heap, especially the basement, where the
sculptors' supplies of wood and scrap metal included many
an object that could have been used, then slipped back where
it came from with no one the wiser. But Dr. Helpern had
identified the cause of the head wound as an implement that
spread the impact rather than concentrating it as a wooden
club or a piece of metal would do. Nor was the skin on the
scalp broken, another indication of a less rigid weapon. In
his expert opinion, the blunt trauma that rendered Benton
unconscious was the result of a blow from a sap.

When Wally emerged fully dressed from behind the
screen, Sheik approached him and identified himself. He
asked Wally for a few minutes of his time.

"Just a few questions, and I'd like to make sure we're not
disturbed," he said as he closed and locked the door of the
now-empty studio. He sat on one of the bench easels and
invited Wally to do the same. Taking out his notebook, he
began by asking Wally's full name and address.

"Have the police spoken to you before about the Benton
case?"

"Yes," he answered. "Officer Gomez, I think his name
was, talked to me last Thursday, the day after it happened.
He and another officer were interviewing everybody who
was in the building that day."

"So you were here on Wednesday?"

"Yeah, I work all day Wednesdays, for the Brackman morning and afternoon classes."

"Where are they held?"

"Down here, in this studio. I finish at half past four."

"Did you hang around after class?"

"Yeah, I had a cup of coffee in the cafeteria, then I went home."

"What time did you leave?"

"I don't know, around five, I guess."

"Anyone who can confirm that?"

"I was sitting with a couple guys from the Brackman class, maybe they could tell you when I left. I wasn't watching the clock."

Sheik rephrased the question. "I didn't mean when did you leave the cafeteria. I meant when did you leave the building. Did anyone see you leave? Did you meet anyone later who could place you somewhere else when Benton was killed?"

Wally stood up, looming over Sheik, a frown on his face. "What the fuck are you getting at?" he said, his tone sharp with indignation. "Why should I have to account for my whereabouts? I thought you figured out that Breinin did it. That Russian asshole had plenty of reason to."

"You don't get along with Breinin?"

"He's a jerk. Full of himself, browbeats the students, treats the models like furniture."

"Sit down, Mr. Green," said Sheik. Impassive now, back

in control of himself, Wally resumed his place on the bench as the detective continued.

"In spite of Breinin's loudly expressed antipathy toward Benton, and some circumstantial evidence, we aren't satisfied that he's the killer. Contrary to what many people believe, the police don't want to railroad someone just because he's the most likely suspect. We have to follow up every lead, one of which has brought me to you."

"I don't know what you're talking about. I wasn't here when Benton bought it. Anyway, why would I kill him? Ask anybody, him and me were kinda friendly. I had nothing against him."

"No, perhaps not," said Sheik evenly, preparing for another outburst, "but your father did."

Instead of anger or consternation, Wally surprised him with a blank stare. For a few moments, he seemed to be frozen in place, his focus not on Sheik but on some distant point far beyond the League's walls. Then his eyes closed.

"Oh, Christ," he murmured, "poor Dad. He can finally rest in peace."

Forty-Five

The result of Sheik's initial interview was a request for Wally to accompany him to Midtown North for more questioning, which yielded nothing. He simply remained silent. They decided to hold him on suspicion pending further investigation.

They confiscated his keys and searched his lockers—he had one in each studio where he posed. The ring also contained keys that fit other locks at the League. He had inherited them from his father, who hadn't turned them in after he was fired. For the staff's convenience, one key unlocked all the studio doors, another opened all the supply closets, and another worked on every prop cabinet. The school's frugality insured that the locks had never been changed.

Not surprisingly, Wally's lockers yielded nothing to link him to Benton's murder. A more thorough search of the building, however, uncovered a brown paper bag full of clothing stuffed behind one of the clay storage bins in the basement. In it was a red velvet jacket with a label from S. Klein, a paisley scarf, a wide-brimmed brown hat, and a pair of cotton gloves. They were taken to the forensic laboratory for hair and fiber testing and analysis of stains on the right-hand glove, which proved to be blood matching Benton's type. Hairs found inside the hat were identical to a sample from Wally's head. Executing a search warrant for his room, the police found the blackjack and clothing receipt in his desk.

Confronted with this evidence, Wally had asked to speak to a lawyer. The Department of Veterans Affairs Office of General Counsel helped him find a pro bono attorney from the Legal Aid Society.

With the promise of attorney-client privilege, Wally told him how he killed Benton, and why.

———

On the Thursday evening in September when Laning first mentioned Benton's name and told the students he'd be coming to visit the following week, Wally was so shaken that he nearly retched. It was, he said, as if the past had come flooding back, drowning him in bitterness. Thank God he was behind the screen on his break, or the whole class would have seen his reaction. As it was, all they knew was that he'd knocked over a stool.

By the time the break was over, he'd composed himself

and had begun to think that Benton's return to the League was really a stroke of luck. Now he'd finally be able to confront the bastard who, as he saw it, had killed his father.

And the more he thought about it, the more determined he became to find a way to pay him back.

It turned out to be pretty easy, once he'd decided that, instead of venting his rage at Benton, he'd befriend him. That was pretty easy, too. The old egotist was a sucker for flattery, so all Wally had to do was sit at his table in the cafeteria and beam with admiration as he droned on about his superiority, then ask if he could go around the Whitney show with him. A few of the others were interested, too, and Benton invited them to his next gallery talk.

The group met at the museum on a Saturday afternoon, the week after the show opened. As his guts churned with hypocrisy, Wally punctuated Benton's running commentary with favorable remarks, praise that simply echoed the artist's own opinions.

As they left the exhibition, Wally confided to Benton that he aspired to paint just like him and would welcome his criticism.

"Anytime, Wally m'boy," Benton had beamed. "Just give me the high sign when you're ready."

On his way out of the museum, Wally stopped in the gift shop and bought a postcard of the Benton painting titled *Retribution*. Although he despised its stylistic mannerisms and simplistic historical theme, it seemed an appropriate metaphor for his plan.

Wally hadn't touched a paintbrush in more than thirty years and didn't intend to pick one up again now. His aim was simply to tell Benton that his canvases were in the racks up in Studio Nine and arrange to meet him there. And that's what he did when he took Benton aside after lunch on November first.

"I'm free after classes finish at half past four. I'll be posing for Brackman until then. My stuff's upstairs in your old studio. Would you meet me there after everybody's gone? I won't keep you long, sir," he assured him, "I just want to know if you think I have enough talent to follow in your footsteps."

Anyone less arrogant would have dismissed such blatant deference, but it was music to Benton's ears.

"I'll be there, son. Maybe I'll go up early and hang around Charlie Alston's class. He won't mind. I'll be quiet as a church mouse."

Not fucking likely, you rancid old fart, said Wally to himself. *The only time you'll be quiet is when you're dead, and we won't have to wait much longer for that.*

Sure enough, eager to escape Benton's bombast, Alston's class emptied out as soon as time was called at four thirty. Alston himself, a bit weary of his old friend's relentless self-promotion, also excused himself and followed suit.

Outside the cafeteria, Wally waited until he was sure everyone had come down, then took the stairs to the fifth floor, where he found Benton alone in Studio Nine.

The artist drew himself up and strutted over to Wally, who towered over him. Not one to be intimidated, even at his advanced age Benton could project the outsize self-assurance that had always defined his public persona. Ignorant of Wally's true intentions, he clapped him on the back and led him into the studio.

"Come on, Wally, show me what you've got."

Courteously, Wally located a chair and set it near the door, facing into the studio and away from the lockers and painting racks. "Why don't you sit here, Mr. Benton?" he suggested. "I'll fetch one of my paintings and set it up on an easel."

Walking behind the chair, he withdrew the blackjack from his right trouser pocket, flipped the latch on the studio door with his left hand, and delivered a backhand blow to Benton's head with his right. The only sound was a dull thump, and Benton toppled sideways onto the floor.

Wally pulled a pair of cotton gloves out of his left pocket. He put them on and wiped his hand along the top rail of the chair where his bare fingers had touched it.

He lifted Benton, carried him to the model stand, and laid him on his back. He unlocked the prop cabinet with his father's key, removed the kinzhal—earlier that day he'd checked it was there—unsheathed it, took the postcard out of his pocket, and stuck the blade through it.

Thanks to his Marine Corps hand-to-hand combat training, he knew exactly where to insert the blade under Benton's rib cage to do maximum damage and cause minimal external bleeding.

You broke my father's heart. Now I'll break yours.

A rapid back-and-forth motion, and the right ventricle

was lacerated. Death would be quick, much more merciful than Benton deserved. But the debt would be repaid.

The rest of the operation took only a few minutes. Wally curled the body into a fetal position, the better to conceal it if someone looked in between classes. He covered it with the tablecloth, which the monitor had folded neatly and stored in the supply closet, according to standard procedure. He opened his locker and removed the bag of clothing he'd placed there ahead of time. He put on the red jacket, paisley scarf, and hat, folded the bag and slipped it under the jacket, and switched off the lights. He unlocked the door, wiped the lock and doorknob with his gloved hand, checked that the hall was empty, and left the studio.

He quickly descended the stairs to the basement, ducked into the sculpture supply room, took off the disguise, put the clothes into the bag, and hid it behind the clay bin. It would be safe there until Breinin was arrested and the cops went away. Then he could dispose of it properly. He took the stairs up to the cafeteria and ordered coffee.

He couldn't be sure that Breinin didn't have an alibi, but since the Russian let it be known that he worked alone in his studio at home, with no assistant and only the radio for company, Wally assumed he'd have a hard time proving he couldn't possibly have met with Benton in Studio Nine at around five, argued with him, and killed him.

Of course they couldn't indict Breinin, there was no way to prove he did it. Any number of people could have taken the knife out of the prop cabinet, days or even weeks before.

Just because it belonged to Breinin didn't mean he'd used it on Benton. And, like a gift from God, Bill Millstein had laid another false but very plausible trail.

So Wally figured he was in the clear. As far as anyone knew, he had no reason to want Benton dead. Unlike many others at the League, hadn't he gone out of his way to be friendly to him?

Then somebody made the connection between him and Johann Gruen—probably Brackman, in whom he'd foolishly confided—and took it to Klonis, who knew what Benton had done, at least that's what Wally assumed. That's when everything fell apart.

———

Wally's attorney told him that, since the crime was premeditated, he would be charged with first-degree murder. He advised Wally to plead not guilty, and said he'd try to get a plea bargain to reduce the charge to manslaughter.

"It's a long shot, but I'm counting on your war record to weigh in your favor," he said. "I hope we can go before a judge who's a veteran. Many of them are. If he doesn't take the deal and it goes to trial, the DA is likely to get a conviction, but the jury may not want to impose the death penalty on a highly decorated marine. Still, if they don't give you the chair, you're looking at a long prison sentence."

Walter Gruen Green turned his face to the wall. "Semper Fi, Dad."

Forty-Six

The opening of Alfonso Ossorio's solo exhibition at the Cordier & Ekstrom Gallery, in the blue-chip art complex at 980 Madison Avenue, was already crowded with art-world luminaries when the Fitzgerald family and Ellen arrived at seven p.m. Several of Ossorio's newly minted assemblages, which he called Congregations, were on display. He had indeed been hard at work since he spoke to TJ in early October.

While the term "Congregation" was a deliberate allusion to a religious gathering, the imagery itself was defiantly and irreverently grotesque, far beyond even the most flamboyant Spanish baroque decoration. In *Eagle and Palette*, for example, Ossorio had arranged a collection of found objects—including shells, driftwood, curtain rings, bones, glass eyes, and a set of false teeth—embedded them in a plastic matrix, and topped it off with a cow's pelvis and a brass bird-shaped finial probably designed for a flagstaff. This was one of his more restrained creations.

Having followed their friend's evolution over the past decade from expressionist painting to this hybrid form of relief sculpture, Nita, Fitz, and TJ were neither surprised nor shocked by his bizarre constructions. Ellen, on the other hand, was visibly taken aback. Given to expressing herself frankly, she was uncharacteristically at a loss for words, which made TJ, usually the tongue-tied one, grin behind her back as she moved around the gallery.

She stopped in front of *Horned Juggler*, a rectangular box surrounded by rounded extensions, studded with menacing eyeballs, among other curiosities, and bristling with real animal horns. "Help me out here, TJ," she pleaded, turning to him in confusion. "What am I supposed to make of this?"

"Whatever you like, my dear," said a resonant voice to her right. The patrician figure of the artist himself approached, and he greeted her warmly with the impeccable manners and charming English accent he'd acquired as a boarding-school student at St. Richard's School in Malvern.

"You must be the lovely Miss Jamison. Señor TJ has been singing your praises over the telephone, and now that I see you in person I know he didn't exaggerate." Ossorio kissed her hand in courtly fashion, which both delighted and slightly flustered her.

"Ted Dragon to the rescue," said Ossorio's companion as he embraced Nita, Fitz, and TJ in turn, introduced himself to Ellen, and put a hand protectively on her shoulder.

"We mustn't monopolize Alfonso," he advised as he led them to the bar, "he has to work the room. You're not the only one who's perplexed, lovely Miss Jamieson. Believe me, the collectors and critics need explanations, too. Besides," he leaned in confidentially and took TJ's arm, "I want to hear all about how you solved the Benton case. Let's get some drinks and go where we can talk."

Before TJ could object, Ted snagged two glasses of wine and steered him out to the lobby, where they found an upholstered bench. Ted handed him a glass, and raised his in a toast. "To our very own Sherlock, following in his mother's footsteps. Tchin-tchin!"

"Honestly, Ted, I'm not the one who brought Walter Green to justice. In fact, if you want the truth, I was kind of against reporting him to the cops. I know that was wrong. War hero or not, he killed Benton in cold blood and even tried to pin it on someone else. I let my feelings get in the way of my judgment." He lowered his eyes. "Plus, I committed a crime to get the goods on him. I don't think I'm cut out for the force."

Ted was all ears. "What crime?"

"I broke into his apartment. I, sort of, borrowed Mom's lockpicking tools, and I searched the place. Almost got caught in the act, too. But that's what put me on to the disguise."

"From what the papers said, he wore an outfit like the one the Russian painter wore, so in case he was spotted people would think it was the Russian."

"They got that part right. I found what I thought might be a receipt for the clothes in his desk. The problem was, I couldn't tell the cops about it, and anyway, like I said, I wasn't sure I wanted to turn him in. So my friend Chris went to them instead. He told them that Wally—that's what everybody at the League calls him—thought Benton was responsible for his father's suicide, so maybe they ought to question him."

Ted gave TJ a long, hard look. "But you're the one who put it all together. Don't shake your head, Nita told me all about it. She and Fitz are proud of you, TJ."

"And so am I, very proud indeed," said Ellen, who had detached herself from the reception. Sliding onto the bench next to TJ, she threw her arms around him and, much to Ted's delight, gave him a big wet kiss.

"Don't you think he'll make a great detective?" she asked rhetorically, as TJ tried to hide his flush of embarrassment. The warmth of her body against his also sent blood coursing in the opposite direction, and he was glad he was sitting down.

"Maybe," Ted replied coyly, displaying his famous dimples to effect, "though Alfonso and I think he has the makings of a great artist." A mischievous grin spread across his face. "But I bet he'll also make a great lover. Don't you agree?"

Ellen winked at him and returned his sly smile. "That bet's already been won."

ACKNOWLEDGMENTS

According to the comedian Charles Fleischer, "If you remember the '60s, you really weren't there." Well, several of the characters in my tale really were there, and others weren't—in fact, they didn't exist. Brian Fitzgerald and Juanita Diaz were invented for my first mystery novel, *An Exquisite Corpse*. Their son, Timothy Juan, known as TJ, came to life, fictionally speaking, in my second one, *An Accidental Corpse*. In this book, they interact with a cast of actual denizens of the New York art world and anti-war movement. Many of them will be recognizable to those who, like me, lived through that turbulent decade and do remember it. I attended the Art Students League and performed at The Bitter End and have vivid recollections of my formative experiences in both places.

Fortunately for those who don't have firsthand

knowledge, the era has been well chronicled, and several of those accounts have been invaluable to me in my effort to evoke its spirit. I am especially indebted to *POPism: The Warhol Sixties*, a personal view of the Factory scene by Andy Warhol and Pat Hackett; Paul Colby's memoir, *The Bitter End: Hanging Out at America's Nightclub*; and *Max's Kansas City: Art, Glamor, Rock and Roll*, edited by Steve Kasher.

Specific inquiries were graciously answered by Henry Adams, Ruth Coulter Heede Professor of Art History, Case Western Reserve University; Sarah Bean Apmann, Director of Research and Preservation, Greenwich Village Society for Historic Preservation; Joshua Brown, Executive Director, American Social History Project/Center for Media and Learning and Professor of History, PhD Program in History, The Graduate Center, The City University of New York; Anna Canoni, Senior Operations Manager, Woody Guthrie Publications, Inc.; Stephanie Cassidy, Archivist and Editor, Art Students League of New York; and Robert J. Singer, MD.

Among the many real people woven into this work of fiction, Thomas Hart Benton is the most fully imagined, though I have taken quite a few liberties. His remarkable story is well told in Justin Wolff's biography, *Thomas Hart Benton: A Life*, and in Benton's own memoirs, *An Artist in America* and *An American in Art*. Those sources will confirm that he was not murdered in 1967 by a man named Walter Green, who is a figment of my imagination, as is his father, Johann Gruen. After putting the finishing touches on his mural *The Sources of Country Music* for the Country

Music Hall of Fame and Museum in Nashville, Benton died in his studio in Kansas City, Missouri, on January 19, 1975, at the age of eighty-five. His property is now a state historic site.

ABOUT THE AUTHOR

Helen A. Harrison, a former art reviewer and feature writer for *The New York Times* and visual arts commentator for National Public Radio, is the director of the Pollock-Krasner House and Study Center in East Hampton, New York, and an authority on twentieth-century American art. A native of New York City with a bachelor's degree in studio art from Adelphi University, she also attended the Art Students League, the Brooklyn Museum Art School, and Hornsey College of Art in London before receiving a master's degree in art history from Case Western Reserve University. Among her many publications are exhibition catalogs, essays, book chapters, reviews and articles, and several nonfiction books, including *Hamptons Bohemia: Two Centuries of Artists* and *Writers on the Beach*, coauthored with Constance Ayers Denne, and monographs on Larry Rivers and Jackson Pollock. She and her husband, the artist Roy Nicholson, live in Sag Harbor, New York. You can visit her website at helenharrison.net.

Enter the first book in the
Art of Murder Mystery series!

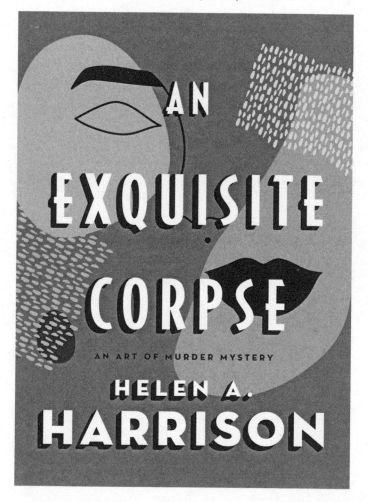

AN

EXQUISITE

CORPSE

AN ART OF MURDER MYSTERY

HELEN A.
HARRISON

Continue with the second artful tale
from Helen A. Harrison.

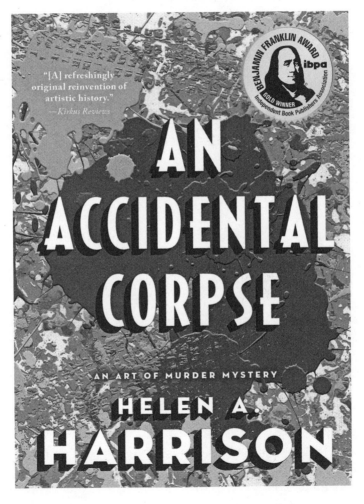

"[A] refreshingly
original reinvention of
artistic history."
—*Kirkus Reviews*

BENJAMIN FRANKLIN AWARD
ibpa
GOLD WINNER
Independent Book Publishers Association

AN ACCIDENTAL CORPSE

AN ART OF MURDER MYSTERY

HELEN A. HARRISON